KNIGHT
of
DESTINY

#5 Sisterhood of Secrets

BY
JENNIFER MONROE

WOLF PUBLISHING

Knight of Destiny by Jennifer Monroe

Published by WOLF Publishing UG

Copyright © 2022 Jennifer Monroe
Text by Jennifer Monroe
Edited by Chris Hall
Cover Art by Victoria Cooper
Paperback ISBN: 978-3-98536-122-9
Hard Cover ISBN: 978-3-98536-123-6
Ebook ISBN: 978-3-98536-121-2

WOLF Publishing - This is us:

Two sisters, two personalities.. But only one big love!

Diving into a world of dreams..
   ...Romance, heartfelt emotions, lovable and witty characters, some humor, and some mystery! Because we want it all! Historical Romance at its best!

Visit our website to learn all about us, our authors and books!

Sign up to our mailing list to receive first hand information on new releases, freebies and promotions as well as exclusive giveaways and sneak-peeks!

WWW.WOLF-PUBLISHING.COM

Also by Jennifer Monroe

The Sisterhood of Secrets

There is far more for the women at Miss Rutley's Finishing School than an education, for their secretive headmistress will assure her pupils find the happiness they each deserve.

#1 Duke of Madness

#2 Baron of Rake Street

#3 Marquess of Magic

#4 Earl of Deception

#5 Knight of Destiny

#6 Captain of Second Chances

Prequel: Gentleman of Christmas Past

KNIGHT
of
DESTINY

Prologue

Chatsworth 1825

Lady Louisa Kirkwood had a dream. In it, she was a young schoolgirl standing beside a large oak tree in the front garden of Courtly Manor. Yet, she was not alone. Her closest friends and schoolmates, as well as the headmistress of Mrs. Rutley's School for Young Women, were beside her. Joined hand in hand, each shared her innermost secret.

They had been called the Sisterhood of Secrets. Not only for what was shared that day, but for all the time after that fateful day each enjoyed at the school.

Yet as she opened her eyes and stared at the initials carved in the trunk of the tree, she reminded herself that it had not been a dream. The very incident had taken place twenty years earlier.

She had been so young then, the youngest daughter of a wealthy merchant and not yet eighteen. Her honey-blonde hair had no silver as it did now, and there had been no crow's feet at the corner of her eyes. And all her hopes and dreams lay before her.

Because of the help she had received from Mrs. Agnes Rutley, most had come true. Her headmistress reared her students not only to become young ladies ready to enter into society but also to be better women—intelligent and confident. Lessons that Louisa had experienced and used in her life since leaving the school.

Her headmistress, whose health was failing, recently requested Louisa's attendance and likely that of the others from the Sisterhood of Secrets. Louisa had not hesitated to pack a trunk for the journey.

Her youngest child, Meredith, had heard many stories about Mrs. Rutley, yet she still could not comprehend why her mother would make such a fuss over a woman who was no longer in Louisa's life.

"I know she helped you, Mama, but why must you leave?" her twelve-year-old daughter had asked. "She was just your headmistress. It's not as if she's family."

Placing a hand on the girl's shoulder, Louisa brushed away a strand of golden hair. The girl was beautiful and always curious. With a smile, Louisa replied, "Because I gave my word—as a lady and a friend—that if any of my friends were in need, I would come. And I cannot break my word now, can I?"

Meredith had sighed dramatically—a common reaction to most situations that did not go as she wanted. "I suppose not. But you mustn't be gone long, Mama. Please say you'll return soon."

Louisa had kissed her daughter's cheek and replied, "I promise, my dear. And you must give me your word that you'll follow all Miss Readsy's instructions and work extra hard on your lessons."

"I always work hard on my lessons, Mama," Meredith said with a jut to her chin. "So, I see no reason to promise." After a quick arch of Louisa's eyebrow, however, she quickly added, "Yes, Mama, I promise."

With a firm shake of her head to clear her mind, Louisa turned and walked back toward the house. It was not just a school for young girls, for it had also been their home. A place of refuge, their headmistress as loving as any parent.

Judging by the carriages that lined the drive—and the crests that adorned them—several of her old friends had already arrived. Such a pity they had not been better about exchanging letters, but life tended to break old ties.

A smile broke across her face when a familiar figure opened the door after she rang the bell. Mrs. Shepherd had touched Louisa's life in so many wonderful ways but had changed little in the last twenty years. Granted, gray now peeked out beneath the kerchief she wore where dark once had reigned, and more lines showed in her round face, but otherwise she had changed little since Louisa had last seen her. Especially her smile.

"Hello, Mrs. Shepherd," Louisa said. "You haven't aged a day." She leaned in close and added in a whisper, "What is your secret?"

"Now, I won't have you telling fibs," Mrs. Shepherd said, although she beamed at the compliment. "Or I'll send you to the kitchen to wash dishes."

Louisa laughed and embraced the cook. How many times had she heard Mrs. Shepherd make this same threat during her years at the school? Too many to count. Yet Louisa had never witnessed any of the students receiving such a punishment. It might have happened but not in her time there.

A wave of guilt washed over her for not returning to Courtly Manor sooner. "It's been too long," she said, unable to hide the regret she felt. "Time passed so quickly, you see. And then came the children—"

Mrs. Shepherd grabbed Louisa's hand and give it a gentle squeeze. "You did exactly what Mrs. Rutley hoped you'd do—raise a family and be happy." She tilted her head. "You are happy, aren't you?"

Louisa nodded. "Very."

"And you're here now," the cook said. "That's what matters most. You'll find Mrs. Rutley upstairs in bed. Go on up and see her. I'll see your things are settled into a room."

With a grateful smile, Louisa stepped into the foyer and came to a stop. She could almost see Unity Ancell and Theodosia Renwick laughing as they hurried up the stairs, both wearing dresses they had ordered to be exactly the same.

And there was Julia Wallace scolding Ruth Lockhart for her mischievous behavior, a regular occurrence when both girls were together. Jenny Clifton was donning her pelisse, Emma Hunter at her side, chatting away about which shops they would visit during their time in the village of Chatsworth.

They were all so young then. The world ahead of them was uncharted.

Stepping off the top step, Louisa walked down the corridor that led to her headmistress's room. A sliver of light glinted on the floor as she approached. When she opened the door, she was immediately engulfed by Jenny's arms.

"I knew you would come," her friend said. "How long has it been since we last saw one another? Six years? Seven?"

"Too long," Louisa said. Her grin widened when her eyes fell on the others—Julia, Emma, and Diana. Each embraced her, whispering welcomes in her ear.

As she looked over her Sisters, her heart was near bursting, for she loved each and every one of them. Yes, it had been far too long since they were all together.

Mrs. Rutley lay propped up by numerous pillows. Age and sickness had taken their toll on her headmistress, so much so that Louisa wanted to weep. Yet there was something in the older woman's eye, a twinkle Louisa would always recognize, for every time she saw it during her time at the school, it always brought her a sense of hope.

Louisa took Mrs. Rutley's hand in her own. "I came," she said simply.

"I knew you would, my dear," Mrs. Rutley replied. Her voice was barely above a whisper. "My heart told me you would."

Her friends drew close, and Louisa was at a loss for words. She was never sure what to say to someone lying on a sickbed. "And the others?" she asked. "When are they expected?"

Julia placed a comforting hand on Louisa's arm. "Unity and Theodosia are in America, so I doubt we'll be seeing them."

"And Ruth?" Louisa asked. When all her friends cast their eyes to the floor, she knew the answer, for that was the same look that came when she had been informed of her uncle's passing. "No," she said, her voice choking. "It cannot be."

Julia nodded, and Emma wiped at her eyes. "No one has heard from her in many years. Not even Mrs. Rutley. The prevalent rumor is that she's dead."

It took Louisa all her might to hold back tears. She and Ruth Lockhart had grown close during that final year at the school together and more so in the final months. To learn that the vivacious and precocious girl was gone, only made the pain and hurt she had felt upon learning of Mrs. Rutley's illness intensify.

"I received word two years ago that she died and nothing more," Mrs. Rutley said, drawing the attention of everyone. "But we can discuss Ruth later. For now, I must make a request."

"Of course, Mrs. Rutley. Ask anything of me, and I'll do what I can."

The headmistress's smile put Louisa's worries at ease. Just as it always had. "Tell me the story of how you found love. It's a wonderful story that I witnessed firsthand, but I wish to hear it nonetheless."

Louisa wet her lips. Where should she begin? Her thoughts drifted to the many days she had been at the school. Any one of them could have been a starting point for her story. Should she begin with the first time she learned that a handsome knight had moved to Chatsworth? Or when she sought him out only to be hurt by his demeaning words?

Then she smiled as another memory came to mind. The Chatsworth Theater. That was where it all began.

"It was not long after Jenny left the school. Perhaps no more than two weeks. As she did every year, Mrs. Rutley took us to the theater as a treat for the new students. It was there where I saw the man who would forever change my destiny."

Chapter One

Chatsworth 1806

Every spring, the students attending Mrs. Rutley's School for Young Women were treated to a tour of the local theater. Although it could not compare in size or elegance to those in London, Miss Louisa Dunston did not care. Like most of the village of Chatsworth, the theater had a quaintness—an almost innocence—about it that appealed to Louisa's senses.

Yet that was not the only reason she was intrigued by the place. There, a woman could enter equal to a man. Well, at least to a certain, yet marked, degree when compared to the reality of life. In some of the plays, the lead role was a woman. Granted, not often, but it did happen.

Both men and women performed in various productions at the tiny establishment, and the roles they played were often equal in importance. Therefore, in Louisa's eyes, that placed them in an unusual predicament—it balanced the scales.

Not only were the students given a guided tour of the theater by the proprietor, Mr. Neil Barker, but they also stayed to watch whatever dramatization was offered at the time.

The outing was meant to provide the pupils with the opportunity to experience the finer things life had to offer. Louisa, however, believed it also gave the students an escape from the humdrum of lessons. Not to mention too many days forced to remain indoors during the winter weather.

Forgoing a muffler, Louisa slipped on her pink spencer jacket and gave herself one final inspection in the mirror.

"We're only going to the Chatsworth Theater, not having tea with the Royal family," Ruth said as she fixed the last button on her shoes. "Your vainness knows no bounds."

With Jenny now off to begin a new life and new students in need of beds, Ruth had been given an ultimatum—either move in with Louisa or make room for one of the new girls in her room. As much as Louisa adored her, which was as much as her other Sisters who had made the vow around the great oak tree, Ruth tended not to care much for rules. After four years, she still had not learned how to conduct herself as a lady.

No, that was untrue. With flaming red hair and a pretty smile, Ruth could act as the politest young lady in society when she chose to do so. She could speak with a honeyed tongue to get anyone to do her bidding. Yet as quick as a spark in a meadow of dried grass, she would transform into a shrew who spoke her mind without thought of the consequences. Today, it seemed she had chosen to act the latter rather than the former.

"I'm not vain," Louisa said with a great deal of indignation. "And the theater is exciting to many of the new girls. We're meant to be an example to the younger students."

Turning this way and that, she pinned up a stray strand of blonde hair and smiled at her reflection. She was beautiful; a fact she had learned over the last few years. If it were not true, men would not spend so much time looking at her. In a world where men ruled, was it a crime for a young lady to use her smile to get what she wanted? In her opinion, no. They used money and their power to get what they wanted, so why could she not do the same with the one commodity she possessed?

"I don't understand why it nettles you so," she continued. "If you don't enjoy it, why go?" She turned to face her friend and sighed. Ruth cared nothing about her looks. She had donned a nondescript black coat that made her look... well, dowdy.

"I do it for Mrs. Rutley," Ruth said. "And no one else."

Louisa smiled at her reflection one last time before applying a dab of perfume to her wrists and behind her ears.

"I must admit," Ruth said, "you do look beautiful today."

Louisa gaped at her friend's reflection. Ruth never offered anyone a compliment. Was this a sign of change? Yet before she could ask, Ruth had to ruin it. As usual.

"Mr. Barker will appreciate the extra effort you're spending on yourself today. Just be certain Mrs. Rutley isn't hurt by it."

Unable to stop herself, Louisa laughed, and Ruth joined in. Mr. Barker was a tall, thin man of an age with Mrs. Rutley. Whenever he was in the presence of their headmistress, he had a propensity to stutter and trip over his own feet. Just last year during the tour, he was in the middle of a speech when he caught sight of Mrs. Rutley and stopped talking midsentence.

As he gawked at her, Ruth had burst into a fit of giggles, making Mr. Barker's cheeks grow so red that one would have thought he had spent too long in the sun. Ruth had earned herself a weekend restricted to her room while the other students made their weekly visit to the village the following weekend.

Louisa paused and strained to listen. "We'd best hurry. I can hear the others downstairs."

Indeed, the foyer was already filled with a dozen wide-eyed young girls. Louisa's heart went out to the new students. She remembered how difficult it was to be away from home and alone for the first time. Therefore, she had taken it upon herself to help them in any way she could.

Unity and Theodosia stood beside Mrs. Rutley in their matching deep-blue jackets over pale-blue walking dresses. With their curly brown hair, large brown eyes, and high cheekbones, they considered themselves twins. It did not matter to them that Theodosia was far taller and Unity's nose was larger. Or the simple fact they were not related. Either way, neither was seen without the other. Even their life plans were the same—to travel to America. What they would do there remained to be seen.

Mrs. Rutley gave two sharp claps, and the students fell silent. "It appears we're all here. Now, remember. You're to be on your best behavior. If you have questions for Mr. Barker, reserve them for the appropriate time. And do keep them relegated to the theater." She gave Ruth a sharp glare. "Asking what an actor wears beneath his robes is highly inappropriate."

Several of the girls tittered at this.

Louisa had to stifle a laugh. Ruth made no attempt. She was the reason Mrs. Rutley gave that warning, after all.

With long strides, Sir Aaron Kirkwood moved swiftly through his home of Hearsely Estate. He had purchased the home six months earlier but had taken up residence only two months ago. With seven bedrooms, a ballroom, and an impressive library, the estate would be his home for the foreseeable future. If all went according to plan.

Aaron wished to open the finest gentleman's club outside of London, and Chatsworth seemed the perfect location. With a growing population and an ever-expanding High Street, he wished to use the village as a way to make a name for himself. One not associated with his being a knight. Or how he had received such a commendation.

After receiving his knighthood into one of the most prestigious orders, he had found his new position complicated to navigate. At first, he had bragged to anyone willing to listen—after all, that was what his betters seemed to do at every turn. But it was not long before he realized that his ramblings drew nothing more than a polite smile from those of the aristocracy. They had not been as impressed as he had hoped.

Yet as the rumors surrounding how he had earned his title became more and more exaggerated, his betters began to change their tune. It was believed that Aaron had fought off a band of highwaymen in order to protect the Princess. That the version so many had come to believe was far from the truth mattered little to Aaron.

Oh, he had encountered the Princess as she was being escorted by the Royal Guards. And yes, he had "rescued" her... in a sense. An overexcited, inebriated man had yelled out and reached for her. Aaron, having reacted faster than the guards, subdued the man. Everything that followed was a blur—and soon entered into the realm of folklore.

After being knighted for his "bravery," the stories of his heroism began to spread. One man became five. A drunkard became thieves who then became a band of highwaymen. The streets of London became a dark forest. Swords, blood, and corpses lay in the wake of a battle, and a kingdom was forever grateful.

And Aaron was named a hero.

Aaron shook his head as he entered the library. He went to stand before a white marble fireplace. Above it hung his most prized posses- sion—the Sword of Destiny. The old piece of steel was said to be more than three hundred years old and was assumed to have belonged to a distant relative of Aaron's. It was used at Bosworth Field during the final battle of the War of the Roses when Henry Tudor and those who rallied with him had prevailed. Thus, changing the destiny of England forever.

Aaron's ancestor, a man whose blood flowed through his veins, was a true knight and had fought in that battle. It had been he who led the charge that ended the life of Richard III.

Yet gazing upon that sword, the symbol of bravery for the man who had wielded it, Aaron often wondered about his own destiny. His father was a brilliant businessman who had earned the admiration and praise of his peers. They hailed him even after his death. And although Aaron managed his family's wealth quite well, he had nothing of which to boast.

Well, besides the exceptionally handsome looks with which he had been blessed. As men of means used their wealth to get what they wanted, Aaron had come to rely on his strong jaw and straight nose. Being dubbed a knight, and the story that surrounded it, had helped to heighten his fame.

And as the story changed and grew, so did Aaron's pride.

He had entered into societal circles of men he never thought possible. Barons, earls, and even a duke had invited him to several gatherings. An impossibility without his new title. One thing all the men had in common was their arrogance. And Aaron quickly understood that the more self-assured a man was, the more respected he became. Power came with his newfound sense of self-importance.

There were times, however, when his arrogance left him feeling empty. Not when it came to his looks, of course. His mother had praised his handsomeness from a young age, and he had no reason to doubt that truth.

Yet what good was an alluring face when most ladies could not be trusted? He had learned early on that their ways were dubious at best. Flirty smiles, blushing cheeks, all were traps to lure a man into their lives and make them weak. Once a woman had her hooks in a man, the suffering began.

Thankfully, his mother and sister were honorable women who lived a moral and just life. Never had he witnessed them acting coquettishly to get what they wanted. Nor did they speak with a sharp tongue. They made their requests with integrity and virtue. And Aaron missed them terribly. Regardless of what he thought of his family, Aaron's idea of marriage contradicted the emerging trend. Love? Grown men speaking of their wives as equals, walking around wearing broad grins akin to those of drunkards, was outrageous. They might as well sell their brains to Luigi Galvani—or whoever performed such studies these days. After all, they no longer had any use for that organ! The wedded state was meant to bring in the next generation and nothing more. He was far too intelligent to fall for the feminine wiles. Instead, since the age of fourteen, he had used their tricks against them. A smile, a light touch on a lady's arm, and they were close to fainting. His goal was never to get them into bed but for any other type of gain that would lead him to an introduction to someone who could give him what he needed. Whatever that was.

But his gift of good looks was only made better by his new title. That and the new moniker that had been bestowed upon him. One he had accepted with pride.

The Knight of Destiny.

"The carriage is ready, sir," his butler said, breaking him from his thoughts. The man was thin, nearing the age of sixty. His shiny head had not seen hair in many years. At least that was what Scriven had shared with Aaron when he had hired him two years earlier.

"Thank you," Aaron said with a dismissive wave of his hand. Once Scriven had left the room, Aaron took one last look at the sword. Today, he would begin to carve out his own destiny, and that could only happen once he was able to complete the purchase of the Chatsworth Theater.

Making his way outside, Aaron ignored the driver's greeting and stepped into the exquisite carriage. Gray cloth benches and ornate wood stained a dark brown decorated the interior, but he paid it little mind as he focused his thoughts on the task before him today.

The proprietor, Mr. Neil Barker, was a plain-looking man whose love for the establishment was nauseating. Yet Aaron had heard about the man's financial struggles, which had led him to offer a more-than-reasonable price to purchase the building outright. There, Aaron would redecorate the interior and turn it into a respectable gentlemen's club.

Two problems stood in his way, however. The first had to do with the proprietor himself. Mr. Barker had yet to fully commit to selling the building. But Aaron would see that remedied today by having the man sign a contract. Once that was done, he could not renege on the agreement.

The second would be a bit more difficult to overcome. Although Aaron had the funds to see the venture completed on his own, a single man could stand to lose a great fortune. What he needed was a way to minimize the risk to himself. Therefore, he was in need of investors.

Despite his lack of acquaintances in Chatsworth and its surrounding area, he had spoken to a Harold, Lord Canton at a small dinner party the previous week. The elderly baron had shown a great interest in Aaron's endeavor but refused to commit. Regardless, Aaron needed more than one gentleman investor. Not only for the theater but also for other ventures in the future.

The vehicle came to a stop, and Aaron found himself standing outside the theater. Located in a two-story, angular building where two roads came together, the Chatsworth Theater had a set of white-painted double doors at the entrance. By far the largest single building in the village, it would be perfect for what he wished to accomplish.

A choked sob made him turn. In the entrance to a nearby alleyway stood a woman with unkempt hair and a colorless burlap dress that appeared not to have been washed in several days, if not weeks. Beside her stood a young boy of perhaps six, his trousers far too short and his toes sticking out the ends of his shoes.

A sudden memory entered Aaron's mind that made his stomach clench with regret. He'd been no older than ten when he encountered one of the young maids weeping out in the courtyard.

A pretty blonde girl of perhaps thirteen, Fara was rarely found without a smile whenever Aaron encountered her. Today, however, she was clearly upset about something.

Wanting to console her, Aaron took a step forward, but his father caught him by the shoulder, forcing him to a halt. "Whatever has her crying like a child, I've no doubt she's brought it upon herself. She's not your problem, Aaron, but rather Mrs. Coplin's."

She had been the housekeeper of his childhood home.

"People like her don't need our charity, boy. They need to learn to do for themselves. Just like we do. If she was berated by Mrs. Coplin for not doing her job—or for whatever misdeed she committed—then she's got no one else to blame but herself."

Later however, doubt still plagued him, and he went to ask his mother about Fara. He found out that the young maid had received word that her father had passed away. The fact he had not ignored his father's request to keep away had filled him with guilt.

Seeing this woman now, sobbing and wiping at her dusty cheeks, was too much for Aaron to bear. His father could not always be right.

"What is wrong?" Aaron asked as he approached the woman.

She jumped, pulling the boy closer to her. "Me 'usband, 'e left us last night, milord. Took every last farthin' we 'ad. And why? 'Cause 'e done found some young baggage..." Her eyes widened. "Beggin' yer pardon, milord. I di'n't mean to use such crude language in front of a gentleman like yerself. It's jus' that I wanna go 'ome to me family, but I ain't got the money. And walkin' with me boy all the way to Canterbury? It'll take us weeks!"

"I won't leave you, Mama," the boy said in an attempt to console his mother.

Aaron drew in a deep breath. Contrary to what his father had tried to instill, he knew better than to blame women for every situation that had gone awry. And this was one example. A man who left his family in dire straits to chase another skirt was dastardly. And referring to him as a man was stretching the meaning of that word to its limits. Grown men took care of their responsibilities, not shirked them.

Reaching into the pocket of his coat, he took out several pound notes. "I'm not a lord, but I want you to use this to help you to return home," he said, placing the notes in her hand.

She looked up at him with those glistening eyes. "Are... are ye sure, me... sir?"

Aaron smiled. "Most assuredly."

"I'll pay it back to ye somehow, sir. I swear. What's yer name so I can send it to ye?"

Although the idea of having his good deeds whispered among the villagers, using another's tragedy to improve how others saw him just did not feel right. "My name is of no consequence. Now, go and feed yourself and the boy."

The woman thanked him again and hurried away, her son in tow.

Aaron shook them from his thoughts. He was not there to wonder what would happen to a woman and her child. Thus, he turned and entered the theater. Passing through the foyer, he entered the dimly lit auditorium.

Mr. Barker was on the stage, surrounded by a group of young ladies. Aaron nearly groaned in frustration. Women were prone to talking without ceasing. At least that was what he'd been taught, though it had only confused Aaron further. His mother and sister, neither of them was a prattler. Still, what was meant to be a polite call for a few minutes' chat with Mr. Barker would likely take hours. He had believed the proprietor marginally competent. Perhaps he was wrong. After all, the man was wasting his time entertaining a gaggle of gossipmongers.

I just hope they leave soon, he thought with annoyance. He was far too busy to have his time taken by a bunch of silly and young females.

Chapter Two

The headmistress opened the door, and the students began filing out into the bright spring day. They strolled down the drive, in clumps of twos and threes, and Louisa, Ruth, and the twins brought up the rear.

Unity tilted in closer to the others. "Do you remember when we came last year? Mr. Barker was awfully familiar with Mrs. Rutley. Do you think he'll be as friendly this time?"

"She's pretty enough for her age," Theodosia offered. "I see no reason why he would not."

Louisa laughed. With her chestnut hair mixed with a bit of gray, blue eyes, and a kind smile, Mrs. Rutley would indeed be considered a beautiful woman. But she was old, and Louisa conveyed as much to her friends.

"Men may remarry at an old age," Unity said with a sniff. "I see no reason a woman cannot."

Ruth yawned. "Because they want young brides, not old women. Sadly, Mrs. Rutley falls in the latter category."

"What you say may be true, Ruth," Unity said. "But certainly a man may take exception to her age."

Theodosia sniffed loudly. "You all act as if the only time they see each other is during these few visits to the theater. Has it never occurred to you that perhaps they spend more time together than we know?"

The discussion of older women marrying continued for the remainder of the trek into the village. Each offered a different opinion, which was not uncommon.

The High Street of Chatsworth hosted the same type of shops one might find in larger villages across England. Mrs. Alton's millinery, Mistral's Booksellers, Mr. Finch's butcher's shop, and Mr. Hill's cobbler's shop, just to name a few.

The village was bustling for a Tuesday afternoon. Most of the nobility were off in London for the Season, which left the working and merchant classes the freedom to shop to their hearts' content. Or as far as their purses would allow.

Mrs. Rutley signaled for the group to stop, and the students formed a half-circle around her. "I expect nothing less than your best behavior," she said. "We represent our families and the school, but more importantly, we represent ourselves. Now, let's enjoy the afternoon."

The outside might have been deceiving in what lay inside, but the interior was much different. The foyer dripped red. Red carpet, red velvet curtains, red-painted walls, it was a mass of crimson. This made Louisa smile. There was a sense of elegance, a regality that made it a crown jewel of the village.

"Mrs. Rutley," Mr. Barker gushed as he walked up to them. His ill-fitting coat drooped over a thin frame as he ran a hand through unruly dark-brown hair. "I've been looking forward to your visit. In fact, I've thought of nothing else." His eyes flew open wide. "I mean... That is, you and your students, of course. Not just you... or rather..." He cleared his throat.

Louisa and Jenny had happened upon the theater owner several weeks earlier. And just like that encounter when he had only mentioned their headmistress, his cheeks went red to his ears.

Yet Mrs. Rutley was ever the lady who presented herself with decorum and propriety. "Thank you, Mr. Barker. We've been exceptionally excited to take your tour this year. Have we not, ladies?" Several of the students nodded in agreement. "If you're ready, please proceed." She gave him a smile and took a step back to stand beside Ruth.

Mr. Barker nodded. "Y-yes. Yes, of course." He cleared his throat again. "Thank you, Mrs. Rutley."

Louisa covered her mouth to keep the laugh that bubbled up inside her from erupting. If he was not enamored with Mrs. Rutley, she would eat her shoe!

"I see a few new faces," Mr. Barker said as he surveyed the group of students. "I'm Mr. Barker, the owner of the Chatsworth Theater. We may not be as grand as those in London or even Yorkshire, but we've hosted some prominent guests during its hundred years. Even members of the Royal family have graced our humble establishment."

Two years earlier, Louisa learned that King George I had visited the tiny theater during one of his few visits to England in 1724. Although he spoke only German, he had said through a translator that it was the finest performance he had ever seen. Or so said Mr. Barker.

When Louisa had asked Mrs. Rutley why the king would visit Chatsworth, let alone its theater, the headmistress had offered a bit of advice.

"Sometimes it's best to smile politely and keep those sorts of questions to yourself."

Mr. Barker continued his usual speech—including the mention of a visit from a king—and soon, they entered the auditorium. More red filled this room, from the main curtains that flanked the stage to those on either side of the balcony seats. Even the fabric on the seats was a deep, almost-black crimson. A center aisle separated two stalls of twenty-five seats each, and below the stage was a pit where a small orchestra sat during each production.

Louisa was always impressed at how large the interior was once she was inside. By all outside appearances, it should not have been able to hold so many people at once.

The backdrop on the stage consisted of numerous buildings that resembled those in Chatsworth. Two men no older than thirty were sweeping the stage, stopping long enough to give a polite bow before Mr. Barker dismissed them.

"Now for a rare treat, ladies," Mr. Barker said, grinning widely. "I would like to invite you to come onto the stage. Few have the privilege of ever seeing the auditorium from this perspective."

A wave of excited whispers flittered through the students. Louisa smiled, remembering the thrill of going on the stage for the first time during her first year at the school.

Ruth, of course, rolled her eyes and remained offstage. She had never been interested in the theater tour, and Louisa often wondered why she bothered to come.

"Isn't this wonderful?" Amy Felton whispered, her round cheeks rosy with excitement. A new student to the school, the young blonde girl showed the most potential of all the new arrivals—or at least as far as Louisa was concerned. "To think we'll stand where the performers bring their characters to life! Upon where King George I once watched!"

Recalling the advice Mrs. Rutley had given her, Louisa gave a polite smile and followed the others up the stairs at the side of the stage— stage left, if she recalled correctly. Mr. Barker led them to center stage, *oohs* and *aahs* erupting behind him.

Mr. Barker turned to face the students. "I'll welcome any questions you may have."

The stage fell eerily quiet.

Mrs. Rutley addressed the girls. "Mr. Barker has a vast knowledge of this theater. Don't be afraid to ask anything you'd like."

Mr. Barker's cheeks could have lit the candles at the front of the stage. "Thank you, Mrs. Rutley. Now, who would like to ask the first question?"

Frances Cunningham, a new student with two brown curls hanging down either side of her face and wearing a nervous smile, lifted a finger. "I have a question, sir," she said in a voice so quiet that Louisa had to strain to hear her. "Where do you find the performers for your plays?"

Mr. Barker clasped his hands behind him in a self-important manner. "A most excellent question. Some journey from across the country for a chance to perform here. But we do allow those who live here locally to audition, as well."

Other girls raised their hands, and soon, all were asking questions. A humorous thought entered Louisa's mind. As she had heard every question and answer imaginable over the past four years, she turned to speak to Ruth but found the girl gone. She had moved to whisper to the twins.

"What is today's presentation, Mr. Barker?" Amy asked.

Mr. Barker's heavy sigh made Louisa frown. Why did he suddenly appear sad?

"Our spring play, entitled The Summer of Destiny, tells the story of the founders of Chatsworth. It will be our next—and possibly final—performance here at the Chatsworth Theater."

Gasps filled the stage, and even Mrs. Rutley appeared taken aback.

"We received a generous donation recently from a Mr. Stonebrook —I believe one of your students is acquainted with him, Mrs. Rutley." He shook his head. "Sadly, the funds were enough to allow this year's production to be produced and not much more."

Louisa recalled a Mr. Peter Stonebrook, a vile man who had attempted to woo Diana, using an act of charity as a means to win her over. In truth, he cared nothing for charity, the theater least of all. Thankfully, she had fallen in love with Lord Barrington, a much better-suited gentleman for her friend.

"Is there nothing that can be done to save it?" Mrs. Rutley asked.

The proprietor sighed again. "I'm afraid not. We have used whatever funds were left from that donation to repair the roof. As you can see, the chairs need to be replaced, and there are tears in some of the curtains. What's worse is we no longer fill the seats as we once did. Even during our summer production, few come."

Louisa shook her head. How could this happen? She had seen every production offered. Sometimes more than once if it was done well. But even she had to admit the number of attendees had shrunk significantly over the past year.

"Once this play has run its course, I've considered selling the theater to a man who wishes to turn it into a gentlemen's club. He's assured me that the integrity of the theater itself will remain, but he will have to make some significant changes to the interior."

Louisa pitied this man. Whether a king had ever visited the theater was of no consequence, but it was clear the imminent loss pained Mr. Barker terribly.

As badly as she felt for Mr. Barker, however, her ire grew much quicker. There was no integrity in owning a gentlemen's club. After all, not only did such an establishment disregard women, it also left those of the lower classes with no place to find any form of entertainment. Unless this man planned to allow in the working class, which was highly unlikely.

"Ah, and speaking of the gentleman," Mr. Barker said, his jolliness returning. "Here he is now. If you'll excuse me a moment, I believe he wishes to speak with me."

Louisa turned, and her jaw fell open in disbelief. Sauntering down the aisle was the most arrogant, detestable man she had ever met in her life. To make matters worse, he was devilishly handsome with his blond hair and piercing blue eyes. Granted, she could not see his eyes from this distance, but she remembered them from their encounter at the tobacconist's shop. Remembered them quite well, indeed.

Hurrying to her friends, she whispered, "There he is! The knight who was rude to me. Do you remember me telling you about him?"

Six weeks prior, after hearing from the tailor that a gallant knight had moved to the area, Louisa and Jenny had gone into the shop for a glimpse of a renowned hero. Oh, fine! The idea was Louisa's. Jenny had vehemently protested against going in search of the man.

Either way, Louisa had found herself instantly smitten with the brave knight. But when she offered to pay him for his bravery with a kiss, he had scolded her. Scolded! As if she were some sort of child!

And now seeing him again, she once again recognized his arrogance. If only she had been thinking clearly during that initial encounter, she would have not been so foolish. And now he believed he could take away the only place anyone—rich or poor, young or old, male or female—could enter if they had the coin to pay? Well as far as she was concerned, he was sorely mistaken on that point.

And she planned to outright tell him so.

Aaron made his way down the center aisle, took a right, and ascended the staircase. At the edge of the stage, he stopped to wait for Mr. Barker to complete whatever it was he was doing.

A moment later, the proprietor hurried over, a smile breaking his face in half. "Sir Aaron, a most welcome surprise."

Aaron forced a smile. "You look incredibly cheerful today, Mr. Barker. I take it all is well?"

"Oh, quite, sir," Mr. Barker replied. He motioned toward the girls on the stage. "The local school for young women is here for their annual trip to the theater. It's an exciting time in their young lives, for many have never been beyond the seats in the auditorium."

Although Aaron gave a polite nod, he was anything but interested. A woman should be working on practical skills, such as the running of a household, sewing, or flower arranging. Even learning to play an instrument was a better use of one's time. Watching a performance was far different from understanding the inner workings of a production.

As Mr. Barker continued his usual monologue, Aaron felt someone staring at him. When he turned to look at the group of girls, he found it was not his imagination. Was that disdain he saw in the young lady's eyes, or were the shadows cast over her face playing tricks?

Then she took a step to the left, and the light lit up her features. It was the young woman from the tobacconist's shop!

Since that moment a month earlier, Aaron could not get this chit out of his mind. He had been perusing a selection of snuff boxes when the two young ladies had entered the shop.

What happened next could be described as nothing more than foolishness on his part. He had mistaken her for Lady Emmerton, a woman with whom he had scheduled a meeting as a means to get to her father. After wasting time complimenting her on her beauty—well, she *had been very* beautiful, on that he had not lied—he had then learned she was not Lady Emmerton. He never ascertained her name, but she had been a most unscrupulous young lady when she offered him a kiss.

Of course, he had wanted nothing more than to do just that. But after enduring the frustration of being tricked, he had ordered her from the shop. Women such as she were dangerous and could easily ruin a man's name. She was surely clever in her ability to tell lies, gossip, and leave a trail of destruction in her wake.

He snorted to himself. Weren't they all?

Yet there was no denying her blonde locks and blue eyes could make a man's breath catch in his throat, just as Aaron's did now. The way the natural pout of her plump lips begged to be kissed could not be ignored. That sort of temptation began with Eve in the garden, or so his late father had told him.

"Women are untrustworthy creatures who brought pain into the world," his father had said. "Heed my words, Son. Don't allow them to deceive you. Because if you do, you'll have no one to blame but yourself."

Until that conversation, Aaron believed the first man and woman were both guilty of the original sin. Apparently, he had been wrong, for his father told no lies. He might have been mistaken at times, but never did he tell outright fabrications.

"Sir?" Mr. Barker said, interrupting Aaron from his thoughts. "May I have the privilege of introducing you to the students of Mrs. Rutley's school? To be in the presence of such an honored guest here at the theater will surely give them much to talk about over the coming years."

Aaron had no desire to speak to petty schoolgirls, but Mr. Barker had a point. Good could come from these women's incessant prattle. Their good impression of him would quickly spread, thus earning him even more favor, which would benefit him quite well in the end.

"I would like nothing more," he said with a smile.

They walked over to the group of students, and Mr. Barker cleared his throat. "I would like to introduce you to a special guest. This is Sir Aaron Kirkwood, Knight of the Most Noble Order of the Garter. A hero who saved the Princess from harm just last year. Sir, this is Mrs. Rutley and her students."

Whispers of approval rose amongst the young ladies. Except one. The woman he had encountered in the tobacconist's shop dared to stare at a hairpin in her hand rather than show the diffidence due him! He would not be ignored, and most certainly not by a chit of a girl who was likely spoiled by her father at every turn! So many of her sort were these days.

"Mr. Barker is gracious in his introduction," Aaron intoned. "I did save the life of Princess Sophia, but it's not worth mentioning."

These final words brought him the praise he craved. It always did. Women gobbled up a man's attempt at humility like cats at a bowl of cream.

"Not at all, sir," the proprietor said, beaming. "What you did is worthy of praise. Would you please share your story with us?"

Eager smiles erupted around the circle of girls. Except for the lovely blonde, who dared to stifle a yawn.

Aaron decided to ignore the girl. At least he had a captive audience in the rest of the group. "I would love to," he said through teeth he was unable to unclench. "A year ago, I was walking through a dark forest known for two things: wolves and highwaymen, which I'm told are closely related."

This always drew a few laughs, and it did not fail to do so now from all except the blonde chit. She yawned again!

"I came upon five highwaymen attacking the royal carriage." He frowned. Still, the woman seemed uninterested. How dare she! He had never encountered such insolence, especially while telling his story. He hated the idea of embellishing an already inflated story, but she gave him no choice. If he told the truth, he would be laughed out of the village. When he finished, he gave a nod to Mr. Barker.

"Would it be too much if they were to ask questions, sir?" the proprietor asked.

Mrs. Rutley, whom he assumed was the headmistress, smiled. "We wouldn't wish to impose on the brave knight and interfere with his day."

The young blonde woman nodded. "I couldn't agree more, Mrs. Rutley. I would prefer to leave him to his own devices, myself."

A red-haired girl crinkled her brow in thought. "Oh, come now, Louisa. I'm sure we can ask him at least one question." She turned back to Aaron. "How is it possible for one man to fight five?"

The smile the blonde gave—Miss Louisa, was it?—sparked Aaron's ire. "By the grace of the Almighty, I prevailed," he replied. "But I'll not bore you with the particulars. I'm not one to boast about my skills in combat." Let them chew on that!

As more questions rose, Aaron's irritation grew. Not for what was asked but rather for Miss Louisa turning her back on him. He was a knight, for goodness' sake!

Finally, the headmistress said, "Thank you for sharing your time with us, Sir Aaron. We must return to the school."

"Oh, but I have one final question for our hero," came a sweet voice. Aaron turned to face Miss Louisa, and his breath caught. She twirled a finger around a long curl, and he wobbled on legs that threatened to give way at any moment. Then she playfully bit at her lip, which sent his heart to thudding against his sternum in a most delightful way. "You don't mind, do you, sir?"

Her fluttering eyelashes and pouty lips had Aaron gasping for breath. "Proceed," he managed to say, glad the effect she had on him was not evident in his voice.

Miss Louisa dropped her hands at her sides and tilted her head ever so slightly. "Our theater has been in Chatsworth for a hundred years."

"I'm aware of that. What of it?"

"Then why would you wish to turn it into a gentlemen's club?" she asked, that sweet smile still on her lips. "Surely, a knight would want an establishment where anyone could enter."

The other girls began to frown. Drat that Mr. Barker for revealing his plans for the place!

He fixed his gaze on Miss Louisa. She was certainly a great beauty and tempting in every way. Frustration washed over him, and a response would not come.

"I'll do what is in the best interest of my kind, Miss Louisa," he replied lamely.

Her smile was wicked, yet it sent a thrill down his spine that confused him far more than it should have. With a tempting smile, she said, "And I vow to do what is best in the interest of women."

Aaron frowned. The best interest of women? Was that a threat? Or a challenge? Either way, this young lady spoke boldly for *her* kind. He gave Mrs. Rutley an expectant look, but the headmistress made no effort to reprimand her pupil. Instead, she was smiling!

As Mrs. Rutley and her students filed away, Aaron also made a vow —that his and Miss Louisa's paths would cross again. Then he would see her put in her place.

And be able to admire those pouty lips again.

Chapter Three

Louisa returned the last of her painting tools to their place on the shelf in the morning room. She was not very proficient at painting—her attempts at fruit were dismal—but worse still was her singing, which could make a dog howl in fright. Therefore, she decided the slathers of paint on a canvas were much more palatable to everyone, herself included.

The younger students were at their lessons as she made her way to her bedroom. It had been three days since the visit to the theater, and the image of Sir Aaron Kirkwood had not left her thoughts. That arrogant smile, the way he ran a hand through his thick, dark blond hair. How he stood just so with his arms crossed, making his muscles press up against the fabric of his coat...

It should be a crime for a man that handsome to try to entice a woman as he did! His tantalizing ways had put the most unsavory thoughts in her mind.

How dare he?

To make matters worse, he meant to turn the theater into a den of thieves!

Louisa might be young, but she was well aware of what happened at a gentlemen's club. It was a place to which men escaped, where they could boast about their conquests of women. Jenny had confided in Louisa just last year that each member of such a club placed their name on a chart. Beside the names, they would add a tally for every woman over whom they had conquered.

They may attempt to hide their depravity in these clubs, but they were no different from the gaming hells, no matter what they called it. *Gentlemen* in the name simply indicated a higher class of patrons.

There was no better way to say it. Men were vile creatures. Their arrogance, especially that of a certain knight, had angered Louisa no end. If only she had her own money to purchase the theater, she would do so. If only to spite Sir Aaron. The theater was a place of entertainment with a rich history no matter how unverifiable the tales Mr. Barker told. Why did men believe they could simply march into a place and destroy it at will?

That last question had haunted her these past three days. At least she was able to share her frustrations with her Sisters.

As she drew near her bedroom, Louisa slowed at hearing Unity's soft voice drifting down the corridor.

"Now that Theodosia has been permitted to return home with me, we'll have plenty of time to plan for our journey to America."

Louisa entered the room and closed the door behind her. When she turned, three sets of eyes fell on her. "What's this about America?" she asked.

Theodosia rose from her place beside Ruth. "Next year, Unity and I are leaving for America."

"But why must you go so far?"

"Because that is where our future husbands live," Theodosia replied, as if she were teaching a child that mares birth foals.

Louisa smiled. "Why haven't you told me you're betrothed?" she asked, wrapping her arms first around Theodosia and then Unity. "Have you met them yet? And how did your parents make such an arrangement?"

Rather than the quick response she had expected, Unity returned to her place on the bed. "This is the brilliant part of the plan with which Ruth helped us," she said.

Louisa stifled a groan. Ruth having anything to do with anyone's plans would likely lead to victory but would also entail some sort of mischief.

"You see, next year when the Season begins, Unity and I will join Ruth and set sail to America. Once there, we'll begin our search for husbands."

Unable to keep her eyes from bulging, Louisa asked, "Are you saying you're not betrothed, then?"

Unity grinned. "Not yet. But we shall be. You see..."

She and Theodosia took turns explaining what Louisa could only define as lunacy. Each would tell her parents she wished to stay at the other's home until the Season began. To stave off any potential suitors, they would mention that a number of wealthy American gentlemen had shown an interest in them and promised to call when they returned to England the following year.

By the time they completed the bizarre telling, Louisa's head was aching. After all their education, after all they had learned at the school, they would throw it all away to stow away on a ship? Bound for America? She doubted she had ever heard anything so absurd!

"Ladies, I don't think..." Louisa's words trailed off upon seeing Unity and Theodosia's expressions. They were clearly determined to see this plan through, and no words—especially any Louisa had to say —would change their minds. She sighed. "Forget I said anything. But before you begin packing, I need your help in regard to the theater. There must be a way to keep it from being sold. Or at least sold to someone who does not wish to make it into something only a choice few can enjoy. If I were able to, I would purchase it. But I barely have enough to purchase a hat let alone an entire theater."

Ruth barked a laugh. "Why do you want to save that pile of rubble? Think of the poor tortured souls Mrs. Rutley forces there every year."

Louisa pursed her lips. "Because it's a wonderful place where a woman can enter equal to a man. It has a rich history and is an important part of the village."

Ruth's brows rose. "Are you saying it has nothing to do with a particular knight you're enamored with?"

The twins giggled at this but stopped when Louisa shot them a glare.

"Enamored with?" she asked, her cheeks burning. "That is the furthest thing from the truth! He's arrogant beyond reason, and his treatment of me was disrespectful. It would not surprise me to learn that he treats all women the same."

As she said this, an image of the knight came to mind. That wonderful smile would make any woman melt in his presence. He was surely the kind of man who would grab a woman without warning and kiss her if he so desired.

Strange. That thought was meant to make her dislike him more, but she was appalled when a soft sigh escaped her lips.

She shook herself. "What can I do to save the theater?"

Theodosia rose from the bed. "I wish I could help, but I've no idea what can be done about it. I must tidy my room, or Mrs. Rutley will forbid me from going into the village. And I saw a lovely trunk at the haberdashery last week that will be perfect for traveling. I would be greatly disappointed if it were sold before I could purchase it."

Unity followed Theodosia from the room, and Louisa turned to Ruth. "You always come up with all sorts of elaborate plans. Surely, you have an idea?"

Her friend walked over to the vanity table and placed her hands on its top. Sighing dramatically, she replied, "Mrs. Rutley will be attending a party at Lord Walcott's this Saturday. You should ask if you can accompany her."

Louisa frowned. "And how will that help?"

Ruth turned, her hands on her hips. "I can't help but wonder how any of you'll survive without me holding your hand at every step."

Although Louisa disagreed with Ruth on any number of subjects, with this one, she did not. Ruth was wise—in a mischievous way—and all the students had come to her for help at one time or another when they were unable to devise a plan for something they wanted. And her ideas, although a bit... unconventional, worked out quite well. Most of the time.

"Since many of the most prominent families are still in London," Ruth continued, "there will be a select few at his party. Old people in their forties such as Lord Walcott and Mrs. Rutley."

Louisa bit back the retort. Now was not the time to defend their headmistress. After all, Ruth did not mean anything unkind by her words.

"But what does that have to do with what I need?" Louisa asked.

Ruth gave an exaggerated sigh. "Don't you see? Old people love the theater. If anyone would go out of his or her way, it would be them. Get them to donate the funds you'll need to either buy it outright or to give to Mr. Barker to make the necessary repairs."

Louisa's heart leapt in excitement, and she threw her arms around her friend. "Ruth, you're brilliant! Oh, thank you! I'll go speak to Mrs. Rutley now."

Without waiting for a response, Louisa hurried downstairs and to Mrs. Rutley's office. Lifting her hand to knock, however, she paused at hearing a man's voice she did not recognize.

"I beg you to reconsider, Mrs. Rutley. Lord Ezra's offer is quite generous. You would receive a hefty sum for the school, allowing you to relocate. Enjoy a life of leisure or travel if you prefer."

Louisa's eyes widened. Lord Ezra Colburn was the uncle of Julia's husband, the Duke of Elmhurst. Why was he interested in purchasing Courtly Manor?

From what Julia had shared about the man, he was nefarious, to say the least. Of all she had learned, one point annoyed him above all others—he despised the idea of women learning anything beyond the mundane necessities.

It was no secret that he believed teaching women about history, philosophy, or the sciences was a waste of time. Did he intend to shut down the school so young ladies such as herself had one less form of education? If so, he was worse than Louisa had ever imagined!

"I've already considered his offer," Mrs. Rutley said, "and I politely refuse it. We've nothing further to discuss."

The sound of footsteps had Louisa scurrying away from the door. A man of perhaps thirty with spectacles and blond hair stormed out of the room. Going straight to the front door, he opened it and left without another word.

"Did you wish to speak to me, Louisa?"

Startled, Louisa turned to find the headmistress standing in the doorway to her office. "Oh, yes," she stammered.

Mrs. Rutley smiled as if the interaction with the bespectacled man had not occurred. "Then come inside." Once they were both seated— Mrs. Rutley behind her desk and Louisa in one of the two chairs opposite—she said, "Well? What is it, Louisa?"

"I wish to ask a favor, Mrs. Rutley. I heard that Lord Walcott is hosting a party on Saturday. May I attend with you?"

Mrs. Rutley stood and walked over to the window that overlooked the gardens. With her back to Louisa, she asked, "And why do you wish to attend?"

"I want to save the theater from that villain, the knight, Sir Aaron." She went on to explain what they had heard about the financial difficulties the theater was facing. She believed that if she could garner enough sympathy, the donations would come pouring in.

After completing the explanation, she frowned. "Mrs. Rutley, is everything all right?"

The headmistress turned, and although she smiled, something was wrong. Her eyes were not as bright as they usually were. "Everything is better than all right, Louisa. It's wonderful. Now, concerning the party, and more so, the theater. I've a question to ask you first."

Louisa nodded. "Of course, Mrs. Rutley."

"Are you doing this in order to save the theater or to stoke Sir Aaron's ire?"

Leaping from her chair, Louisa scowled and said, "He thinks a great deal of himself, Mrs. Rutley. But worse, he wishes to destroy one of the few places everyone can enjoy. Especially women! Are we to be relegated to our drawing rooms, working on embroidery for the remainder of our lives?"

To this, Mrs. Rutley laughed and came to stand in front of Louisa. "Perhaps today, and even tomorrow, that may be true. But I have hope to one day see that change. Who knows? Maybe you'll be the one to change the minds of men. And this theater just may be the very place to start."

Louisa beamed with pride. "I should purchase it and forbid men from entering! Let them endure being restricted from a particular place."

Mrs. Rutley's smile fell. "If we hurt others as they've hurt us, are we no better?"

Thanking her headmistress, Louisa returned to her room where she explained to Ruth what had transpired.

Yet it was later that night, as she considered Mrs. Rutley's advice of not hurting others, that the surefire grin of Sir Aaron came to mind. Oh, but he was a cocky man!

Clenching her fist beneath the covers, Louisa swore she would not allow him to beat her.

No matter how well-turned his calves were.

Chapter Four

Aaron strummed his fingers on his knee as the carriage ambled along the road. He despised being late to anything, be it be a meeting, dinner, or—as in this instance—a party being thrown by Henry, Lord Walcott.

He had been surprised to receive the invitation. After all, he had yet to meet the Earl of Walcott. Yet he had heard of him.

Was it because the earl had gotten wind of his plans for the theater? Aaron had wondered as he wrote out a hasty acceptance. Or could it be that Lord Walcott wished to invest in Aaron's endeavor? If so, perhaps not all was lost, after all.

Earlier this afternoon, Aaron had met with Lord Wellington, a round man with pudgy cheeks who looked ten years younger than his true age, to discuss the possibility of a joint venture in the gentleman's club.

Aaron had spent the better part of two hours explaining his plan, and although the man had wished Aaron luck, he had refused to take part.

"I'm afraid I've spent far too much time at the Rake Street gaming hell," Lord Wellington had said in a low whisper, as if someone were hiding within the walls of his home to listen in on his conversations.

Apparently, he had been caught exiting the premises with a woman who was not his wife on his arm, which sent him into hiding for the past two months as he waited for the rumors to die down.

Aaron had not visited the Rake Street gaming hell, but he had heard about it. It was no wonder the place was as busy as it was. Gentlemen had no other place to go to get away from the women who otherwise complicated their lives. Which was why the club was so important.

He had returned from Lord Wellington's home in plenty of time to wash and dress for the evening. Yet his cook, Mrs. Pentham had not only burned his dinner but her hand as well. That meant sending for the doctor and eating cold meats.

Stretching the taut muscles in his neck and shoulder, Aaron vowed that the miserable streak of bad luck would end this night. From what he had gathered in his short time in Chatsworth, Lord Walcott was one of the most respected men in all the village. His reach was far, which meant the invitation Aaron had received would put him in touch with other prominent men in the area, thus securing the investments to purchase the building that housed the theater.

Sighing, Aaron recalled his recent visit to the theater, and the unpleasantness he had endured at the tongue of Miss Louisa. Why would a headmistress allow one of her students to be so impertinent? Was that not part of the girl's instruction at the school—how to be respectful of those deserving of it? Apparently not.

His father had once told him of such schools for young women. They were meant to teach their students practical skills. Rumors had reached Aaron's ears that those who attended Mrs. Rutley's School for Young Women learned about subjects expected of their male counterparts, but he had his doubts. Surely, they would not waste time on philosophy or, God forbid, the sciences.

It was not as if Aaron did not like women, for he did. There were some he respected—his mother, for example, who had looked after him and doted on him daily. How many times had she told him his handsome looks would get him far in this world? Would catch the eye of every lady, of every woman, he encountered? Too many times to count.

She worked to make everything in their home perfect in every way. He and his sister wanted for nothing, and that was because of their mother. Oh, their father had provided for his family financially, but his mother had been the one who ran their household and shared her love with her children. Just thinking of her made Aaron realize how much he missed her. He would pay a visit to where she currently lived in Wales, once the gentlemen's club was completed.

Despite how much he respected his mother, however, or how much he admired his sister, so many contemporary women made every attempt to rise above themselves. They had their place in society and the running of the home. But if women were learning about science, soon they would want to discuss—and possibly take over—business as well.

If that happened, all mankind would be doomed. That was one fact about which his father had been adamant. And this had been confirmed when he had overheard too many gentlemen complain about how their wives nearly bankrupted them with their excessive spending. If they could not maintain a household properly, how could they ever be successful in matters of business? Why, such nonsense would likely bankrupt the entire country in a matter of months!

Regardless, Aaron hoped to one day find a woman worthy of marrying him, one who was intelligent but knew her place and had the ability to take care of his household. Yet finding her seemed impossible. Especially after witnessing Miss Louisa's actions.

A headstrong woman was nothing but trouble, and he pitied the man who fell for her charms.

Once he arrived at Foxly Manor, the estate belonging to Lord Walcott, Aaron hurried inside. After the butler took his coat and hat, he made his way to the opulent ballroom where the sounds of a cello and a violin greeted him. To his surprise, there looked to be nearly thirty or so people in attendance, although most were far older than he.

"Sir Aaron?"

Aaron turned as a silver-haired man approached, his smile welcoming.

"Henry Walcott," the man said. "I'm so pleased you accepted my invitation."

Shaking the hand the earl offered, Aaron said, "Thank you for including me. I apologize for my tardiness."

"There are worse crimes committed," Lord Walcott said with a laugh. "So, how do you find our little village?"

"I like it very much," Aaron replied and went on to regale all its wonderful qualities, which were few. A passing footman allowed him to draw his compliments to a close. "Which led me to hear of Mr. Barker's plight," he concluded as he took a glass of wine from the proffered tray. "It then occurred to me. Why not convert the old building into something few villages of this size enjoy—a gentlemen's club? A place where distinguished men may go to relax without the pressures that come with entertaining our female counterparts. Now I'm on the hunt for investors and would like to offer you the opportunity to be among the first."

Lord Walcott took a sip of his wine. "I must agree that many gentlemen enjoy such establishments." This made Aaron smile. Until the earl continued, "I, however, am not one of them. But I do wish you luck in your endeavor, Kirkwood." He looked past Aaron and smiled. "Well, look who we have here. Mrs. Rutley, please, join us."

Aaron frowned as the woman from the theater walked up to them. Her gown was green with yellow flowers, and gray sprinkled her otherwise brown hair. She was a lovely woman despite her advanced years.

"Thank you for having us," she said with a polite nod.

"May I present Sir Aaron Kirkwood," Lord Walcott said. "Sir Aaron, Mrs. Agnes Rutley."

Mrs. Rutley gave him a polite smile. "It's good to see you again, Sir Aaron."

Aaron forced a smile. He did not have time to waste speaking with a headmistress of a woman's school. "You, as well, Mrs. Rutley."

Why would the earl invite this woman to a party? Granted, a man of title would be acquainted with a headmistress, but inviting her to a gathering meant for the titled folk was another matter altogether.

"Well, I'll leave the two of you to speak," he said, giving a small bow. Mrs. Rutley seemed pleasant enough, but he had more important matters with which to take up his time. He was here to find investors, not make friends.

"Before you go," Lord Walcott said. "The thin man with the crimson coat there beside the wall. That is Nathaniel, Lord Talbot. He may be someone interested in your endeavor."

Thanking him, Aaron gave a quick nod and hurried away. "I beg your pardon. Lord Talbot? I am Sir Aaron Kirkwood."

"Ah, the knight I've heard so much about," the gentleman said, the lines on his face deepening with his smile. "What a treat to have you with us this evening."

Retreating to his humble personality, Aaron lowered his head. "I'm nothing more than a simple man, my lord. One who came to the aid of the Crown, just as any good Englishman would."

"Simple man?" Lord Talbot said with a snort. "I'd say you're far from simple. You're a true hero. One deserving of recognition."

Aaron's pride swelled, but he tempered it. He had a mission to complete. "Have you heard about the troubles the proprietor of the theater is having?"

Lord Talbot frowned. "I have. Mr. Barker is not alone. Many are suffering in these difficult times."

"I could not agree with you more, my lord," Aaron said with an exaggerated sigh. "It pains me that such a well-respected man is suffering. Which is why I've decided to lend him my aid."

"Oh?" Lord Talbot asked. "And how will you do that?"

"By seeing him receive enough money that he'll not have to work again," Aaron replied. "You see, I hope to purchase the building and turn it into a gentlemen's club." He went on to explain his plans in full, earning him a wide grin.

"If you can get Barker to sell that theater to you, I'll surely invest. We men need a place to call our own!"

Aaron smiled. This invitation had been well worth his time. And the evening became better when Lord Talbot added, "You know who may be interested in such an enterprise? Zacharias, the Earl of Brayberry." He pointed across the room. "He's always looking for new ways to invest his money. He's the curly-haired man standing beside the fireplace."

As Aaron turned his gaze on the man Lord Talbot had pointed out, it did not remain on that gentleman more than a moment. His attention immediately shifted to Miss Louisa who stood nearby. What she was doing was apparent. She was undermining his carefully laid plans.

Yet it was the manner in which she implemented her actions that sparked his ire.

From the small distance that separated them, he could hear her polite laugh as she placed a gentle hand on the arm of a rotund man of around sixty years of age. If that action was not forward enough, her attire bordered on the obscene. Her yellow dress had white ribbons woven through the hems of the puffed sleeves and of the bottom of her skirt.

Her blonde hair was held back by ribbons that matched those on her dress, and seductive curls covered her ears. But what completed her look was her beautiful face and pouty lips, both of which drew the eyes of every man there. Including Aaron.

It clearly defined the feminine contours of her body. And she displayed a goodly amount of bosom...

His heart thudded as his body heated with desire. How dare she cause his thoughts to become impure! If she had acted like a lady and refrained from offering him a kiss at the tobacconist, he would not be thinking of her as nothing short of a harlot!

If she wished to stoop to such levels, he would show her how it was done properly. With grace and dignity.

He returned his attention to Lord Brayberry, a rather tall man in his middle years with black, curly hair. Beside him stood a young lady who was clearly his daughter. No older than twenty, she wore a brown gown that matched her hair. Her face was freckled, and her looks were plain. Extremely plain.

One of the benefits of being handsome was the ability to distance himself from homely women. That did not mean he could not speak to her father, however.

The poor girl's destined to marry a penniless viscount, he thought.

"Pardon me, Lord Brayberry?" Aaron asked as he approached the pair. "Allow me to introduce myself. Sir Aaron Kirkwood, newly arrived in Chatsworth."

The young lady gasped. "Father, this is the knight I told you about. Do you remember?"

Lord Brayberry frowned. "Calm yourself, Hannah. Don't embarrass me. Of course I recall. Who can forget the tale of a brave man willing to put his life at risk to save the Princess? What can I do for you, Sir Aaron?"

Aaron explained his plans for the theater, and the earl puckered his lips in thought. "I'm unsure that such an investment is wise," he replied. "Here, let me get us another drink. Where's a blasted footman?" He took Aaron's empty glass and went in search of another, leaving Aaron alone with the daughter.

Now Aaron would teach Miss Louisa a lesson. That he would win in matters of using subtle seduction to get what he wanted.

Seizing the opportunity, Aaron grinned at the young lady. "I imagine you're already spoken for. Is that not so, Lady Hannah?"

Lady Hannah giggled, which sounded like old iron hinges in need of oil. "No, sir. But I'm hoping for more prospects come next Season."

"Perhaps telling your father how wonderful I am may help you," he whispered, adding a wink. "If you would like me to call on you, that is."

The young woman gave a vigorous nod, her cheeks reddening.

Lord Brayberry returned and handed Aaron a glass of brandy, and Aaron could taste the victory. The lovestruck girl would all but beg her father to invest in the gentlemen's club, thus doing Aaron's work for him.

To say he was tempted to tell Miss Louisa of his victory was an understatement. But he was a man of dignity and would refrain from gloating and instead continue to seek investors.

He moved on to another gentleman, who refused outright, as did the next. By the third rejection, he was growing suspicious.

"I've already promised that courteous young lady I'd donate to save the theater, not ruin it," the hunched Lord Montgomery croaked as he clutched his cane. "I'll not help build a house of debauchery!" This he said with the added wave of a gnarled finger, reminding Aaron of his tutor during his time at Eaton's College.

Excusing himself, Aaron moved across the room to where several couples he had yet to meet stood. What young lady had Lord Montgomery meant? It was clear the word "courteous" did not describe Miss Louisa. And given his advanced years, any woman below the age of forty was likely a young lady to him.

As he continued to make the rounds, Aaron's ire began to grow. Twice more he was rejected for the same reason as Lord Montgomery had given—a mystery lady had spoken to them first.

Could it be Miss Louisa?

As Aaron scanned the room, he realized there was no other explanation. Across the room, Miss Louisa was speaking with one man whilst smiling at another! Apparently, she was using her feminine wiles along with a mixture of carefully crafted words to convince the man that her plan for the theater was better than his.

He downed the remainder of his brandy in one gulp. Whatever game she was playing, he would put a stop to it! This party was a collection of proper and greatly respected gentlemen and certainly not a place for a young lady to flounce about and entice men, no matter their ages!

For a moment, he was tempted to confront her for her behavior but thought better of it. Instead, he crept away to wait for her to leave. Then he would pounce and see her put in her place!

Chapter Five

The timing of Lord Walcott's party could not have been better as far as Louisa was concerned. She intended to speak to every gentleman in attendance, petitioning them to do their part in saving the theater. Once enough funds were pledged, she would then go to Mr. Barker to inform him that there was no need to sell. At least not to that knight of all people.

After the first hour at the party, Louisa was teeming with confidence. Two men, both likely older than England itself, had spoken at length about the necessity of a theater in Chatsworth. With the promise to donate twenty pounds each, she was well on her way to reaching her goal. What that goal was remained to be seen, but the cost of a theater could not be all that much, could it?

Louisa knew her lack of knowledge when it came to intricacies of business could be a hindrance. As would her limited understanding of men and the inner workings of their minds. After expressing her concerns to Mrs. Rutley, her headmistress had promised to speak to Lord Walcott about lending her a book on the best methods for conducting business.

Well, she had work to do. So, she returned to presenting her idea to the guests.

After three gentlemen in a row politely declined, however, disappointment began to settle on her. With her confidence waning, Louisa considered what to do. The idea of more rejections did not sit well with her. But how could she ensure success?

She paused. There was one strength she possessed on which she could always rely. Flirting. Of course, it had to be done in a respectable manner—she was no harlot to throw herself at any man just to get her way. If she could have gotten the investors without coquetry, she would have chosen that avenue. But what choice did she have? The theater had to be saved. And it was not as if she were making promises that would later place her in hot water.

Having consumed one glass of wine thus far, she chanced taking a second. This time, she took polite sips rather than full gulps as she had done previously. The last thing she needed was to become drunk and make a ninny of herself.

A young man of an age with Louisa approached. He had two prominent front teeth and wild blond hair that looked as if it had never seen a brush. But his smile was hearty, and kindness rolled off him in waves.

"Are you Miss Dunston?" the man asked.

She nodded. "I am."

"I'm so pleased," he said with a relieved sigh. "Lord Walcott told me about your endeavor to save the theater."

"Did he?" Louisa asked with a smile.

"He did, indeed. Oh, my apologies. My name is Rupert Scarsdale. My father is Baron Hollinsworth. I had intended to go to London for the Season but chose to wait another year. After all, why would one wish to endure the continuous rejections?" His smile broadened, and his teeth reminded Louisa of a mule owned by a neighbor near her family home. "At least there are still lovely young ladies such as yourself here in Chatsworth."

Louisa felt sorry for him. He was unfortunate-looking and would likely catch the eye of few young ladies. What a terrible way for anyone to live.

Well, she had been blessed with comeliness. Perhaps she could use that gift to aid him with his confidence. And if she was able to convince him to help her reach her goal with the theater... well, it would be nothing more than a reward for her benefaction.

"I can assure you, Mr. Scarsdale, that many young ladies will be more than pleased to have you send a card requesting a call." She lowered her voice and batted her eyelashes. "I know I would."

He let out a nervous chuckle. "I'll certainly remember that. And I may just take you up on that offer and send a card to the school."

School? How did he know she attended the school?

As if reading her thoughts, he added, "Mrs. Rutley and I met earlier."

Giving him a flirty smile, Louisa rested a hand on his arm. There. Now he would feel better about himself. But it was time to collect her reward. "I would love to tell you about my plans for the Chatsworth Theater." For several minutes, she repeated her rehearsed speech, just as she had earlier. Upon finishing, she let out a breathy sigh. "Do you think you can help me?"

Flushed to his ears, Mr. Scarsdale nodded. "What a kind gesture on your part. Yes, of course I would like to contribute to the arts. Let's say ten pounds? I don't have it on me now, but if you send word when you'll need to collect it, I'll see it gets to you."

Promising she would, Louisa excused herself. Mrs. Rutley was alone alongside a far wall, and she walked over to join her headmistress.

"So, are you having any success?" Mrs. Rutley asked. "I saw you speaking with Mr. Scarsdale. He appears to be smitten with you."

Louisa grinned. "He was, and he's promised to donate to my cause. Two others have, as well. By the end of the night, I may have more willing to help."

"Then I wish you luck." Mrs. Rutley glanced at the glass in Louisa's hand. "And do be careful with the wine. I would suggest you drink that one slowly. Make it last the rest of the evening. You don't have a head for wine."

After promising she would, the women parted ways. Louisa stopped in front of the string quartet and sighed. The music was lovely, and the ballroom was such a romantic setting. Too bad only two men of marrying age were in attendance.

Well, three if one counted Mr. Scarsdale, which she did not. The problem was that the other two both had a young lady on their arms. That meant no romance for her this evening. Not if she hoped to catch the eye of a man without a hunched back or carrying a cane.

Her eyes fell on Lady Hannah Brayberry. A sweet young lady Louisa had met once before, Lady Hannah wore a dress the color of dried grass, a very unbecoming color for her in Louisa's estimation. Beside her stood a gentleman that could only be her father.

Louisa had heard of Lord Brayberry. According to Jenny, he spent a great deal of time at the Rake Street gaming hell—he and his mistress. If she had not seen it for herself, Louisa would have chalked it up to pure rumor. Yet the previous summer, she had indeed seen the good earl helping a woman who was not his wife into his carriage.

How must his daughter feel knowing her father was disloyal to her mother? It had to be a terrible situation for anyone concerned. Perhaps she should go to cheer up the girl. Yes, that was the right thing to do.

Halfway across the ballroom, however, she came to an abrupt stop. That knight was here? Why on earth would Lord Walcott even consider inviting such a scoundrel to his party? Well, she would learn what sort of lies the man was telling that poor, innocent girl!

Louisa sneaked behind a large potted tree, straining to hear what the knight and Lady Hannah were discussing. What she heard made bile rise in her throat. Sir Aaron was *flirting* with the poor unsuspecting Lady Hannah! And he dared to make a promise to call on her in exchange for her helping him secure her father as an investor in his club? At least with Mr. Scarsdale, her reasoning was sound— approaching him would help improve his confidence.

To her horror, Sir Aaron flashed Lady Hannah a smug grin.

With her blood boiling and her fists clenched, Louisa swallowed a growl and stormed away.

How dare he use his handsome looks to lure an innocent young lady such as Lady Hannah. And all so she could betray her father! A gentleman with such a chiseled jawline, deep-blue eyes, and overtly masculine voice was too much for any woman to resist.

Retreating to a far corner, Louisa continued her observation. Lord Brayberry returned and handed the knight a glass of wine. As he lifted the glass, the fabric on the sleeve of his coat tightened. Were his arms that muscled?

What would it be like to touch them?

Just the thought sent Louisa's head spinning. Yet like raindrops filling a puddle, more filled her mind. Only a rogue would flaunt himself so callously in public! It was just as she had suspected upon encountering him at the tobacconist's shop. Sir Aaron was no gentleman but rather an uncouth beast.

Angry at the man for causing such unwelcome thoughts, Louisa glanced at the massive fireplace on the opposite side of the room. As warm as she felt, she could have been standing beside it. And her throat was dry. She took a rather large, unladylike swallow of her wine in an attempt to stave off the heat. If she had any hope of gaining more donations, she would have to compose herself.

And that meant averting her eyes from temptation.

She caught sight of a gentleman with round cheeks and a robust laugh. Mr. Walter Fernside owned several of the buildings in the village proper, which he rented to the various shops. She had met Mr. Fernside the previous winter at the bakery, which he also ran. Like many of the townspeople, Mrs. Rutley had known the man for years.

"Good evening, Mr. Fernside," she said, giving him a pleasant smile. "I don't know if you remember me, but I'm Miss Louisa Dunston. We met last year." When he frowned, she added, "At the bakery?"

A light of recognition lit up his face. "Ah, yes, of course. You're one of Mrs. Rutley's students. I hope you're not here to complain about my bread." Before Louisa could reply, he gave a hearty chuckle. "I'm only joking."

She gave a small laugh. "I've actually come to you for another reason. I'm sure you've heard that the theater is in dire straits. Well, I wish to seek your help." She went on to explain her plan.

When she was done, Mr. Fernside gave a sad nod. "Sadly, I haven't any money to donate. But I do have a wonderful story about how Mrs. Fernside and I met there."

Louisa gave him a polite smile and listened as he told a wonderful tale of falling in love. Several times, he had her laughing outright, his telling was so humorous. Or perhaps she had consumed too much wine.

"By the time she was gone, I realized I hadn't given her my name!" he said with a loud guffaw.

Louisa tittered and patted the man on the arm. "Well, it seems it all worked out since she's now your wife. But thank you for sharing your story with me. I can see that what I'm doing is well worth the effort."

Excusing herself once more, Louisa returned to Mrs. Rutley, keeping an eye out for Sir Aaron. When she could not catch sight of him, she sighed with relief. Good, he had left the party. Civility had returned.

"Lord Walcott has offered to loan you a book from his library," the headmistress said. "I understand that he has a nice collection of books on the best business practices of the age."

"Oh, I must thank him!" Louisa said. Then she caught sight of the earl speaking with several of his guests. "When he is not occupied, of course. Do you mind if I go now?"

"I don't see why not," Mrs. Rutley replied. "And take your time. Once you've found what you'd like, we can leave. Unless you would prefer to remain?"

Giving one last survey of the room, she replied, "I wouldn't mind remaining a while longer." After all, now that Sir Aaron was no longer in attendance, she could continue her requests for donations.

After receiving directions to the library, Louisa made her way down the corridor to a candlelit room filled with dark-stained oak shelves on every wall but one. Two windows sat in that wall, a sideboard between them. Deep leather chairs had been placed in various spots around the room, a side table with an oil lamp beside each, allowing readers a variety of choices to enjoy their books.

Being in such a masculine sanctuary gave her a thrill. It was as if she had entered a sacred place closed off to her at any other time.

A single candle sat on the sideboard, allowing just enough light to see by. She lifted it and moved along the bookcases, peering at the various titles until she came to a particular shelf. There, she perused the tomes until one caught her eye. *The Wealth of Nations* by Adam Smith.

Setting down the candle, she removed the book and flipped through the pages. Yes, this was exactly what she needed.

"What is this?" a deep baritone demanded, causing her heart to stall. She turned as the wretched knight stormed toward her and pulled the book from her hand. "Have you any idea how angry Lord Walcott would be if you were to steal from him?"

"Steal?" Louisa asked, snatching back the book. "I'll have you know he permitted me to be here. How dare you accuse me of thievery!"

He narrowed his eyes at her. "Oh, you're far more than a thief, Miss Louisa. I've seen you toying with the various gentlemen in attendance this evening, using your flirtatious ways to coax coins from their pockets! Why are you working so hard to sabotage my plans? You know I'm searching out investors for my club, and you're stealing them from me!"

Louisa stared at him in utter shock. His arrogance knew no bounds! Other women might endure such maltreatment, but she certainly would not.

"First of all, we are not acquainted well enough for you to address me in such a familiar manner. I am Miss Dunston to you. Second, I've stolen nothing." She poked a finger into his chest, which was a mistake, for she met a solid mass that made her legs wobble. "And I was not flirting. I was merely speaking with them."

A sudden image of Mr. Scarsdale came to mind, but she dismissed it. That had *not* been flirting!

"And how dare you accuse me of churlish behavior," she said with an indignant raise of her chin. "You promised to call on Lady Hannah if she influenced her father." Sir Aaron's gaping mouth had Louisa smiling in victory. Narrowing her eyes, she whispered, "Oh, yes, *noble* knight. I heard it myself. And I saw how you smiled at her so don't bother denying it."

"I deny nothing. But can you honestly say you would not have done the same to me?"

Blood pounded in Louisa's temples. "You can only you pray I would do so!" she countered.

"Ha! And what about your pouty lips? Your feminine wiles? Admit it! You use both to draw the attention of men."

He stepped closer, their bodies only an arm's length apart. The pounding in her heart became stronger and her throat parched. Yet she managed to whisper, "And what about the way you wear your smile like a trophy?"

"Oh, ho! What say you about how your eyes call to me? Not to mention how you fingered your hair at the theater." His voice had dropped to a near whisper, a caress on her spine. "Have you any idea what that did to me?"

Louisa had never been one for fainting, but she was certain she would do so now. He had stepped close, their bodies a mere few inches apart.

His masculine fragrance of orange and sandalwood overwhelmed her senses. His broad chest was tempting her to touch him.

Yet through it all, she found the strength to speak. "Well, you should search out a better tailor," she retorted. "Your coats need to be better fitted. I see how you use your well-formed arms to tempt women. And you're well aware of what they do to me!"

He reached for the book in her hand, and she made no attempt to keep him from taking it and placing it on the shelf beside them. Nor did she offer any resistance when he placed his hands on her arms. In fact, she welcomed his touch.

"You're a beautiful woman, there is no doubt about that. But your unwillingness to remain silent must be rectified."

Jutting her chin, Louisa looked into his piercing blue eyes. "No man will ever silence me," she breathed. "No matter how handsome he may be."

He tightened his grip on her arm. It was not enough to cause pain, but it sent a thrilling shiver down her spine.

"No woman, no matter how tempting she may be," his eyes raked over her, "will ever command me."

Then to her shock, he pulled her against him. The touch of their bodies ignited a fire inside her she had never experienced before. Shame should have filled her. But instead, desire did.

"You beast!" she said without conviction. "Release me, or I'll scream!"

"If you do, I'll silence you with this, for I'll never let you go." Before she could react, he pressed his lips to hers.

Louisa had often dreamed of her first kiss. It would happen while standing beneath a tree with a flower in her hand. Her suitor would be a respectable gentleman, and his kiss would be soft and sensual, just enough to stave off her desire for him.

This kiss was nothing like that.

Powerful, possessive, it turned her body into soft clay in his hands. Her mind told her to push him away, but her heart would not allow her to do so. Instead, she placed her hands on his arms. Just as she had imagined, firm, strong muscles lay beneath.

She found herself wanting more—more kisses, more chances to touch him. And she secretly wished he thought the same.

Yet as suddenly as the kiss began, common sense returned. She pushed against his chest and pulled away. It was the most difficult thing she had ever done in her life, but it was what she had to do.

"I should alert the magistrates about your roguish behavior!" she said, grabbing the book from where he had left it. "Pray we never see one another again."

His soft chuckle warned her insides as she hurried to the door.

"Admit it. You're smitten with me, Miss Dunston. And I've bested you into silence with a single kiss."

Louisa stopped at the door and turned to face him, her eyes narrowed to slits. Sir Aaron was leaning against the bookcase, his arms crossed over his chest in that infuriating manner that made her body heat once more. Pushing aside the distracting thoughts, she took a deep breath. "I'll remember this night always, Sir Aaron, for it was when I realized how much I despise you!"

And with that, she hurried down the corridor to return to the ballroom.

"Did you find anything interesting?" Mrs. Rutley asked as Louisa joined her.

Louisa nodded. "I did, thank you. But I'm much more tired than I realized. Do you mind if we leave? I'm afraid I've spoken to all the remaining gentlemen."

Chapter Six

"You've no idea how much I feared for my life!" Louisa wailed as she sat with Unity, Theodosia, and Ruth. "I attempted to break his hold on me, but he was too strong. That was when he—much to my horror—kissed me! And I must say, it had to be the worst kiss any young lady would ever receive. One would think a rogue such as he would have enough practice, but alas, that was not the case."

It had taken her two days to work up the courage to share with her friends what had taken place at Lord Walcott's party. Not because she feared them learning the predicament in which she had found herself but rather because she was afraid they would sense how much she had enjoyed it. To her relief, no one interrupted her. Even Ruth remained silent until she finished her telling.

"I'm no longer frightened, though my trust in men has lessened further." She sighed heavily. "I pray that other innocent women are not held against their will as I was."

"I don't know," Unity said, frowning. "Your blush is far deeper than it should be for one with your sentiment. I think you enjoyed it more than you're letting on."

Ruth barked a laugh. "Of course, she liked it. She's just unwilling to accept that fact."

Louisa gasped. "I'm accosted—and nearly kidnapped!—and you believe I enjoyed it? Not only was I betrayed by Sir Aaron, but now I'm being betrayed by those closest to me! Theodosia? Surely, you don't agree with them."

Theodosia sighed. "I think Ruth is right."

"Unity?" Louisa asked, shaking her head in disbelief.

Unity stood and walked toward the door. "My opinion is that you believe you're being truthful. But Ruth is correct. You're enamored by him. But I must go. Amy's expecting me to help her with her Latin."

"Wait for me," Theodosia called after her.

Once the door was closed, Louisa sighed. "Well, although my innocence was nearly torn away from me by a vile man, I must push on. I have other more important matters with which to concern myself. And now I'm more determined than ever to solicit more donations. I can't allow that man to purchase the theater. It means too much to me."

Ruth walked over to the vanity table, chose a hairpin from those Diana had left for them, and placed it in her red locks. "Are you sure you wish to go into battle with this man?" she asked. "He is a knight, after all, and the village respects him."

Louisa snorted. "I'm scared of no man or beast, and he's both," she said with a firm nod. "I must find a way to stop him."

She had never been to battle, of course. The mere sight of a spider, which she thought to be the ghastliest beast on earth, sent her into instant panic. But this was more than defeating the knight. She wished for the theater to remain, and so it would.

"Why not ask Mrs. Rutley if he may call on you."

Louisa's brows rose in horror. "Why would I do that?"

"It's clear he's attracted to you," Ruth said, undaunted by Louisa's harsh tone. "Do what you typically do—use your feminine wiles on him."

Louisa gasped. "My feminine wiles? Am I to blame for the attractiveness with which I was gifted? When I smile at a man, he believes I've taken some sort of interest in him when I simply wish to be friendly. That means the fault lies with him and not with me."

Ruth took a wrap from her bed and placed it around her shoulders. "No, I meant nothing like that. You don't do those things." She smiled. "I saw how you used them to distract Sir Aaron at the theater. It worked then and will do so again when he calls on you." She patted at her pockets as if searching for something and nodded. "The sooner you accept it, the better off you'll be."

Once Ruth was gone, Louisa thought of the day at the theater. It was true. She had pushed out her lower lip, had battled her eyelashes at him a bit more than usual. Ruth was right. Sir Aaron had even lost the ability to speak.

Yet her actions had been justified. How else was she to distract a rogue from tempting impressionable young schoolgirls? Therefore, Louisa was certainly not the flirt Ruth claimed her to be.

And why squander what can be used for good? Even if it was for her own gain.

What if she invited the knight to tea? Would she be able to appeal to his sense of self-righteousness and get him to stop his antics?

She smiled. It truly was a brilliant idea. Yet where did the knight reside? Well, if anyone knew the goings on in the village, it would be Mrs. Shepherd.

Making her way to the kitchen, Louisa stopped in the doorway to watch as the cook kneaded a ball of dough, whistling a merry tune.

"You know, it's impolite to stare, even at a cook," Mrs. Shepherd said without looking up from her work. Louisa laughed, and the cook wiped her hands on a cloth. "Now, what can I do for you?"

"Are you familiar with Sir Aaron Kirkwood? He's recently moved to the area."

"The knight?" Mrs. Shepherd asked as she returned to her kneading. "I am."

"Do you happen to know where he resides?"

The cook grunted as she pounded a fist into the dough. "I do."

Louisa sighed. "May I ask where that is? I would like to write him a letter to... thank him for all he's done."

She had meant to say that the correspondence had been due to the story he had shared at the theater. Instead, she recalled the way he had kissed her. Which could not happen again. Regardless, she certainly could not tell Mrs. Shepherd she hoped to invite him to the school so she could flirt with him.

"I'll tell you, but you'd best be careful with that one," Mrs. Shepherd said, placing a floury hand on her hip. "There are all sorts of rumors about him."

Despite Mrs. Rutley's insistence that one should never listen nor share rumors, Mrs. Shepherd spent a great deal of time doing both. Which was why most of the girls went to the cook rather than the headmistress when it came to learning the truth about someone.

"Oh?" Louisa asked, pulling her brows up innocently. "What sort of rumors?"

"I've heard he likes to have his way with women," the cook replied. "He's one of those men who thinks he can kiss any woman he wants whenever he wants."

Louisa sighed. He was as vile as she had suspected. When he had kissed her, her body had taken on a life of its own, but that did not mean *she* enjoyed it. Granted, her thoughts were muddled for several hours afterward. And she could still feel his hands gripping her arms two days later. But that was a natural reaction to a man's touch.

Should she have fought it? Of course. Was that not the very reason she had fled the library when she had? Plus, she had consumed more wine than usual. Alcohol also erased one's senses.

"He bought the old Yeats' estate on the other side of the village. I imagine you can write him there."

"Thank you, Mrs. Shepherd," Louisa said. "I believe I'll do that now."

Soon, she was sitting at the small desk in her room, a piece of parchment in front of her and a quill pen in her hand. She would have to balance flattery with propriety. It seemed like ages before she felt ready, and once she began, the words flowed freely.

When she finished, she read over the correspondence once more. Satisfied, she sealed the letter and went in search of Mrs. Rutley. When she was unable to find her, Louisa returned to the kitchen. Mrs. Shepherd was just dropping a dollop of jam on the tarts she had baked.

"Have you seen Mrs. Rutley?" Louisa asked. "I can't seem to find her."

"She had to go into the village," Mrs. Shepherd replied. "Won't be back for at least another hour is my guess. What is it you need?"

"To send off this," Louisa replied, showing the letter. "Oh well, I suppose it can wait until tomorrow."

"Leave it on her desk," the cook said. "She'll see it sent." With a grunt, she leaned over and picked up her dropped spoon.

Not wanting to bother the cook any longer, Louisa went to Mrs. Rutley's office and set the letter on her desk. Then her curiosity piqued upon seeing a letter with a familiar postmark. Conflict rose in her. Her nosiness had gotten her into trouble over the years. One particular instance had revealed a terrible secret she wished she could forget. A secret that made her the person she was today.

A person she did not always like all that much.

Worry filled the pit of her stomach. These were Mrs. Rutley's private things. To go through them was a betrayal.

But what if she learned something important just as she had all those years ago?

With a glance over her shoulder to make certain no one was nearby, Louisa pulled the document from its place and unfolded the parchment.

It was from Unity's father. He would be arriving to collect her in just over a fortnight.

Sighing, Louisa refolded the letter and returned it to its place. This was not new information. Unity had already announced as much. It would be a sad day having another sister leave. But for now, there were more pressing matters to consider.

Returning to her bedroom, Louisa began to plan a way to handle a roguish knight who needed to learn a lesson.

Later as she lay beneath the covers, the plan complete, a smile crept onto her lips. Not only would she win over the knight, but she might also get just one more kiss.

All to save the theater, of course.

Chapter Seven

Aaron had never engaged in acts of war, at least not on a battlefield or with weapons other than his fists or tongue. The occasional disagreement during a hunt, in the fine negotiations for the purchase of property, or an agreement in trade was where his experience in warfare lay. But suffering a woman as stubborn —or as tempting—as Miss Louisa Dunston was a new experience altogether.

As the carriage ambled toward the school, he unfolded the letter he had received the previous day and reread it for the fifth time. Its words were simple, yet he could not shake the feeling that there was more behind their simplicity.

Sir Aaron,

After we spoke at the party held at the home of our mutual acquaintance, Lord Walcott, several things came to mind. It is my hope that we may discuss what transpired so we may eradicate any ill feelings that we may hold against one another.

. . .

The rest of the letter requested that he call to the school today and thus why he was en route there now.

Having read a variety of books on warfare, Aaron was well aware that a letter such as this was meant to make him drop his guard. He had to give Miss Dunston her fair due. She was both beautiful and wise. He imagined picnicking with her, laughing, sharing stories, and enjoying one another's company. Afterward, he would parade her around the village so everyone could see. He could not help the grin that spread across his lips as he pictured such a thing. He did not doubt the villagers would stop and gawk in admiration at the striking couple they made.

"Look how happy she is!" some would exclaim.

"How can a man be so handsome?" would say others. *"She is so lovely. No other woman can compare!"*

Women would whisper behind their hands because of their jealousy of them.

Yet as these thoughts filled his mind, he had to ask himself whether the imagined strain Miss Dunston would put on him was worth being able to parade her. She already dared to read books meant for men. What if she wished to discuss the topic?

What a pity Mrs. Rutley's School for Young Women had not taught that women had their place in society. And that did not mean in the affairs of business. What could they possibly know about signing contracts or enticing investors? Miss Dunston might understand the intricate games of netting a husband, but that compared in no way to the complex dance of charming a man to dig deep into his coffers for an investment in which he initially had no interest.

The only explanation Aaron had for this particular invitation was that the young lady was smitten with him. Well, he would use it to his advantage. If Mrs. Rutley was not willing to provide proper instruction, it would be up to him to see that she learned that particular lesson.

Strangely, the idea did not seem as burdensome as it should have. Instead, it sent an exciting bolt down his spine. This could be quite entertaining. Plus, being in her presence would mean the opportunity to feast on her lovely features.

The carriage made a violent lurch, and Aaron swore. "Watch it, you fool!" he shouted, although the driver could not hear him. It could not be all that difficult to keep the wheels from hitting the various holes left by the fierce winter. Perhaps it was time for him to find a new driver.

No, he did not enjoy wasting his time. It was not as if he spent a great deal of time in his carriage. Next time, he would take his horse. At least then, he would have control over where the animal stepped.

Glancing at the letter once more, he sighed. Before he could even consider teaching this girl her place, he first had to learn why she wished to meet. Perhaps she already recognized her mistake, and his energy could be better spent on what he had to accomplish in Chatsworth.

When the vehicle came to a stop, Aaron returned the letter to his breast pocket, adjusted his cravat, and waited for Milton to place the steps. For a moment, he prepared his mind for the duel he was certain would take place. One he was far better equipped to win.

Stepping from the carriage, he was surprised—and dare he say pleased?—to find Miss Dunston waiting for him on the portico. She wore a lovely lime-green dress with yellow stitching. Her long, honey-colored hair was made more alluring by the glowing rays of the sun that shone down on her.

A strange sensation coursed through him—a warmness that began in the pit of his stomach and radiated to his limbs. He had been attracted to lovely women before. Had even availed of several from time to time. But Miss Dunston produced a far different—and quite foreign—feeling, one that was much more pleasant than he would have expected.

But what made his breath catch were her soft blue eyes and her perfectly sculpted face. He had to fight the urge to take hold of her and kiss her as he had before. This time, however, it would not be to silence her but rather to show his appreciation for her beauty. To express his desire for her. What better compliment could a man give a woman?

Blast it! Why had that kiss come to mind? How would he never be able to defeat her if he was thinking about intimacies with her? Plus, he had allowed her to charm him. A hero did not fall for the enemy's tricks!

"Sir Aaron," she said, performing a low curtsy. "And I believe you have yet to meet my friend, Miss Ruth Lockhart?"

Aaron nearly started at the introduction. He was so caught up in the web Miss Dunston had weaved that he had not noticed the red-haired young woman at her side. "A pleasure, Miss Lockhart," he said curtly before returning his attention to his target. "I appreciate the invitation, Miss Dunston. Though, I must admit it was quite vague in its intention."

She came to stand directly in front of him, and his breath caught. Those eyes seemed to penetrate his very being. "Some things should not be put into writing, sir," she whispered. Oh, but her voice was like a soft caress, making his skin pebble with anticipation. "I thought it would be best to say what I wish in person."

Clearing his throat, Aaron glanced at the building that housed the school. "Will we go inside?"

"I thought we would take a stroll around the gardens," she said breathily. "We should take advantage of the warm weather. One never knows what tomorrow may bring." Her brows rose innocently. "But we'll do whatever you would like."

Aaron sighed with relief. So, the girl did understand life far better than he first realized. That a man's responsibilities and comfort far outweighed that of a woman. Perhaps he had been too quick to dismiss any hope for her.

He had intended to go inside, but instead, he said, "Yes, I would enjoy taking a stroll." When her hand came to rest on the arm he offered her, a sudden urge to protect her washed over him. "I say we begin at that large tree."

The redhead... what had been her name? Miss Lockhart. Yes, that was it. Miss Lockhart followed behind them as they strolled down the drive and came to a stop at the oak tree. Several sets of initials marred the smooth surface left by the removal of a branch, but before he could inquire, she spoke.

"Thank you for calling here today. I realize that men of your level of importance are often occupied with work."

"Indeed, we are," Aaron replied, smiling down at her appreciatively. Perhaps she would make a very good wife.

He nearly choked. Where had that thought come from?

"I've thought often about what happened in the library at Foxly Manor," Miss Dunston whispered.

Aaron glanced over his shoulder and was relieved to see Miss Lockhart several steps behind them. "Are you still angry with me?" he asked. "What word was it you used? Oh, yes, you said you despised me. That is a bit different from simply being angry."

Miss Dunston clasped her hands together at her breast. "I did. You see, I've never been accosted like that before. But I must admit... Oh, how do I explain this? It calmed the rebellion in me, so thank you."

Unable to help himself, Aaron grinned in victory. Another woman conquered with a simple kiss. If she was this easy to control, perhaps he would be parading her around sooner than he expected.

"I also wish to apologize," she continued. "I was angry and spoke rather harshly."

His breath caught. She had placed a hand on his arm. Not as she had when he walked her to the tree. No, this was more familiar, more intimate. And what was that? A sigh?

A beast roared inside him, and he had to fight it down. It was one thing to kiss her in the library where no one would see, but out here in front of the school? Absolutely not!

Walking her fingers up his arm, she smiled up at him. "Are we at peace now, sir? In regard to the silly argument we have over the theater?"

"Of course," he managed to say through a throat so parched, he could have swallowed a mouthful of sand. "I hold no ill will toward you, Miss Dunston. And please, don't feel bad. Many women experience streaks of rebellion from time to time. As long as you realize the trouble it can cause, that is what matters. I'm just glad to have been the one to help you see a better way."

She smiled up at him and placed her hand on his arm as before. "Shall we stroll a while longer?"

They continued past the right of the tree toward an open field.

"I've thought about the theater," Miss Dunston said.

"So, you've decided to put aside your foolish notion?"

She shook her head. "No, I wish to continue my quest to save it."

Aaron came to an abrupt stop. She had not invited him here to apologize! "So, I was right all along. You asked me here so you could use your feminine charms to make me change my mind. Well, your coquettish ways have been exposed for what they are, Miss Dunston. I, for one, shall not fall for them!"

Miss Dunston looked up at him, her eyes glistening with unshed tears, and confusion clouded his mind. "It appears you've misinterpreted my intentions, sir."

His mind told him to keep his guard, yet he could not stop the pounding of his heart against his sternum. *Listen to her,* it said.

"I'm listening." He sighed. It appeared the battle was already lost.

"Well, it occurred to me," Miss Dunston said, "with so many of the more affluent residents off in London for the Season, my attempts to raise the necessary funds to see the theater restored have not been as sufficient as I expected. What good is the two of us scurrying about when those who can provide the most money are not here to show their support?"

Aaron went to argue, but she placed a hand on his arm for a brief moment. Why did her touch make him feel so alive?

Miss Dunston's eyes twinkled as she continued. "I understand that there are a number of families without daughters returning to their country estates at the beginning of next month. The others will return in July and August, so why not wait until then to begin the arduous task of gathering allies?"

Aaron considered her words. "Do you mean to say that you intend to continue with this endeavor of trying to save the theater?"

"I do. But I propose that for the next thirty days, neither of us engage in any sort of solicitation of funds for our particular cause. Once those with the financial ability to help have returned to their country estates, we can begin again."

Aaron frowned in thought. Her idea was sound. Had he not considered the difficulty of approaching the few who remained in the country? Yet he would never admit he had felt defeated at times. How could he? Especially in the presence of this young lady? Doing so would only open him up for annihilation.

Yet, she saved him from confessing the truth.

"I'm sure a strong man such as yourself has already considered this." Her gentle hand on his arm sent his chest to roaring once more. "I have. In fact, I had hoped to present this very idea to you today."

"Then we have an agreement?"

A smile crossed his lips for a brief moment, but he withdrew it. He had nearly agreed outright. Yet if he did so, the pride this young lady possessed would grow to the point of being unwieldy. Perhaps it was best to make her wait for his response.

"I'll consider it," he replied.

A yelp made them both start, and a brown dog came limping up the drive from the main road. It had big, floppy ears, a wrinkly face, a panting tongue, and a tail that wagged when he caught sight of them.

"A hunting mastiff," they both uttered as one.

The sound of Miss Dunston's laugh was more melodious than any orchestra Aaron had ever heard. And for the first time since he could remember, his joining laughter was genuine.

"You know hunting dogs?" he asked. "How?"

"My father and his friends enjoy hunting a great deal. Our mastiff was named Quinton because he was the last of a litter of five. I adored him." She laughed. "Mother would not allow him into the house, so I used to sneak food from my dinner plate to feed him."

"Did no one else feed him?" Aaron asked.

"Oh, yes, but he was so big, I thought for sure he needed more food. I was only a child at the time."

Aaron clutched his side as he laughed. "My father's dog was named Lazarus. I, too, sneaked food out to him for that very reason."

Miss Dunston arched an eyebrow. "Lazarus? What an odd name for a dog."

"I couldn't agree more," Aaron said. "He was named for my father's brother, whom he despised."

This had them both laughing again, as the mastiff limped toward them, his head hanging low and his tail between his legs.

"Perhaps we should continue this conversation later," Aaron said. "It appears our friend here is in need of aid." He offered her his arm, which she once again took, and they made their way toward the dog.

How odd it was that he, a knight, shared a love of animals with a simple schoolgirl. Which begged the question, what else did they share?

What difference does it make? he asked himself. By the end of the following month, he would win this strange battle they had waged with each other, and the building that housed the theater would be his.

Chapter Eight

Louisa had never felt more satisfied than she did at this moment. From Sir Aaron's sharp intake of breath, her accolades had him lowering his guard. He needed time to think, or so he had said, but his smile told her all she needed to know. He was malleable enough to get him to agree to her terms. Terms she had no intention of honoring. After all, saving the theater was much more important than keeping to an agreement she had had not meant to comply with in the first place.

Sometimes acts of war call for deception to reach victory. Had Odysseus not built a wooden horse to sneak into Troy? Had the Normans not drawn the English off Senlac Hill by feigning defeat and fleeing? Had the Turks not dressed as bird sellers to infiltrate the Frankish camps at the Field of Blood? No one thought twice about their cunning, so why could she not use similar means to win this battle between them?

The sight of the injured dog, however, had her putting aside her thoughts of victory. Sir Aaron's laugh made her feel comfortable, as did the arm he offered her. What was it about this man that brought about a sense of safety? Of being protected? That no man—nor beast—could harm her in any way? Not once had he mentioned providing her protection, yet here she was accepting it outright.

Life had a peculiar way of changing one's opinion of a given situation. It had nothing to do with his height nor his well-defined arms. She had admired the taut muscles through the sleeves of his coat only moments ago. The touch had been spontaneous, calling to her, tempting her. Who was she to deny herself a simple pleasure that would cause no harm to anyone?

If men such as Sir Aaron chose to flaunt themselves at women, sometimes they had no choice but to give in to the temptation. Even if society dictated otherwise. At least, that was how she justified her decision.

Yet their shared conversation was what had given her greater pause. The stubborn, arrogant man just might have some decency in him. Of course, most were likely eroded away by his immense pride and that cocksure grin he always flashed, but there seemed to be a little left within him.

As they approached the mastiff, its sad brown eyes tore at Louisa's heart. He stood panting at them, one paw lifted several inches off the ground. Each time he lowered it, a harsh whine erupted from his throat.

"What is hurting you, my friend?" Sir Aaron asked as he lowered himself to one knee. Taking the injured paw in his hand, he studied it for several moments. "Ah, that is a nasty thorn you have there. But don't worry. I'll remove it for you. You'll feel much better once it's gone."

Louisa let out a dreamy sigh. No, he was not as vile as she had first thought. If he showed such great care and spoke in soothing tones with an animal, he would have an even better consideration for his fellow humans.

"Ah!" Sir Aaron shouted as the dog snapped at his hand, sending him toppling onto his backside.

Louisa stifled a giggle upon seeing the knight's crimson cheeks of anger. Instead, she offered him a hand. "Here, allow me to help you stand."

A scowl crossed his lips, and he snorted at her offer. "I'm not feeble," he murmured. "The grass is wet and thus slippery." He pulled himself up and brushed at the legs of his breeches, drawing Louisa's attention to his well-turned calf. "Now, let's try this again."

Louisa frowned. "Won't he snap at you again?" she asked.

"Only a man can tame a beast, Miss Dunston." He crossed his arms over his wide chest and arched an eyebrow at her. "Unless you believe you are more capable?"

Louisa swallowed back a retort. This man's arrogance knew no bounds! Yet looking over his face, she understood why. He was handsome, devilishly so. That coupled with his newly bestowed title, what more could his pride do than swell?

She might have enjoyed the way he had grabbed hold of her and kissed her during their time alone together at Foxly Manor, but this Knight of the Most Noble Order of the Garter needed to be taught a lesson. A little bit of humility went a long way when dealing with a man's vanity. And if he learned that a woman was as capable as a man, then all the better.

Without a word to Sir Aaron, Louisa squatted beside the poor dog and began stroking its head. "My friend here wishes to help you," she whispered. The dog whimpered. "Yes, I know he has a terrible temper, but don't worry. He'll not harm you."

"The dog doesn't understand you," Sir Aaron growled, sounding like a dog himself. "Surely, you know that!"

Louisa ignored him and put out a hand. "Your paw, please."

The dog stood panting at her for several moments before raising his paw. "You were saying, Sir Aaron?"

Sir Aaron's look of astonishment as he lowered himself beside her made the afternoon worth every moment.

"Now," she continued, "I'll move away, and you can remove the thorn."

She moved to the dog's side, petting its head and neck and speaking soothing words.

The knight shook his head and set to removing the thorn. Once it was out, he tossed it in a nearby bush and said, "There. It's gone. But now he's bleeding." He removed a handkerchief from his pocket and wrapped it around the dog's paw.

Louisa could only stare in incredulity. How could a man possess the mannerisms of a pig one minute and be so gentle the next? It was no wonder women struggled to understand their male counterparts. They were such a fickle lot.

Once the cloth was tied, Sir Aaron stood. "That should help protect the wound until it heals."

"That was kind of you," Louisa said. "To give up your handkerchief for a dog. And one you've never met even more so."

His brow knitted. "Do you think me cruel?"

Louisa went to nod but stopped herself. There was no reason to be rude.

The sound of hoof beats had Sir Aaron staring past her, his eyes narrowed. A blond gentleman in his mid-thirties with a fine brown woolen coat and black leather riding boots came riding up to them. His frown told them he was displeased.

"What's that on Rollo's foot?" he demanded, grunting as he dismounted from the chestnut mare. "You there, woman. Is this your foolery? And you, sir, you allowed her to do this? This is a dog, not a child. And he's certainly nothing to either of you."

Louisa could not help but gape. They had gone out of their way to tend to his animal, and he was angry? If that was not ingratitude, she did not know what was.

A movement made her glance to her side. Ruth was walking up to them, her hands clenched into fists. This was the last thing she needed, Ruth challenging this man to a bout of fisticuffs. What was absurd about the entire situation was that the girl likely would if Louisa did not stop her.

Waving off her friend, Louisa went to speak, but Sir Aaron did not give her the opportunity.

"An animal feels pain as much as any human," he said. "And her name is Miss Dunston, not 'woman.' Speak to her so disrespectfully again, and we'll have words."

Each man glared at the other like a pair of bulls squaring off to lock horns. That was shocking in itself, but what surprised her more was how Sir Aaron had come to her defense! Hers!

"He's not worth the trouble, Sir Aaron," Louisa whispered.

The man's eyes went wide, and he threw back his head and laughed. "So, this is the brave knight I've been hearing about. Sadly, your title is barely above a trinket sold on High Street. Unlike mine." He gave a mocking bow that had him sweeping an arm behind him. "Ashton, Baron of Lenten. Now *that* is a title to be honored."

Louisa frowned. She had never heard of this man. But witnessing two men fighting was not anything she enjoyed. Therefore, she smiled and said, "You must be new to Chatsworth, my lord, for I've never seen you before."

Lord Lenten smirked as he squatted beside the dog and removed the cloth from its paw. Peering at it, he threw it aside. "I've taken up residence in the area at the request of a friend," he said. "Perhaps you've seen him? Lord Ezra Colburn."

Louisa was unable to stop herself from gaping. Oh, she knew well who Lord Ezra was, for he was the very man causing problems with Mrs. Rutley. What had him inviting this friend to Chatsworth?

As if hearing her thoughts, the baron said, "I've heard about your headmistress, girl. Why anyone would send his daughter *here* is beyond understanding. But she'll not corrupt any more young ladies. I'm here to see that school shut down by the end of the year."

"Ruth, no!" Louisa said, grabbing her friend by the arm to keep her from pummeling the baron.

"You'll do no such thing!" Ruth shouted. "You're not welcome here, *my lord*." She used the address as a curse. "And if you return, I promise your next visit will not end well."

"Silence, both of you," Sir Aaron hissed before turning back to Lord Lenten. "Let us bid you a good day, my lord."

With a snap of his fingers at the dog, the baron leapt onto his horse and galloped away. Louisa's heart went out to the limping animal that followed in his wake, hoping its paw healed quickly.

Ruth grumbled a threat under her breath before storming away toward the house, leaving Louisa and Sir Aaron alone.

Louisa looked up at the knight and was surprised to find his eyes searching her face. "I'm sorry you were forced to witness such uncouth behavior, Miss Dunston. If he were not a baron, I would have struck him for the harsh tone he used with you."

Louisa's heart raced, and her mouth went dry. So, her earlier thoughts had been correct. He would protect her. The very idea sent a tingling down her spine, much like the kiss he had given her.

And suddenly, she wished he would kiss her again.

"Thank you," she whispered, but he made no move to draw closer to her. She retrieved the handkerchief from where Lord Lenten had thrown it and offered it to Sir Aaron.

Sighing, he returned the cloth to his pocket before offering her his arm once more. They walked over to a nearby tree and stopped.

"I must go," he said. "But first, we must discuss this truce you've offered concerning the theater. I don't typically make such agreements with women, but after today, I can see I have little choice."

Louisa had been so taken by Sir Aaron that she had nearly forgotten her plan. Now, her heart leapt with joy. He was finally seeing the error of his ways by recognizing that women were equal to men in more ways than he once believed. After all, she had been the one to calm the dog in order for him to remove the thorn from its paw. If not for her actions, the poor animal would still be in pain.

Getting him to admit this truth outright, however, would not be easy. Men were not willing to give up even an inch of their position of superiority, even if its infallibility was proven as it had been today. And his good looks would make doing so all the more difficult. If he was not careful, he would be unable to walk with the amount of pride he carried on his shoulders.

"I realize it makes little difference that I was correct," she said, choosing her words carefully. "What is important is that we were able to remove the thorn. You've grown wiser today, and that is what matters most."

His eyes narrowed, and his brows lowered. "You make it sound as if you're somehow victorious in all this, but was it not I who removed the thorn?" He took a step away from her. "And I was not speaking about the dog—or you, for that matter. Lord Lenten is the one who was lucky today, for I was close to pummeling him for his rudeness! And because I could not act so callously in the presence of a young lady, or rather in the presence of "—he gave a small nod to the returning Ruth—"I'll do the honorable thing and accept your offer of a truce. I'll make no requests for investors for thirty days." He pushed out a hand. "I suggest we shake on it."

He pushed out a hand, and Louisa gaped at it. The gall of the man! It was clear it was because of her that the dog had been saved, for if she had not calmed it, he would not have been able to remove the thorn. But being the kind woman she was, she had allowed him to take some credit for the rescue so he could take some of the praise. Even if he did not deserve it.

As the knight stood with his arms crossed over his chest, Louisa allowed herself one more look. He truly was alluring. So much so that he could tempt any woman. But she was not just any woman. She could fight her urges. Especially when the man to whom she was attracted was so full of himself.

Louisa took his hand and gave it a firm shake. "Yes, Sir Aaron," she said, batting her eyelashes and causing his grin to widen. "We do have an agreement."

Chapter Nine

L ying on her bed, several pillows behind her back, Louisa read the book on business she had borrowed from Lord Walcott's library. It had been two days since the incident with the mastiff, and she continued to struggle with her emotions when it came to Sir Aaron.

Part of her wished the knight would call on her again. His handsome gaze made her feel as if she were the loveliest woman on earth. That, to him, she mattered. Yet how was it possible to be attracted to someone she despised?

The encounter with the dog had given her a glimpse of a decent, admirable man who had earned his knighthood. Or so she had believed. After all, anyone willing to save a wounded animal was worthy of admiration. Yet then he had to open his mouth, allowing his haughtiness to come pouring out as easily as water from a pitcher.

His brain—if he indeed had a brain—was as thick as custard. Oh, how she had wanted to slap him! How could anyone as attractive as he lack any sense, whatsoever? It was as if he had been blessed with good looks at the expense of common sense.

Well, he had ruined any chance for a truce about the theater. No matter what promises were made.

Louisa sighed and turned the page in her book. She was nearly halfway through and never had she read anything so tedious in her life. Why could men not simply say outright what they wanted from one another? The writing seemed to focus more on a man's pride, or rather the history of such. Granted, there were a few nuggets of wisdom she found useful, but who cared about Smithian Economics and the division of labor?

Perhaps it was not the book itself that made her struggle to maintain her attention, for the thought of Sir Aaron flitted into her mind unbidden. She should have informed Mrs. Rutley that he had accosted her in the library that night. If anyone would have put him in his place, her headmistress could!

Yet much to her shame, she found herself relishing the memory. It had been a thrilling experience. What if the knight kissed her again but this time kept quiet?

Or better still, she could silence him with a kiss of her own...

A gentle knock on the door preceded the entrance of Mrs. Rutley. "I understand you were looking for me."

Louisa set aside her book and moved to the edge of the bed. "Oh yes, but you didn't need to come to me. I would have gone to your office."

Mrs. Rutley waved a dismissive hand and sat beside Louisa. "I don't mind. Plus, I believe we'll have much more privacy here. No one will think to look for me in a student's room. Now, what is it you wished to discuss?"

"I wish to speak about Sir Aaron."

The headmistress smiled. "Very well. I'm listening."

Louisa considered how to approach the subject. After all, it was not the typical conversation one would have with a headmistress. "I realize he was knighted for bravery, and what he did was indeed gallant. But I cannot help but find him vexing."

"Vexing? How so? Did he say something in particular that irritated you?"

"It's everything he says, Mrs. Rutley. I've never met a man so full of pride. His arrogance knows no bounds. But I cannot lie. He's handsome. I'm sure even you at your age can appreciate that."

Mrs. Rutley laughed. "Indeed. Even we old women can appreciate a handsome man from time to time."

Heat rushed into Louisa's cheeks. "I didn't mean—"

"I know. You meant no ill will, and no harm was done. Go on."

"Well, how does a woman tame such an arrogant beast? Especially one as feral as Sir Aaron?"

Taking Louisa's hand in hers, Mrs. Rutley gave it a gentle squeeze. "I believe you're asking the wrong question. Have you considered why you believe you feel the need to tame him?"

"For the survival of the theater," Louisa replied without hesitation. "I must quell his pompous behavior before he ruins that lovely place." Upon seeing a frown settle on the headmistress, she quickly added, "And taming him will only help him in the years to come. Someone must protect the innocent women he's bound to entice with his devilishly good looks."

She would not mention that she was one of those women. Nor would she tell about the kiss in the library, or how she had enjoyed the feel of his taut muscles beneath the fabric of his coat.

It was likely best that she kept her actions about the other afternoon to herself, as well. A proper young lady did not twirl her hair around a finger or push out her lower lip when speaking to a gentleman. Or any man, for that manner.

"And I suppose you are innocent in all this?"

Louisa gaped. Emma had once said Mrs. Rutley could read her students' thoughts, but Louisa never believed it. Now she was not so sure.

What was worse, her headmistress's use of the word "innocence" now tugged at her conscience. Indeed, she had done much that some would consider unladylike. Yet it had been thrilling to watch men stumble over their words when speaking to her. As had the knight's sharp intake of breath when she had touched his arms.

No, she was not at fault. She was justified in her behavior, for the knight had tempted her, as well. Therefore, she had committed no crime.

She replied to Mrs. Rutley's question with a firm nod. "Yes, I can say that in the particular instance, I am innocent."

"And in other instances?"

Louisa bit at her lip. How could she explain her reasons for flirting at other times? "Well, women have certain... abilities, and they must learn which are more useful for their needs. Even you have said as much."

This was a misrepresentation of the headmistress's words, and Mrs. Rutley's expression said as much. "We've discussed how easily men can be enticed by a playful look, Louisa. A proper lady never tries to entice men using the tricks of indecent women. You're far better than that."

Louisa blinked back tears. *I'm not better,* she wished to say. It was why she conducted herself as she did around men. But she could not say as much. It was her secret to hide in hopes it would lessen its hold on her. Voicing it aloud would only make it truer. At least the words were merely thoughts at the moment, and thoughts were not always truths.

"What am I to do about Sir Aaron?" she asked.

Mrs. Rutley smiled. "I suggest you lead by example, Louisa. You're a bright, intelligent young lady. Show him the proper way to conduct himself, and perhaps he'll see the error of his ways."

Louisa considered this sound advice. "I'll do the best I can, Mrs. Rutley. But I'm hoping never to see him again. Being in his company is taxing, and his behavior... well, it would not be considered acceptable in any circle of people."

"Just in case, then," Mrs. Rutley said with a light chuckle. "But I'd like to give you a word of warning. Take care. When we set out to change others, we often expose that which we, ourselves, are hiding."

"I'll be careful," Louisa said.

Although Mrs. Rutley's words were wise, Louisa had nothing to fear. She was nothing like Sir Aaron Kirkwood. Her reasons for all she did were warranted, unlike his. Everything she did was for the greater good. He only did what was best for himself.

As her headmistress walked toward the door, another thought came to Louisa's mind.

"Did Ruth tell you that Lord Ezra called today?" she asked.

Earlier when Mrs. Rutley had left the school, the gentleman had arrived. Ruth had let the man know in no uncertain terms that he was not allowed on the property.

Mrs. Rutley paused, her hand on the door handle, but she did not turn. Nor did she respond.

"What does he have against you, Mrs. Rutley?" Louisa asked. Then she dropped her gaze. "I'm sorry. It's not my business."

The headmistress sighed and turned to face Louisa. Although she wore a smile, it did not reach her eyes. "No, you have a right to know. Lord Ezra and I were... involved many years ago. We parted ways, but he has not been happy with that separation since."

Louisa stood. "So, that is why he and Lord Lenten want to close the school. What will you do to stop them?"

This time, Mrs. Rutley's smile lit up the room. "Nothing. Those who seek to harm others only bring trouble upon themselves in the long run. Now, enough about the past, Louisa. You have a theater to save." Louisa followed the headmistress's gaze to the book on the bed. "And I'd recommend keeping your attention on that rather than on a long-forgotten romance of an old woman." The last she said with a wink.

Once Mrs. Rutley was gone, Louisa returned to her book. It was not long before new questions began tickling her mind. Although the headmistress had said she was not concerned about Lord Ezra, Louisa doubted it was the truth.

It was no business of hers—and Louisa was not one for gossip—but when had that ever stopped her from wanting to learn more? The simple fact was that she just had to know.

That would have to wait, however. She had more important matters to see to, the first of which was Sir Aaron. Although she had said she did not wish to see him again, that had not been completely true. Yet how could she be in the company of a man working in opposition with her in regard to the theater?

Well, she may not have the answers she sought just yet, but she did have her memories. Memories of a possessive kiss in a library during a party at Foxly Manor. Memories of the feel of his arms. Of the feel of being *in* his arms. Of how breathless he had made her.

And of how she had never wanted to be apart from him ever again.

Chapter Ten

One never knew when an opportunity would strike. Yet it had been the case in the letter Sir Aaron Kirkwood received the prior day. A Mr. And Mrs. Arthur Bagwell had invited Aaron to their country home for tea. And to discuss Aaron's plans for the theater. From his understanding, Mr. Bagwell was an apparently wealthy man who dabbled in various forms of speculation.

Of course, Aaron had pledged to refrain from soliciting funds for thirty days. Although he had meant to keep that promise, some rules were meant to be broken. Especially when an occasion as favorable as this arose. Plus, he was a man—a member of the Most Noble Order of the Garter!—and thus could override any pact made with anyone.

The carriage jostled ever so slightly as Aaron considered a different letter. Two days earlier, he had sent word to Miss Dunston, inviting her to dine with him. Granted, he had sworn to keep his distance from the temptress, but the idea of not seeing her again in a social sense did not sit well with him.

The lovely young woman had consumed his thoughts on too many nights, making sleep difficult. During the day, he could not shake the image of her from his mind. Perhaps if he spent a few hours with her just one more time, then he could assuage the desire to be in her company. Once that itch was scratched, he would then go on with what needed to be done to get what he wanted.

The vehicle came to a stop, and Aaron went to the front door of Thinhollow Estate. A grand home covered in green ivy with white-trimmed windows and a front garden filled with several varieties of roses, Mr. Bagwell had done quite well for himself indeed.

Aaron pulled the bell cord, giving the bell three quick clanks, and the door opened to a brown-haired liveried butler of perhaps thirty.

"Sir," the man said with a bow before stepping aside to allow Aaron entry.

The large foyer was tastefully decorated with marble flooring. In the middle of the circular room sat a round oak table with a bouquet of roses in a famille rose and blue porcelain vase. Qing Dynasty, Aaron was certain.

Aaron was well studied in spying items that demonstrated wealth, and that particular vase had to have cost Mr. Bagwell a great deal. The oriental rug—Kangxi with blue blossom palmettes—on which the table sat was worthy of St. James's Palace.

"If you will follow me, sir," the butler said.

To their left was a hallway, and Aaron was directed to the second door on the right. A young woman with blonde hair, no older than twenty, stood at a far window with her back to the door. She wore a yellow day dress with white lace around the bottom hem and sleeves. When she turned, she offered him a smile.

"Sir Aaron, it's an honor to have you here in our home."

Aaron stifled a frown. He recalled someone mentioning that the Bagwells were an older couple with numerous children. Yet the wife appeared no older than twenty. Well, who was Aaron to judge? Perhaps Mr. Bagwell had remarried, and like so many wealthy men, he had chosen a far younger woman as a second wife.

"The honor is all mine," Aaron said. The door clicked behind him. The butler had left them alone. So, this was the young wife of the man with whom he was to meet. The daughter would never be allowed alone with him. "I admit that your invitation to tea was unexpected yet welcomed." He glanced around. "And Mr. Bagwell?"

"He'll be here soon enough," she replied. "Please, sit. There is no need to stand on my account." She directed him to a cream-colored couch before walking over to where several decanters sat. "When I heard our Chatsworth had a new resident, and no less a brave knight such as yourself, I must admit I was delighted. I knew I just had to meet you."

She poured him a measure of brandy without asking him first, followed by a glass of wine for herself. How strange that the butler had not remained behind to see to the drinks.

"And now, we finally meet," she said, offering him the brandy.

He nearly choked when she took the place beside him rather than one of the other chairs.

"The letter I received mentioned the theater," he said, hoping to move along the meeting even if the husband was not yet in attendance. She was pleasant enough in looks, but he would not receive any funding if he was caught in a compromising position with the wife of a man he hoped to gain as an investor.

"Oh yes, of course," she said with an air of disappointment. "What do you plan to do with it once you've purchased the building?"

Aaron cleared his throat. "At the expense of sounding rude, should we not wait for Mr. Bagwell to arrive? I would not want him to miss anything I say."

The woman took a drink of her wine and then motioned to a side table behind him. "Would you be a darling and set this aside for me?"

He did as she bade only to turn around and find that she had moved closer to him in the interim.

Two things came to mind at once. The first was that a married woman was clearly flirting with him. Some lines he would not cross, and this was one of them. The second was that he felt conflicted about being here. Not only in the presence of another woman but also in that he was breaking the agreement he had made with Miss Dunston.

Coming here had been a mistake, yet the damage was done. "I would like to convert it into a gentlemen's club." He explained his plans, and with each word, Mrs. Bagwell smiled, nodded, and sometimes even sighed. When he was done, he reached for his brandy, which he had placed beside the wine glass, and finished it off in one gulp.

"I think your plan grand, Sir Aaron!" she said as she clasped her hands together at her breast. "So much so, in fact, that when Father returns... I mean my husband..." She laughed. "I'll tell him he should invest with you."

The warning bells pealed in his head, and he glanced at her hand. No wedding band. Then he realized the truth and quickly stood.

"You're his daughter?"

The young woman leapt from her seat. "Yes," she said enthusiastically. "I'm Susanna. My parents are away for the week, you see, and I heard so much about you that I just had to meet you. This was the only way!"

Aaron's heart was close to bursting from his chest. He was alone with an unmarried young woman! Not only would her name be ruined, but his would be as well! Not only that but he would have to explain this situation to Miss Dunston if word got out!

Why would I have to explain anything to her? he thought. Miss Dunston was a spoiled child at best. He was an honored knight. Had her tempting ways truly muddled his mind to the point that he could be so easily tricked by this young woman?

"Miss Bagwell," he said, slowly backing toward the door, "my being here with you without benefit of a chaperone is inappropriate, as much for me as for you."

She sniffed. "And who will tell?"

"Surely, your butler will say something!" he said, mustering as much incredulity as he could into his tone.

As Miss Bagwell moved toward him, he felt like a rabbit being stalked by a fox. No, he could never compare himself to a rabbit. Perhaps he was a fox, and she was a hawk. Yes, that was better. Either way, he was the prey and she the predator.

"Coleman has been paid well for his silence, Sir Knight," she cooed. Cooed!

His back hit the door, and he grasped the handle and turned it. "Nevertheless, I must leave. Perhaps we'll speak another time."

Without waiting for a response, he hurried from the room, down the corridor, and out the front door to his waiting carriage.

"Mistrals!" he shouted to the driver before leaping into the carriage and blessedly slamming shut the door. Thankfully, Miss Bagwell had enough sense not to chase after him, but he drew shut the curtains all the same.

It was not much later when he entered Mistral's Bookshop. Mercifully, the pounding in his heart had subsided by then. He had nearly been eaten alive! Or at least nibbled upon. If Miss Dunston ever learned of that encounter, she would laugh herself silly! As well she should. He had put himself in a precarious situation, all so he could gain an investor. Knight or not, he should have noticed the signs before the butler had closed the door.

Mr. Mistral was a thin, bespectacled man with a long, straight nose. On his head sat a brown cap that many said hid a balding pate. The proprietor stood hunched over a book behind the counter. He looked up when Aaron approached.

"Ah, Sir Aaron, it's a pleasure to see you again. How may I assist you?"

Aaron glanced around to make certain no one was nearby. "A Lady Mathison is to collect a book from you tomorrow, correct?"

The proprietor nodded. "Indeed, she is, sir."

"May I ask that you give her a message from me?"

Mr. Mistral nodded again as he closed his book. "Yes, of course."

"I need a place, somewhere private, where she and I may speak without fear of anyone overhearing. Have you any suggestions?"

Rubbing his chin in thought, Mr. Mistral replied, "I believe I do."

After receiving directions, Aaron wrote a quick note and handed it to the proprietor. "See that she gets this, but please be discreet. I'm sure I can trust you to keep this to yourself?"

If Lord Mathison learned that she and Sir Aaron were meeting, they both would be in a great deal of trouble. But Aaron did not care. He had to see her. And like so many other things in life, Aaron understood one thing that his father had taught him.

Some rules were meant to be broken.

Chapter Eleven

L ouisa stared at the letter for the tenth—or was it the hundredth?—time. It had arrived the day after her talk with Mrs. Rutley, and now two days later, she had yet to respond. He had invited her to dine with him, but did she wish to do so?

A familiar dilemma had risen inside her. Dining with the handsome hero would be enjoyable. Enduring his arrogance, however, would spoil what could be a lovely evening.

Yet that was not what bothered her most about the arrangement. Although she had known when she had offered the truce the previous week that she would not keep her word, Louisa was riddled with guilt. She had sought out and collected donations from two shopkeepers in the village.

Well, her actions were justified. After all, Sir Aaron had refused to acknowledge the part she had played in helping the mastiff. If she had not calmed the poor animal, the knight would not have been able to remove the thorn. It was that simple.

Yet if he were standing before her now, she was unsure if she could look him in the eyes. She had not been well trained in the art of deception. Her ability to eavesdrop was second to none, but she never did so without a good reason. It was one thing to be inquisitive and altruistic and another to be outright nosy.

Sighing, she slid the letter under her pillow just as the door opened, and Ruth entered the room.

"I have a bit of news concerning your knight," the redhead said. Her hands were on her hips, which said the news was not good. "You'll not believe what the twins heard."

Louisa nearly launched herself from the bed. "What did you hear?"

Ruth waved a hand at her Louisa. "It'll have to wait. We're due to meet in the drawing room for our history lesson."

Louisa groaned. Mrs. Rutley had arranged for a special guest to come and speak to the students. With all that was going on at the moment, Louisa had no interest in any lessons, and history least of all. Who cared about what had already happened? But she had only one choice. Attend or endure the wrath of the headmistress. And that could mean any sort of punishment, none of which Louisa wished to endure.

"Why can't you tell me as we go?" Louisa demanded in a harsh whisper. "What did you learn? Was he soliciting funds from someone in the village?"

He had best not be! she thought with vehemence. They had agreed to a truce. If she learned that he had gone back on his word, so help her...!

Ruth shook her head. "Not that I'm aware. But he was overheard saying he is to meet a Lady Mathison at Yeats Park tomorrow at midday."

Louisa's heart dropped. Why would the knight, or any gentleman for that matter, meet a lady at the park? Such covert meetings were meant for one thing, even in a village the size of Chatsworth.

Her jaw tightened as she imagined Sir Aaron taking hold of and kissing this Lady Mathison as he had done to her. What gave him the right to manhandle a woman in such a despicable way? And what if that lady, like Louisa, was innocent, and the knight merely wanted to prey upon her vulnerability? Louisa was strong enough to resist his charms, but what if this Lady Mathison was not? She could not allow another woman to endure what she, herself, had!

There was only one thing to do.

"Ruth, tomorrow I'd like to go to Yeats Park to see what I can learn. Will you go with me?"

A strange malevolent grin spread across Ruth's face. "I'd love nothing more than to go and spy on them! Just think of the things we may overhear. Or see!"

Louisa frowned. The idea of seeing the knight do anything as simple as a kiss with another woman made a clump of sadness form in her chest. Now, that was odd. She despised Sir Aaron with all her heart. Why should thinking of him with someone else make her melancholy? It made no sense.

When they entered the drawing room, the murmur of just over a dozen students filled the room. Amy Felton, her cheeks becoming more rounded when she smiled, patted the place beside her. Louisa and Ruth lowered themselves onto the settee just as Mrs. Rutley called for quiet.

"Now that we're all here," Mrs. Rutley began with a sharp look at Louisa and Ruth, "I would like to introduce Mr. Hugh Jennings. Mr. Jennings is a historian who specializes in the local history of the area. I know I've no need to remind you that we should be on our best behavior." That sharp look was directed at Ruth.

Mr. Jennings ran a hand through his curly, dark hair as he thanked Mrs. Rutley. A rather short man with nervous brown eyes that darted hither and thither as if he were tracking some sort of flying insect, he could not have been younger than forty years of age.

"Thank you for that warm welcome, Mrs. Rutley," Mr. Jennings said in a voice one would expect from a man twice his height. "Our story of the founding of Chatsworth began nearly five hundred years ago in the once grand village of Hensworth."

Louisa recognized that particular name, for it was located nearly two hours away by carriage. Once a thriving place, it touted a handful of residents after the dozen or so mines in the area had dried up and closed. Because of its rocky soil, farming the land was out of the question.

"It was there," Mr. Jennings continued, "that Philip, Marquess of Artemus wished to expand his land holdings. Thus, he began what is known as the Great Expansion. Lord Artemus began purchasing as much land as he possibly could with the hope of developing it into a small village. Each month, he gathered up more and more land—farms, grazing land, forests, whatever anyone was willing to sell for the right price. There is no record to say from where those funds came, but soon, he owned enough to create what he considered his 'kingdom.' But it was what happened next that is the most fascinating."

Louisa, who found most history lessons a bore, suddenly found the lecture interesting. So caught up in the story, she clung to every word.

For some time, the historian explained how the lord had continued building small villages in the area, producing jobs for those willing to work whilst also gathering up even more land. The final village was christened Chatsworth, named after a childhood friend, a servant by the name of William Chatsworth.

"Once he had enough villages scattered across his lands, Lord Artemus wished to build a house. No, the term *house* is not the best descriptor. Perhaps we should call it a castle. Regardless, he built a home so grand it's rumored that even King Edward III himself traveled to gaze upon it."

Louisa's mind began to drift. What would it be like to live in such a magnificent house? Perhaps with Sir Aaron as her husband. She shook that thought out of her head as soon as it entered. The stress over the last few days was clearly making her lose her mind.

But what about Sir Aaron? How could he tell Louisa she was beautiful and then plan to meet another woman in the park after? She nearly snorted. Oh, she knew the answer to that question and did not like it in the slightest.

"Now, have you any questions?" Mr. Jennings asked. When no one responded, he added, "Come now. There's no need to be afraid. It's through our ability to question that we gain more knowledge."

Still, no one spoke, and an awkward silence filled the room. Louisa glanced at Mrs. Rutley, who gave her a nod. Being one of the older students, it would be up to her to lead by example.

"What of Lord Artemus's castle?" Louisa asked. "Do his descendants still live there today?"

Mr. Jennings sighed. "Sadly, due to a number of factors, the title and most of the land were lost over the last century. A single descendant remains, a Mr. Abraham Artemus."

Well, at least he had a grand home in which to live. Perhaps one day, Louisa would visit the area.

Her bravery sparked others to make more inquiries. Eventually, the questions came to an end, and Mrs. Rutley dismissed the students, each thanking Mr. Jennings before she left the room.

Once returned to her room, Louisa sat on the bed beside Unity, Theodosia, and Ruth across from them.

"I found it all rather interesting," Theodosia offered. "I never realized how fascinating the village history could be."

Ruth, of course, snorted derisively. "Of course it was fascinating. Most lies are."

Louisa rolled her eyes. Why did Ruth have to argue about everything?

"I don't know," Unity replied. "What he said made a lot of sense."

As the others argued over which points Mr. Jennings had made were truth or lies, Louisa found her patience running thin. Did her friends not realize she had an important task tomorrow? That she had to learn what Sir Aaron was doing in the company of another woman, in a park rumored to be a meeting place for lovers?

Unable to stand it a moment longer, she scooted off the bed and leaned her back against the door. "Enough!" she said in a whisper far harsher than she intended. Well, perhaps she did wish it to be that harsh. They were arguing about things that were unimportant. Or at least less important than what she wished to discuss! "What exactly did Sir Aaron say?"

Unity smoothed her cream-colored skirts and sighed. "He said he wished to speak to Lady Mathison alone, someplace private where they could not be overheard."

Theodosia clicked her tongue. "He said no such thing. I was the one who heard him, not you."

"What did he say?" Louisa demanded again. This was worse than getting a child to confess to putting his finger in the icing on a cake! Drawing in a deep, calming breath, she leveled her voice. "Please, just tell me what he said."

Theodosia closed her eyes, a habit she had whenever she wished to recall something. "Unity and I were at the bookshop. Sir Aaron was inquiring of Mr. Mistral about a place where one could have a private discussion without concerns that someone might eavesdrop. Mr. Mistral suggested Yeats Park."

"But have you any idea what he plans to talk about with Lady Mathison?" Louisa asked.

"I do," Theodosia replied, opening her eyes. "But I've told no one, not even Unity or Ruth."

"Well?" Louisa demanded, her annoyance barely controlled.

Theodosia shook her head. "No, I think it would be best that I didn't say."

Louisa's heart was near to bursting from her chest. If Sir Aaron planned to kiss this lady, it was best if she learned about it now rather than later.

"No, please do."

With encouragement from the other two, Theodosia gave a small nod. "Very well, but I'm merely the messenger." She glanced at Louisa before taking a deep breath. "He said he adored the lady for looking after William."

Louisa's jaw dropped. "Who is William?"

Theodosia gave her a level gaze. "It's quite obvious." She blew out her breath in vexation. "Don't you see? The knight has an illegitimate son!"

Chapter Twelve

With Ruth at her side, Louisa began the short trek down the main road that led to the village. Their destination was a particular section of Yeats Park. Or as rumor had it, the Lovers' Nest. Many nights were spent with the students of Mrs. Rutley's School for Young Women whispering at the goings on there, which included plots of murder to married lovers and their secret rendezvous. Of course, most of what they had heard came from second- or even third-hand knowledge, and often the girls added their own interpretation to the less eventful stories.

As far as Louisa was concerned, there could only be one reason Sir Aaron and his mystery lady would meet in secret, and it was the very same reason any other clandestine couple might use. Just the thought of what they would be doing made Louisa's stomach roil. She had thought there was hope for the arrogant knight, but now she had no doubt there was none. To father a child out of wedlock was an appalling act. Had he no sense of decency?

Oh, who was she fooling? Too many men found this type of behavior commonplace. In fact, he would likely celebrate the results of his indiscretions in the gentlemen's club he wished to build. Why,

Louisa would guess he had more than a dozen poor illegitimate children scattered throughout the country!

Louisa paused her thoughts. Why did it matter to her? What difference did it make if he sired a dozen or a hundred children to women he refused to marry?

And why would the very idea hurt her as it did? After all, they were not a couple in any sense of the word. They were not courting. He was not even a suitor. She knew very little about the man, and certainly not enough to have any sort of admiration for him.

Well no, that was untrue. He was brave. Even the King himself had established that as truth when he bestowed the knighthood upon Sir Aaron. Not just any man was given such distinction. Therefore, who was she to argue with the King?

The sounds of the bustling village reached Louisa's ears before she and Ruth entered the village. The warmer weather had brought out the merchants hawking their wares. The villagers chatted, and the voices of children playing joined those of their parents. Horses whinnied and snorted, and the wheels of the carriages they pulled clambered by.

Just past High Street, Louisa and Ruth made a right. From there, it was a short stroll to the park. And at the back of the park was their destination. The Lovers' Nest.

"I wonder how many children he has," Ruth said thoughtfully. "If it's fewer than five, I'd be surprised. Men like him have at least ten. Even a dozen."

Louisa, whose temper had been on edge all morning, snapped, "And what makes you think I give even the slightest care? Now, let's please change the subject."

Ruth narrowed her eyes, and Louisa braced herself for a harsh warning. It was one thing to be castigated by their headmistress, but to have a fellow student act as if she knew more about the world in which they lived was insulting.

To her shock, however, Ruth took hold of her arm and pulled her into a small alleyway beside the cobbler's shop. "I realize you're upset, Louisa. Now, don't give me that look. You're smitten with the man, so don't try to deny it. Here is my suggestion. Let's go and see what is happening. You can't make an educated decision until you have the truth."

Indignant, Louisa jutted out her chin. "We've nothing to debate here, Ruth. Yes, the man kissed me. And although his actions were roguish, I'll admit I enjoyed it." Her cheeks heated recalling the memory of his lips upon hers. "Beyond that, my only objective is to save the theater. My life would be far better off without him in it. Plus, what business is it of yours? None whatsoever! I knew I should have asked someone else to accompany me!"

Perhaps it was the shadow cast by the buildings on either side of them, but Ruth suddenly appeared older and far wiser than Louisa had ever seen her before. It was at that moment that Louisa realized how different Ruth was from the other girls at the school. That the tales she told of the adventures she wished to take were not just stories. They were who she was meant to be.

"You're lucky I like you, Louisa," Ruth said, her fist raised. "Most of the girls would never get away with the way you just spoke to me." The gleam in her eyes belied her tone, and Louisa could not help but laugh. Ruth grinned and pulled Louisa by the arm. "It's about time you spoke up for yourself. Come on. We're already late. We may miss the show!"

"I'm sorry for speaking so harshly with you, Ruth." She paused to glance at her friend. "Why did you not get angry with me?"

They reached the end of High Street, and still, Ruth did not respond. Perhaps she would not. Ruth was not one to explain her actions to anyone. Well, anyone but Mrs. Rutley, of course. And even then, it was a toss-up as to whether she would remain silent during a disagreement with the headmistress or if she would speak her mind.

They entered the park and made their way to the farthest corner behind a hedgerow. What would they hear? Or see, for that matter? Before they reached Lovers' Nest, however, Ruth came to a sudden stop and grabbed Louisa by the arm.

"Do you truly want to know why I'm not upset with you?"

Louisa nodded. "I do."

"Because you are my friend, just as the others are. We've become Sisters through the oath we made. I would never hurt any of my Sisters." She balled her hand into a fist and lifted it menacingly. "But mark my words. If someone were to hurt any of you, in any way, I'd see that person pay."

Besides the day when they had made their blood pact at the tree, Louisa had never before heard Ruth stand up for anyone with such fervor. This begged a question.

"How is it you know how to fight like a man?" Louisa asked. "Or the other tricks you know. Who taught you these things?"

Ruth gave a rueful laugh. "Sometimes one must learn what's necessary for certain situations, Louisa. It's as simple as that. Now, come on or we'll miss the meeting."

They made their way down the small path. The nearby trees created shade to wash away their shadows as they edged closer to Lovers' Nest. A single bench sat in a glen of sorts, surrounded on three sides by hedges and backed against rose bushes that filled the air with their sweet scent. Behind the roses was a wooded area that created a back wall to the natural room. Louisa had always thought it a romantic place—if it had not been for the couple who sat on the bench.

She could not make out the features of the couple, but somehow, she could *feel* the knight. Having him so close gave her a warm, pleasant feeling that she cherished. Yet it was not she who sat beside him.

"I can sense his vanity," she whispered with a sniff.

"Let's go around to the other side," Ruth replied in an equal volume. "The woods will supply cover, and we'll be behind them. They'll not see us, but we'll hear every word they say."

With a nod, Louisa followed her off the path. Underbrush grabbed at her skirts, and more than once, she had to pull loose the fabric when it caught on a branch. Her dress would be ruined by the time this was all said and done.

Yet, the journey was well worth it. As Ruth had said, they were able to sneak up close enough to overhear the conversation taking place.

Indeed, Sir Aaron sat with a woman who had to be Lady Mathison. They were facing one another, their knees nearly touching.

Just as lovers would.

Louisa could not deny the lady's beauty. Her deep-brown hair and heart-shaped face would have turned any man's head, as would the jewels that glinted in the sun on her fingers and around her neck.

"Once my work is completed here," Sir Aaron was saying, "I'll likely move on. Though I've no idea where. Have you decided where you'll be next?"

The lady sighed. "Peter will be dead soon enough. The doctor believes he'll not last through the summer. Once I'm free from the bindings of marriage, I'll make a decision. But whatever I decide, I know I'll be happy."

Louisa's eyes widened in shock. What kind of woman wished her husband dead?

"Just know that I'm here for you," Sir Aaron said as he placed an all-too-familiar hand on her arm. "If you need anything, all you need to do is ask."

Louisa shook her head in disbelief. This lady had to do nothing more than play to his sympathies, and the knight was almost leaping to her aid. What an arrogant, selfish man!

"Tell me how William is doing," Sir Aaron said. "I do miss him."

Lady Mathison gave another breathy sigh. "You should not have spoiled him as you did, you know. He now follows me around everywhere I go, and he thinks he has the right to eat my food! I've considered making him sleep in the stable as a form of punishment."

They both laughed at this, but Louisa was horrified. Who would treat a child so abhorrently?

"I can arrange for you to see him if you'd like," the lady said.

Sir Aaron gave a wave of his hand. "I'm far too busy at the moment. But if Mathison does die, I'll visit both of you."

Louisa had heard enough. Disgusted, she signaled to Ruth, and they tiptoed away. When they reached the entrance to the park, Louisa halted.

"Forcing a young boy to sleep in the stable because he wants proper food?" she demanded of Ruth. "Have you heard anything so despicable?"

Ruth nodded. "And what is equally bad is their hope her husband dies. No one would believe it if I told them."

Louisa pursed her lips. "I knew he was a foul character, but to learn he would allow the mother of his child to treat him so terribly only adds to why I despise him as I do!"

"Miss Dunston?"

Her heart leapt into her throat, and Louisa spun around to find that very deviant man approaching. She raised herself to her full height and jutted out her chin. "Sir Aaron."

"What brings you to the park?" he asked as he came to a stop in front of her.

Fully determined to give him a proper tongue lashing, she looked into his deep-blue eyes... and melted. Sadness mixed with awe washed over her as the rays of the sun fell over his face, making him more handsome than ever. She wished to touch his cheek and tell him what a shame it was that he was so vile. That his good looks had been wasted on such a disgusting man.

That she would allow him one more kiss so she would be able to relish it forever. A gift to remind him of what he would never have.

But she had never been that brave, so instead, she said, "We are here to stroll. Why else do people come to the park?" She gave him an innocent smile. "Is that not why you are here?"

He swallowed visibly and nodded. "Oh yes, well, I just completed my walk, but would you like me to join you in yours?"

"No thank you," Louisa replied. "Miss Lockhart and I have matters to discuss. Of a feminine nature." She gave him a wicked grin. "But perhaps another time."

He bent his head a fraction. "Then I'll leave the two of you alone. Oh, and concerning dinner tomorrow evening. I've yet to receive a reply."

Louisa considered what to do. Having dinner with Sir Aaron was the last thing she wanted to do. But a new thought came to mind. She now had information that would cast aspersions on his name. Perhaps if she accepted his invitation, if she asked the right questions or searched the right areas, she could learn more. And then use said knowledge to end his silly idea of funding a gentlemen's club.

"I'll be ready at four as you requested," she replied, batting her eyelashes.

Sir Aaron bid her farewell. Louisa watched him walk away. Yes, this dinner would prove to be a wonderful way to find more to use against him. Then the theater would be saved, and the vile knight would be run out of the village. Let him find another village to terrorize!

But even as she considered this, the very thought of hurting him, even after all she had learned thus far, left a bitter taste in the back of her throat.

Chapter Thirteen

The sun's rays lit up the dining room at Hearsely Estate, highlighting the occupants of the table. Miss Dunston sat at Aaron's right, and beside her was Miss Lockhart. But Aaron took little notice of the redheaded companion.

He took a sip of his wine, allowing him a moment to admire the lovely features of Miss Dunston. Her honey-blonde hair gleamed, and her soft blue eyes shone. Not for the first time, he considered how perfectly shaped her face was. Even her slender nose had been crafted to perfection.

She and Miss Lockhart had arrived some twenty minutes earlier. Although they exchanged polite greetings, Miss Dunston had remained otherwise quiet, which had raised his suspicion. The otherwise opinionated and outspoken young woman had never been this reserved, not in the time he had known her.

Cutting into his duck, Aaron lifted a bite to his mouth only to find her gaze upon him. Her eyes glimmered, not in the usual flirtatious manner she tended to use but rather in a knowing way. She was hiding something, and he was determined to learn what that something was.

"How do you find the meal this evening, Miss Dunston?" he asked. "Is it adequate?"

She placed her utensils on the plate and said, "Most adequate. The mint sauce complements the meat quite well."

"I'll be sure to pass that along to the cook. She'll be pleased." Taking a final bite of his food, he motioned to one of the footmen to take away his plate. "You are unusually quiet this evening. May I be of assistance in any way?"

Dabbing at her mouth with a napkin, Miss Dunston lifted her glass to her lips. When she pulled the glass away, her lip held a lovely pout.

This had been one of the reasons Aaron had invited her to dinner —so he could feast upon her beauty. His other motive had been to use his good looks and charm to convince her to drop the silly competition.

Granted, they had agreed to postpone their bout, but their arrangement to postpone any gathering of funds would soon come to an end. A fine dinner and expensive wine would be the perfect way to loosen her inhibitions, to weaken her stubborn mind, thus quashing any further resistance on her part.

Aaron snapped his fingers, and a footman hurried over to refill her glass.

"I heard a terrible story earlier this week," Miss Dunston said, pausing long enough to give the footman a small nod of thanks. "It seems a well-respected man in the village ignores his son. An illegitimate son, to be sure, but a son, nonetheless. What's worse, the boy is forced to sleep in the stables as a form of punishment."

"How awful," Aaron said, taken aback. "What kind of person would do such a thing?"

Miss Dunston sniffed. "Only the most despicable person in all of England." She wore a tiny yet odd smile. "One who must believe himself better than the King himself to be so cruel."

The footmen cleared the remaining plates and returned to their places along the wall, but Aaron paid them little heed. He was missing something, an important detail of some sort, but he could not seem to work it out. And that was not like him.

"You have a lovely home," Miss Dunston said. "May I have a tour? Maybe beginning in your study?"

Did she always leap from subject to subject in such a jarring manner? Aaron would have thought she would have received better training at that school she attended. Well, what did he know of that particular establishment? For all he knew, it was less renowned than others. Given their faulty instruction, it was no surprise why.

The house was grand, far grander than the school. Plus, if he was to change her way of thinking, granting her request would put him on the right path.

With a wave of his hand, the footmen hurried to pull out the chairs for the young ladies.

"I purchased Hearsely Estate six months ago. The lack of decoration does not represent my lack of wealth, for I am wealthy. I simply don't see myself remaining in Chatsworth very long, so why bother changing the decor?"

"Why is that?" Miss Dunston asked. "Why purchase an estate only to leave it immediately after?"

The truth was that the gentlemen's club was only one of what he hoped to be many ways of gaining the approval of the nobility. Once he finished here, he planned to go in search of other, larger pursuits, quests that will make him even more renowned. What those pursuits might be or where they would lead him remained to be seen.

Yet saying so would make him seem vain, and he did not want anyone to believe he thought so much about himself.

"I enjoy traveling the country," he explained as they walked down the corridor. "Therefore, I prefer not to remain in one place for very long." He pushed open the door to his study and stepped aside to allow the two young ladies to enter. A single desk of high-polished birch sat in the middle of the room, a single bookcase housing several of his ledgers beside it. A large window looking over the gardens made the otherwise small room bearable. "Why did you wish to see my study?"

"Oh, I find it so fascinating to see where a man works," she gushed, using that same tiny smile she wore when mentioning the mistreated boy. "Here, I can imagine you working late into the night, doing all you can to increase your worth. You must hold the most interesting meetings. And the number of men who are jealous of you must be great. Trust me when I say a lady will find such things captivating."

Her front teeth nibbled her bottom lip, and fire erupted inside

Aaron. In that moment, he wished they were alone, for he would have pulled her into his arms and kissed her again!

But a grunt from her companion dissuaded him of such a thought.

"Oh! My stomach! The pain," Miss Lockhart said, clutching at her abdomen. "I'm not feeling well."

Aaron hurried to the young woman. "Are you all right?"

She doubled over in pain, but her pallor did not change. "I'm so sorry, and I do hate to be a burden, but do you have a room where I may sit and rest a moment?"

"Of course. I can take you to the drawing room and have Scriven bring you tea if you would like. I'm sure Mrs. Pentham has something that can provide a remedy of some sort for you."

"I'll wait here," Miss Dunston said. "There's no need for both of us to accompany her. Once she's settled, we can resume the tour."

"Are you sure?" Aaron asked. "I wouldn't want you to think me rude."

"Not at all. I'm sorry, Ruth. I forgot you cannot eat anything with mint. It bothers her stomach terribly, you see."

Aaron nodded, although he thought it a strange reaction to an herb typically used for indigestion. He led Miss Lockhart to the drawing room. "Sit here," he said, helping her to the couch. "I'll go in search of Scriven. Will you be all right here alone?"

"I believe so," she whispered. "I only need a moment. Please, don't go to any trouble."

Aaron's heart clenched. Many years ago, his mother fell deathly ill, and it began with stomach pain. He sat at her bedside day and night, doing whatever he could to help. Whatever sickness had taken over her had not killed her, but she never fully regained her strength. Since then, seeing any woman in pain caused him distress. "It's no trouble at all. I assure you. I'll return momentarily."

He hurried from the room in search of the butler before remembering he could have rung the bell in the drawing room. Before he could turn back around, Scriven appeared, and Aaron sent him to Mrs. Pentham for the tea.

Relieved to have Miss Lockhart seen to, he returned to the study only to take a quick step back into the corridor. Did he see what he believed he saw? Peeking around the door jamb, he watched a hunched Miss Dunston rifle through the small stack of letters on his desk.

What was she doing? How dare she look through his things! Then to his astonishment, she took one, folded it, and slid it into her reticule.

Clearing his throat, he entered the room. She pulled her hands behind her back with a gasp.

"What are you doing?" he demanded.

She flushed. "I was... it's just that I saw how disorganized your desk is, so I thought I would tidy it up for you." She straightened up the letters and placed them in the center of the desk. "You see? Much better, would you not say?"

Aaron took a step forward and closed the door without taking his eyes off her. "How kind of you. I'm lucky to have such a considerate friend."

"Friend?" she asked. "What an honor to be considered your friend, sir."

Aaron could not help but smile. This young lady was skilled at the art of dodging the truth it seemed.

"May I ask why you closed the door?"

He eyed her for several moments. Then a mischievous idea came to mind. He could counter her game with one of his own. "Because there is something I want from you, Miss Dunston." He looked her up and down. "Surely, you know what it is, for you've made it clear you want the same from me."

Her eyes went wide, and she placed a hand to her breast. "If you think I'll allow you to kiss me again, you're sadly mistaken. Now, I must go see how Ruth is feeling."

"You're going nowhere," he said, placing his hands on his thighs. The game was now over. "Not until you return to me the letter you stole."

Miss Dunston gasped. It even sounded indignant. "Me? Steal from you? How dare you make such an accusation!" She moved to the right of the desk, and he followed suit, blocking her exit. "Don't play games with me, Sir Aaron." She took another step to the right, and he followed her movements again. "I'm warning you. Ruth is skilled in fisticuffs and will come to my immediate aid if you try anything improper!"

Aaron could not help but laugh. "The charade is over, Miss Dunston. Don't you think it's about time you stopped pretending to be an innocent young girl? It's quite clear you're a spoiled child, no doubt placated by your parents at every whimper."

This time, no gasp escaped her lips. Instead, she narrowed her eyes. The girl had a temper, that much was sure, and he found it alluring.

"You know nothing about me or my family," she spat. "So don't act as if you do. And how dare you mock my innocence. I'm far better than you will ever be. You're a beast, Sir Knight, one who ignores his son and believes that sharing the same food as you or his mother is worthy of punishment! You may not have married his mother, but what right does that give you to approve of her maltreatment of your son? Is it not your blood that flows through his veins? Does that not allow him at least the decency to be fed and housed properly? No child, born in wedlock or otherwise, should be treated like an animal!"

Confusion clouded Aaron's mind. His son? He had no son. Miss Dunston's face was red, and she was breathing heavily by the time she finished her tirade. He took a step toward her. As she went to move to the left, he acted as if he would do the same, and she took the bait. Reaching across, he moved right, took hold of her arms, and pushed her back against the desk.

His breathing became ragged, and he struggled to keep from kissing her again. He needed to keep his wits about him if he was to get to the bottom of this nonsense. And to see that whatever she had stolen was returned to him. But having her so close made it nearly impossible.

And although the young woman was a thief, she looked at him through her eyelashes. "You may kiss me," she said, her words breathy.

All hope was lost. The fruit of the tree was too appealing to resist. He pulled her into his arms, a small whimper escaping her mouth as he did as she bade.

The kiss was powerful, his grip on her firm. She made no attempt at escape. With his guard dropped, the pounding of his heart increased, and an odd sensation washed over him. It was not primal like it was before. This time, there was a sense of connecting, as if they were drawing closer together. He relished her soft lips and could not help but smile when she attempted to move past him again while at the same time returning his kiss in equal measure.

"Enough," he whispered, holding her firmly in place. Her breathing was as shallow as his, and her cheeks were bright red. "Why did you take a letter off my desk? And what is this nonsense about my son? I have no children."

Her glare only increased his desire. "You may be able to deceive others," she snapped. "But not me. I was at the park yesterday while you were speaking with Lady Mathison. I heard her say that she makes your son—William, I believe was his name—she makes him sleep in the stables! That is the reason I took the letter she wrote to you. To find more evidence to bring you down."

Aaron had never witnessed such passion from any woman, let alone one so beautiful. Yet, he found her words so humorous, so outlandish, he could not stop himself from roaring with laughter.

"William? My son?" he asked between guffaws. "Miss Dunston, William is my dog, and Lady Mathison is my sister!"

She shook her head. "But you met her in secret. Why would you do that if she's only your sister? And who is this Peter she wishes dead?"

Aaron drew in a deep, calming breath. What she asked was personal, yet he found he trusted her. Why? He could not be sure, but he did. "Horatia is married to an earl far older than she. It was a marriage of convenience. He's cruel and unloving and controls every aspect of her life. He's locked her in her bedroom for days when she's angered him, and he never allows a moment to pass without reminding her that she's only a decoration for his arm. That's why we meet in secret. If the old man learned we even spoke, she would pay dearly."

Miss Dunston hung her head. "I'm sorry," she whispered, removing the letter and handing it to him. "I made assumptions and interfered where I clearly should not have." Her voice was filled with pain, true pain.

Something she had said hurt him deeply. "Do you truly think so poorly of me?" he asked.

She gave him a wide-eyed shake of her head. "No, of course not."

He wanted to believe her, he truly did, but the doubt that emanated from her made doing so difficult. A strange, overwhelming desire to prove he was not the rogue she believed him to be came over him.

"Come with me," he said. "I want to show you something."

"Wait," she said, pulling her hand from his. "My actions, my words... shame is burning inside me. I do truly apologize for what I did. I know eavesdropping is wrong, and I know you'll never understand, but I've always had a strange need to do so. More often than you can imagine. But now, I swear to never spy again."

There was no pride in watching Miss Dunston expressing her regret. This was not a matter of who was right and who was wrong. Rather, it was about a hurt young lady he did not wish to see suffer any longer.

"Don't be ashamed of anything in this life," he said. Strange how easy it was to give advice he was unable to take. "I hold no ill will toward you. All is forgiven. In fact, I admire you for facing your shortcomings."

"You're not lying?" she asked, wiping at her eyes.

"No. I promise I am not. Now please, come with me."

He led her down the corridor to the library and stopped in front of his family's sword. "The Sword of Destiny has been in my family for centuries. I assume you've heard of the War of the Roses?"

"Yes, of course. We learned about it last year. Was this sword used in that war?"

Aaron smiled. "It was. It played an important part." He gave her a brief explanation of his ancestor's involvement. "It's said that whoever wields the sword will do great things. But more importantly, it will lead that person to his—or her—destiny."

Turning to face Miss Dunston, Aaron felt a sudden urge to share everything with her. To tell her about all his worries and his failures in life. But he could not. Not all of it. Not yet.

"Just as those before me, I'll do great things in my life. And although I'm uncertain what those things may be, the gentlemen's club is just a start. As long as I possess the sword, I'll be successful."

Miss Dunston frowned. "But you're a hero. A knight! Is that not enough?"

He stifled a laugh. "No, it's not enough. I must do something great. To prove myself worthy of my ancestors. Of my father. Then that will be enough."

She placed a hand on his arm. This time it was in kindness rather than as a form of manipulation. Somehow, he knew this. "I see you as the hero everyone recognizes you to be, Sir Aaron. You carry the nobleness of your title well. Whatever you wish in life, I believe you can achieve it." She glanced at the sword. "Since you shared with me something so personal, I'll do the same for you."

Never had he wanted to hear words from anyone as he did Miss Dunston at this moment.

"Please, tell me."

Chapter Fourteen

Guilt consumed Louisa. Had Mrs. Rutley not warned her of the dangers of eavesdropping? Of keeping her nose out of other people's business? Indeed, she had. Several times! Now, not only had Louisa assumed the worst, but she had accused Sir Aaron outright of moral malfeasance.

Yet the knight's willingness to forgive her for her actions had somehow alleviated the shame that filled her. In truth, he had every right to despise her, to hold her accountable for her childish behavior, but he chose to be a gentleman.

Silently, she vowed to never spy on anyone again. If she was to become the lady she wished to be, such misconduct would be of no help. In fact, continuing down this current path—one of which she had tried to avoid these past few months—would send any possible suitors fleeing in disgust.

As she stood beside Sir Aaron looking up at the Sword of Destiny, her heart filled with admiration for the knight. She had been correct. Deep down, he was a good person and, like her, wanted something better in life. Through this common need, a bond had formed between them.

How strange that she had despised him before today. Yesterday, she loathed him because as far as she was concerned, he was arrogant and self-righteous. Now, however, she saw him in a different light. What she saw stunned her. Rather than pushing him away, she now wanted to strengthen this alliance.

And she knew what it would take to make that happen.

"Since you shared something so personal with me, I would like to reciprocate if I may."

He smiled down at her, and she was reminded of their chance encounter at the millinery. That smile had intrigued her. Before he had mistaken her for someone else, of course. And had treated her rudely.

No! It was time to put behind her what had already happened. Their future would go nowhere if she allowed herself to dwell on the past.

"Go on," he said.

Louisa dropped her gaze to gather her thoughts. Where did she begin? "I have three sisters, all older than I, and I love them very much. They are all married to men of title and wealth, which has pleased my parents. After all, now their circle of friends has grown. They are now invited to parties for which they otherwise would be passed over. You must understand, they did not use my sisters to insert themselves into society. But they have benefited from those marriages."

She sighed. What she wished to admit was not coming as easily as she had hoped.

Sir Aaron must have sensed her reluctance, for he gathered her hand in his, sending her heart fluttering. "Whatever you wish to say, whatever you wish to share, know that it is safe with me."

Lifting her eyes to look into his face, Louisa did not see just a handsome man. Now she saw a gentleman with whom she could share her heart. Well, perhaps not all that was on her heart, but some. After all, if he learned her darkest secret, he would want nothing to do with her. But there were some things she was willing to share.

"You spoke of your destiny. Well, mine is to marry and have children." She shrugged. "I realize that is not much different from other women like me, but I worry that by doing so, my story will end. I feel as if something is out there waiting for me, but I've no idea what it is.

And I fear that if I don't find whatever that something is, I'll never be as good as my sisters."

The room fell quiet as her mind returned to when she had returned home the previous summer and shared these very thoughts. "My parents believe I'm a fool. My father was angrier with me than he ever had been. He blamed Mrs. Rutley for putting thoughts in my head, and if it had not been for Mother, I would not be here today. To him, it was a waste of his money. 'A place that teaches nothing but nonsense' had been his description. Mother agreed with him to a point. To her, my only duty was to find a husband. I had no business even considering any other path. My sisters made them proud. They had no strange aspirations in life, no thoughts of achieving anything outside of what was expected of them. Instead, they reveled in the idea of marriage. That is why Father does not see me as equal to them."

Sir Aaron frowned. "I'd say that is likely untrue. What father does not love his daughter?"

Louisa wished to say her own but withheld the words. This man would never understand. No man would.

"Nothing I do can compare to what my sisters have done for them. Patricia, the eldest, married a viscount. Georgia is now a viscountess, and Anna a baroness. My parents are now tied to the nobility. They don't need me."

He gently squeezed her hand. When he went to pull away, she tightened her grip. She needed the feeling of protection his hand offered, for it lessened the worry in her heart.

"It appears I've also misjudged you," he said. "You're not a spoiled child but rather a beautiful young lady with dreams. I can respect that."

His words warmed Louisa's heart and soul. She could see a good man behind his mask of arrogance.

"Before I say more," he said, glancing toward the door, the corner of his mouth twitching, "should we see how your companion is faring? Or should I assume her malady was a part of the ploy to give you time alone in my study?"

Louisa flushed. "She was never ill."

Sir Aaron chuckled, a pleasant sound to her ears. She had never thought laughter could be considered handsome, but he proved her wrong.

"Allow me to help you," he said. "Let me aid you in this search for your true destiny."

Louisa smiled. "I would like to learn how to conduct business, how to deal in trade, or how to manage contracts. I want to learn that which so many men spend their lives pursuing."

An image of them sitting on a blanket beneath the shade of a tree appeared in her mind. Birds performed a beautiful melody for them. The blades of grass rustled in the gentle breeze. Sir Aaron was instructing her and voiced his amazement at her ability to learn.

He would gaze down at her, his eyes filled with admiration. "You've proven to me how wrong I've been. Never again shall I doubt you. You've made me see women, in general, in a new light. Now, may I kiss you?"

The choir of birds would sing the agreement that lay on her heart, and Sir Aaron placed a gentle kiss on her lips. She shared more of her newfound knowledge, awing the knight all the more.

Then her daydream came to a crashing halt.

Rather than looking upon her with admiration, Sir Aaron was frowning. "The idea of women studying the intricate strategies that make up all aspects of business really is a waste of time. After all, what could they possibly do with such knowledge? But I believe I can make an exception for you. I would be happy to give you a few basic lessons, ones that can be far more effective than those presented in the book you took from Lord Walcott's library. It's rather advanced. I imagine most of its contents are quite confusing to you."

His words pricked her daydream as efficiently as a needle to a soap bubble. The warmness that had filled her heart dissipated. Did he not hear how arrogant his words were?

Pulling her hand from his, she glared up at him. "Lord Walcott lent that book to me. I did not simply take it."

Sir Aaron closed his eyes and sighed. "You are quick to assume the worst in me, Miss Dunston. I was not implying that you stole it, so allow me to rephrase my statement. The book you *borrowed* from Lord Walcott's library."

Louisa's jaw tightened with anger. A moment ago, she was considering allowing this man to court her. To be romantic with her. Now, she wanted to be away from him. But not before slapping his handsome face!

"Now," he continued, "if you accept my offer, I'd be happy to instruct you in the basics of business." Was it her imagination or was his haughty grin widening? "But if I do this, you must promise to stop with this silly notion of taking it further than our studies. Women have no place in creating contracts or owning an enterprise. But understanding a barter or how to deal with a household account is essential to working with her husband's money."

Louisa clenched her fist. This man was a pigheaded buffoon! "Before I respond to your... generous offer," she put as much derision into the term as she could muster, "why not explain why a handsome knight has no woman on his arm."

Sir Aaron led her to a blue couch with white flowers and waited for her to sit before taking the place beside her. His strong jaw and the heady scent of oak and orange was making her lightheaded, and she prayed this closeness was not a ruse to lower her defenses.

"You are correct," he said. "I am handsome. And although one would believe it is a gift, I'm here to say it is a curse. I've rejected many ladies, and each time I do, I hurt them. But finding a worthy woman is no easy task, I assure you. She must be from a good family, be obedient, and she must allow a man the peace he needs to function in society. That was what my father taught me, and he was right." He let out a small sigh. "If we're honest, Miss Dunston, women tend to be more of a burden than a blessing. Oh, they are necessary for several reasons—like bearing children or seeing to the daily running of a household."

He smiled at her, and she had to swallow back the desire to laugh outright. "And what of their duty to raise these children?" she demanded.

"There are servants who can help, so how difficult can it be? My mother had few problems, and she had only a nanny for my sister and me."

For a moment, Louisa imagined Mrs. Rutley applauding her for taking one of the beast's ledgers off the shelf and hitting him across the head with it. How difficult could it be, indeed!

"I'm beginning to see why you believe women are a burden, sir," she replied, not caring that her words were waspish. "You don't listen. I explained that, like you, I hope to do something great with my life. How am I to learn what that is if I'm discouraged from reading certain books? Why should I not be allowed to study that which I find fascinating, even if it falls outside what custom dictates? Do you truly believe my destiny lies with me sitting in a drawing room working on embroidery? Even the Queen has greater expectations!"

It was not the shake of his head that caused her ire to boil over. Nor was it the laugh that accompanied it. Rather it was the words that tumbled from his lips. "I'm handsome and you're beautiful. Is it not in your best interest for me to continue to call on you? After all, it's what is expected of people such as you and I."

"What are you saying?" she demanded, her jaw aching from how tightly it was clenched.

He patted her hand as if she were a child who needed help in understanding a simple point. "It only makes sense that we marry. I can then guide you in your search for whatever it is you feel you need. Perhaps I'll even allow you access to my ledgers—for study, of course. And as long as you tell no one."

In one quick motion, Louisa pulled her hand from his and stood. "Your arrogance knows no bounds! You believe I would marry—or even allow you to court me—based solely on your appearance?"

Sir Aaron came to his feet. "Surely, you're not saying you wish to marry a plain-looking man? Yes, it's done all the time, but for marriages of convenience. How often are two such attractive people thrown together as we have been? It only demonstrates how intertwined our destinies are."

Louisa groaned and buried her face in her hands. "I wish to marry for love, Sir Aaron. I want someone who will love the woman I truly am." When the knight frowned, she sighed. "I'm sure you've heard the word before. Oh, what does it matter? I don't want your instruction. Nor do I need your guidance in my destiny. I'm more than capable of finding it on my own. And certainly not with a man like you!"

She turned to leave, but he grabbed hold of her arm. "Love is only found in books, Miss Dunston. In fairy tales and novels, all with fictional characters. And don't pretend you are not as arrogant as I." He paused, and a smile crossed his features. "I've just made a wonderful realization."

Louisa's breath caught. Did he finally see how foolish he was being? Perhaps he had seen the error of his ways and would apologize.

"I'm sure you remember our argument in the library at Foxly Manor," he continued. "We disagreed then just as we are now. And I know exactly what you need to help you keep that temper of yours in check."

Louisa gasped as he leaned in to kiss her just as he had at the home of Lord Walcott. This time, however, she pushed him away. With a grunt, he took a step back. She would not be caught in his net again!

"You're correct. This situation resembles that encounter. And I would like to leave you with the same words as I did then. I despise you, Sir Aaron!"

The knight crossed his arms over his chest and barked a laugh. "No, Miss Dunston. Like before, you're smitten with me. You may deny it, but you and I both know it for true."

A growl stuck in her throat, for she could not argue this fact. She did want his kisses, but she wanted to strangle him more! Therefore, she turned on her heel and barged from the room to go in search of Ruth. As they gathered their wraps, Sir Aaron leaned against a nearby wall, that silly grin on his face.

"Would you like me to accompany you back to the school?" he asked.

Adjusting her wrap, Louisa replied in her sweetest tone, "I would rather poke the eyes from my head, sir."

Ruth snorted and quickly covered it with a cough as Sir Aaron opened the door for them. "At least allow me to walk you to the carriage."

The sky was washed in pink as they stepped outside, but Louisa paid the sunset little heed. All she wanted was to be as far away from this beast as she could be. Yet as she lifted her skirts to follow Ruth into the vehicle, he placed a hand on her arm to forestall her.

"I know you think I'm cruel, but I assure you, I'm not. I only wish to save you from the humiliation of me besting you when I purchase the theater."

Louisa placed a hand on his chest. His heart beat against her palm. "I recognize my destiny now. I'll write a book."

"A book? And what will it be about?"

"A knight with a rather large head who was bested by a woman and thus scorned for the rest of his life. Yes, that is exactly what I'll do. I'll save the theater and write a book about it."

Without waiting for his reply, she stepped into the carriage and closed the door. Soon, she and Ruth were heading back to Courtly Manor.

"You'll not believe what he said!" Louisa said.

Ruth laughed. "Oh, I do believe it. I heard everything."

"You spied on me?"

Ruth shook her head. "No, I'm your chaperone. It's my job to see you don't succumb to your passions."

Louisa sniffed. "You mean his passions," she corrected.

"Oh no, I mean yours. I'm beginning to see that your frustration with him stems from the attraction you feel whenever you're in his company."

Crossing her arms, Louisa glared at her friend. "I'm not attracted to him in the slightest! At least not any longer. It has been a terrible mistake on my part, but I'll remedy that situation just as soon as I can."

Ruth shook her head. "Maybe if you tell yourself that enough, you just might believe it."

Chapter Fifteen

Three days had passed since Louisa had last spoken to Sir Aaron. Despite how they had left things, to deny she missed him would be a lie. There was something about that man that seemed to call to her. What that was, she could not name, yet it was there just beneath the surface of understanding. He frustrated her, to be sure, but Ruth had been right. Fighting her attraction to him was a challenge, for he was a walking contradiction. Arrogant one moment, compassionate the next.

After opening her heart to him, after allowing him to see a piece of her soul, she was glad she had not revealed all to him. If he ridiculed her for wanting to learn beyond what was expected of her, how would he have reacted if she had shared more? No, she had made the right choice. He could not be trusted. And winning this feud was the only way to be rid of him for good, so she would be able to find a husband worthy of her.

But she had no time to waste thinking of him. Two of her friends, her Sisters, were now far more important.

Gray clouds dotted the sky as Louisa stood on the portico of Courtly Manor with the remaining members of the Sisterhood of Secrets. Unity's parents had arrived the previous evening, ready to collect the twins so they could return to Unity's home. Their belongings had already been strapped to the top of the carriage, and the girls were allowed a moment alone to say their farewells.

"I've no idea what to say," Louisa said as she blinked back tears. "I'll miss you both so very much. The school will not be the same without you here."

Unity dabbed at her eyes with a handkerchief. "The years passed by far too quickly. I suppose I have no one to blame but myself. And Theodosia." She grinned at her friend. "After all, we both urged it forward because we've so looked forward to the next stage of our lives. Now I find myself in a conundrum. I wish to turn back the clock so I have more time here, yet I also cannot wait to leave. I know I speak for us both when I say that we will cherish every moment of our time here."

Theodosia nodded. "I could not have said it better myself, Unity. It's as if we're leaving behind family."

"That's because you are," Louisa said. "We're all sisters now, remember? We made a pact, which means we're now family. But all children in a family must move on, do they not?"

The girls exchanged hugs and promises to write. Although Louisa knew they would at first, she also understood that life had a way of changing plans. They would all soon be married and raising their children. Days of leisure would be filled with a variety of activities. Replying to correspondences would become less of a priority. That thought made her sad.

Mrs. Rutley's voice made Louisa start. "Whatever you do in life, know that I'm here for you. You've both become very capable young ladies, and I have no doubt you'll be successful no matter what you decide for your lives."

Louisa allowed the words of her headmistress to wash over her and soothe her soul. Mrs. Rutley could always lift her spirits when she was down.

With a final goodbye, the twins stepped into the vehicle. Those who remained stood side by side, the wind growing in intensity around them.

After watching the carriage disappear down the lane, Mrs. Rutley crossed the drive and approached the large oak tree where the Sister-hood had first been formed.

With a nod from Ruth, she and Louisa joined Mrs. Rutley as she ran a hand over the initials carved in the tree's flesh. A chilly breeze from the darkening clouds blew past them, and Louisa wrapped her arms around herself for warmth. She could feel the building storm.

"I remember the first time I saw this tree," Mrs. Rutley said, breaking the silence that surrounded them. "My lady's maid and I stood right here, admiring its magnificence. We could not help but wonder what sort of secrets it may have heard." To Louisa's surprise, tears rimmed the headmistress's eyes.

Louisa frowned. "What is wrong, Mrs. Rutley?"

Thunder pealed in the distance, and the first spits of rain began to fall. Mrs. Rutley took first Louisa's and then Ruth's hands in hers.

"One by one, my girls are leaving me," she said, her eyes red. "And now I have only the two of you remaining. Soon, you'll leave here forever, and I'll miss you so very much." She then smiled. "Oh, I'll have other students, but none will hold such a special place in my heart the way you girls do. The bond we share can never be replicated." She glanced at the tree. "The day we made our vow, I did not share my secret with you. Perhaps I will once we are all together again."

The wind began to howl and flicked Louisa's hair as she glanced at Ruth. She was stunned to see a single tear rolling down her friend's cheek.

"We'll meet again, Mrs. Rutley," Ruth said, her voice raised to be heard above the impending storm. "Not even death himself can stop me from returning."

Louisa shook her head. Ruth's words might be poetic, but no one could defeat death.

Mrs. Rutley embraced Ruth before turning to Louisa and doing the same. "Now, enough of this feeling sorry for ourselves," she said, although her smile could have pushed away the darkness emanating from the storm. "What do you say to asking Mrs. Shepherd to make us some drinking chocolate?"

"Who could refuse chocolate?" Louisa asked as she wiped away the tears that flowed down her face.

As they hurried to the house, they were soon sitting in the drawing room sharing stories about their classmates who had already gone. Louisa's mind began to wander. What sort of secrets did her headmistress keep from them? And which would she share once they were all back together again? Her thoughts were cut short when Mrs. Rutley inquired about Sir Aaron.

Later that night as she lay in bed, rain pelting against the window, Louisa came to a decision. Sir Aaron was a stubborn man, yet she could not deny her attraction to him.

She would do all she could to secure the future of the theater. And once she did, she just might decide to save Sir Aaron after she had saved the theater. It was the least she could do.

Chapter Sixteen

Besides a few odd puddles in the streets of Chatsworth, there was no evidence of the storm that had passed two days earlier. Louisa had gone into the village to speak to several of the shopkeepers in an effort to garner their support to save the theater.

Sadly, most she encountered could spare no more than the odd shilling. Everyone was struggling, and most had so little time or money that availing of the theater was a rare treat.

This meant that Louisa would have to change tactics. Of course, those simply trying to make ends meet would be unable to donate. Yet there were those of the higher class, those who had the means she could approach. Therefore, she would write letters to the various noble families in the area and plead her case to them. They enjoyed the various plays and shows offered at the theater—more often than the lower classes—so they would be interested in saving it, would they not? After all, doing so would keep culture—and a bit of London—in the village.

With Ruth at her side, Louisa exited the tobacconist shop, tucking away the small donation she had received from the proprietor. It was the very same shop where she had first encountered Sir Aaron. That seemed eons ago yet as if it happened just yesterday. The passage of time could be very strange.

"Look over there," Ruth said, tugging at the sleeve of Louisa's pelisse.

"Where?"

"There. At the theater. Is that not Mr. Barker? I wonder where he is going."

Indeed, a carriage sat in front of the theater. Beside it stood the theater's landlord, supervising the loading of two bags onto the back of the vehicle. Was the man abandoning his premises?

Well, I never! she growled to herself. What a scoundrel! And here she had believed they were in a truce.

With these thoughts in mind, Louisa hurried across the street. A young boy sat against the front wall of the theater as he tossed a coin into the air.

Mr. Barker ran a hand through his unruly brown hair. And as always, his coat was easily two sizes too large for him.

"Good morning, Mr. Barker," Louisa said as she approached the man. When he gave her a blank stare, she added, "Miss Louisa Dunston?"

"Ah, yes. One of Mrs. Rutley's girls. H-how's she doing?" It appeared that even speaking of the headmistress caused him to stutter.

"She's well," Louisa replied. "Thank you for asking." She glanced at the carriage. "Forgive me for inquiring, but you're not leaving Chatsworth, are you?"

"Well, isn't that what a carriage is used for?" Mr. Barker replied with a light chuckle.

"Yes, of course, but what I mean to ask is if you're leaving Chatsworth for good. You aren't, are you?"

Mr. Barker laughed outright. "Heavens, no. I'm off to my brother's for a few days. Holidays, you see." He tilted his head. "Is that why you came to speak to me?"

Louisa was unsure if the man was agitated or simply curious. "No, of course not. I wanted to let you know that I've been soliciting donations for the theater. The amount is small at the moment, but I have every faith that it will grow over time."

Mr. Barker let out a heavy sigh. "I admire your dedication, Miss Dunston, I truly do. But I must be honest. If I lose this place, my heart will be forever broken, to be sure. But Sir Aaron has scheduled a meeting with me at noon Wednesday next after I return from my trip. I believe he wishes to increase his offer, and I may be forced to accept his terms."

Her jaw ached with how tightly she was clenching it. So, the knight believed he could break the rules, did he? What gave him the right to go behind her back?

Granted, she had disregarded their thirty-day agreement, but her rationale was far more virtuous. Her goal was to do right by the entire village, not for a select few. Which was what would happen if the gentlemen's club was allowed to take over the building.

"Don't worry, Mr. Barker. I have faith that those of means in and around our village will come to our aid."

Then an idea came to mind. Yes, it was as devious as what Sir Aaron had done, but what was sauce for the goose was sauce for the gander. Or so went the saying.

"Were you aware that Mrs. Rutley adores the theater as much as you do?"

Mr. Barker gaped. "Sh-she does?" he managed to stammer.

Louisa ignored Ruth's snort. "Oh, yes." She leaned in closer and lowered her voice. "And between us, she believes the knight is a selfish man and that real men, worthy men far more deserving should be honored instead. Men such as you. They are the true noblemen. Those who occupy the thoughts of many women.

The poor man was close to fainting. His breathing had become ragged, his face was as red as a tomato, and he had slid a finger into his cravat to pull it away from his throat.

Not wanting to put him through more turmoil, Louisa said, "We must go, Mr. Barker. But I'll call on you after you've returned. I should have enough funds by then so you may begin the repairs."

"Yes," Mr. Barker said as he wiped the sweat from his brow. "I would like that very much, indeed. And do bring that wonderful head-mistress with you."

Assuring him she would, Louisa walked away, Ruth following behind.

The village was bustling by now. Single horses pulled a variety of buggies and carts, teams the more elaborate carriages of the wealthy—of which there were fewer given the time of year. Most of the nobility were still enjoying the diversions of the Season and would not be returning until the end of summer when England became too hot and stuffy.

"Are we done yet?" Ruth grumbled. "You've asked just about everyone in the village. Unless you'd like to visit Rake Street and solicit donations there." She snorted at her attempt at humor.

After making several inquiries, Louisa had painstakingly calculated the cost of the materials, as well as the labor for replacing the roof. Unfortunately, it far exceeded what she would have ever considered before all this began. That meant increasing the amount she needed to collect by at least double.

"Yes, well, I think not," Louisa said. "Besides, if I wanted to converse with the lowest in the village, I would search out Sir Aaron." She glanced ahead of them. "Oh, I would like to stop in at the tailor's shop. It's on our way and will be the last place, I promise. Then we may return to the school."

As they walked, Louisa stewed. It had been nearly a week since she had last seen Sir Aaron. Why had he not called? Or written?

That inflated sense of pride of his is likely keeping him away, she thought wryly.

When they arrived at the tailor's shop, Louisa peered through the front window. Good, no customers.

"I'll meet you here in a few minutes," Ruth said. "I have something I must do."

Louisa frowned. "Where are you going?"

Ruth jerked a thumb behind her. "That way."

With a shake of her head, Louisa entered the shop. A tall man of perhaps thirty with dark-brown hair and a kind smile stood in the far corner. He was handsome in a way, with a straight nose and fine cheekbones. Although he was not the tailor, Louisa had seen him before in passing.

"May I help you, miss?" he asked.

"I'm looking for Mr. Beadle," Louisa replied. "Can you tell him that Miss Louisa Dunston wishes to speak to him?"

The man shook his head. "I'm afraid my uncle is quite busy at the moment. He's making alterations and has asked not to be disturbed." He eyed her up and down appreciatively. "Is there anything I can do for you?"

"Your uncle?"

"Yes. I'm Jeffery Venter, his nephew. He and my mother are brother and sister." His smile broadened. "I'd love nothing more than to be of assistance if I can."

Louisa nibbled her lip. Perhaps his clear attraction to her could be used to her advantage. After all, what good was it to be as attractive as she was and not be able to put it to good use?

She batted her eyelashes and gave him a tiny smile. "You just may be able to help me, Mr. Venter." He beamed at her, and she had to push back her jubilation. "You see, the Chatsworth theater is in dire need of our help."

For several minutes, she went on to explain the situation, emphasizing more than once what a tragedy to the village it would be if the theater were forced to close its doors.

Placing a hand on his arm, she smiled up at him. "Will you be able to help me?"

Mr. Venter drew in a staggered breath. "Why, yes, of course. I would love to make a donation, Miss Dunston, I truly would, but you see"—he leaned in close and lowered his voice to a whisper—"my uncle is a miser. He wouldn't be very pleased with me if he knew I gave funds to something that had nothing to do with helping him make more money."

A curtain behind the small counter fluttered, and Mr. Beadle entered from a backroom. Louisa sighed. All this work for nothing!

"Well, thank you for listening to my plight, Mr. Venter. I suppose I can find someone else willing to help."

Mr. Venter touched her arm. "Wait. There is an alley behind the shop. Meet me there in five minutes, and I'll see you have a donation."

Louisa glanced at the tailor. "Are you sure you'll be able to get away?"

"Most definitely."

Louisa exited the shop. Ruth had still not returned, so she lowered her head and hurried to the small walkway that connected High Street to the alley behind the shops. It was a dark, foreboding place, consisting of a cobbled path in much need of a good sweep—if not a good wash—that ran parallel to the main street and ended in a field at the edge of the village.

As she drew near the back entrance to the tailor's shop—or she hoped it was that shop for there was no signage on this side—Louisa glanced over her shoulder. It was rather quiet here. Too quiet. The tall buildings that flanked the alley muted the sounds of traffic and created deep shadows that made it look like dusk.

What was she doing meeting a man alone in such a place? Good cause or not, a lady did not put herself in such a predicament.

"Miss Louisa!" Mr. Venter called. He stood not ten paces from her, making her start. Did he have to shout?

She glanced behind her again. Perhaps she should make excuses and leave. Running.

"I have five pounds for you."

Five pounds? Not one person had offered her five pounds! The most she received thus far from any one person had been one pound from Mr. Pollard, the jeweler. And that had been a struggle.

Unable to believe her newfound luck, she hurried to Mr. Venter to find a smile that matched hers.

"Thank you so much, sir," she said, extending a hand. "Your generosity is appreciated far more than you can imagine."

She reached for the money, but he refused to release it. When she looked up at him again, her blood ran cold. His once-warm smile was now icy, and his eyes were flames. "I'm a very generous man, Miss Dunston," he said in an oily tone that sent unpleasant shivers down her spine. "But my money does not come easily. I require a kiss in exchange."

Oh, why could she not be like Ruth and simply punch this man?

Yet even the threat of doing so stuck in her throat as he lifted her gloved hand to his lips.

"Now, what do you say? A kiss?"

Indignation filled her. How dare he take such liberties! "You may keep your money, Mr. Venter." She pulled her hand, but he did not release it. "Release me this instant. My friend will be waiting for me."

"Surely one kiss will not hurt?" he said, grinning like a Cheshire cat. "You were obviously flirting with me, Miss Dunston. You cannot tell me you're not experienced with the act of kissing."

Her anger flared. "What do you think you're doing?" she demanded. "Let go of me!"

But rather than doing as she bade, he pulled her closer to him. As he leaned in close, she closed her eyes and turned her head to keep him from kissing her.

Then Mr. Venter cried out in pain, and Louisa landed on her back-side after he abruptly released her. When she opened her eyes, the tailor's nephew was lying on the ground, a figure standing menacingly above him.

Chapter Seventeen

The idea of being lonely was foreign to Aaron, for he had never carried that burden. Yet a week of not being in Miss Dunston's company gave him a sense of longing he had heard described by others. Yet that was not why the feeling was odd.

The fact was Miss Dunston was a strange young lady, flirtatious with a head full of scandalous ideas. Women being educated like men? Preposterous!

Despite all her faults, however, he found that he did admire her. And they did share some commonalities. They both had a love for dogs and the ability to dream. And they were both blessed with handsome features. Beyond those few similarities, however, he could not think of a single commonality that indicated they could be more than simple acquaintances.

Granted, he could admire her beauty all day. And when he had confessed his dreams to her, a spark had ignited between them. A bond of sorts had formed, and he wished to see it grow. If he so chose, he could pursue her.

But did he want to be mixed in with the kind of trouble she offered? After all, she had a fiery temper, which would make her a difficult wife. Men who saddled themselves with disagreeable wives deserved their lots. Each time he considered calling on Miss Dunston, he remembered how irksome she could be, and he was cured of that thought. Even the three letters he had written her had been ripped in half and tossed into the fire before they were posted. All they did was make him look weak.

No, the girl had to come to her senses on her own and realize the mistake she had made. He was a handsome knight and therefore the best man for her. After all, if he had to choose the woman for him, he would pick her. After she recognized her wrongdoing, of course.

As the carriage trundled down the road, Aaron closed his eyes and pictured himself at Hearsely Estate. Miss Dunston had just arrived.

"Sir Aaron," she would say, her head hanging low, "I don't know what came over me when I last was here, but my actions were half-witted and unreasonable."

He placed a finger beneath her chin and lifted her face. Gazing into her blue eyes, he sighed. "Don't be ashamed, Miss Dunston. Women are prone to outrageous bursts of nonsense from time to time. If you're ready, I'll teach you."

They would be in his study as he lectured her on the finest points of business, Miss Dunston watching him in awe.

"Your brilliance is matched only by your handsomeness!" she would exclaim. And because she had recognized and commended him on his abilities, he would reward her with another kiss.

"Sir?"

Aaron started and his eyes flew open. Claremont was five years younger than Aaron with orange-red hair and so many freckles he looked as if he had tanned while wearing a net.

"Sorry, sir. Din't mean to wake ya, but we've arrived."

"I wasn't asleep," Aaron snapped. "Just resting my eyes."

"Yes, sir. If you say so, sir."

Clearing his throat, Aaron exited the vehicle, his eyes falling immediately on the front door of the theater. "I may be awhile, Claremont.

If you'd like to get yourself something to eat, you may. Just be back here within the hour in case I'm ready to leave."

The man bowed. "Thank ya, sir. I won't be gone long."

Although he had given his word to keep away from anything to do with the purchase of the theater, Aaron had decided to break that promise again. After all, Miss Dunston was not a business rival, not in the true sense of the phrase. She would have to be a man to be a rival. Therefore, not only had he secured an appointment with Mr. Barker next Wednesday, but he had also found another gentleman willing to invest in the gentlemen's club.

Mr. Walter Bolt was a wealthy merchant who dealt in linen. He was a recent arrival to Chatsworth just as Aaron was, which created an immediate bond between the two men.

As Aaron approached the theater doors, a young boy no older than ten with a dirty face squinted up at him. "Mr. Barker jus' left," he said, scratching at the mop of blond hair on his head. "He's off to 'is brother's."

"Is he?" Aaron asked. "Have you any idea why?"

The boy shrugged. "Said somethin' to that woman 'bout needin' a rest."

"And what woman was that?"

The youngster's grin had several missing teeth. "It'll cost ya a copper if ya wanna know."

Aaron dug a copper coin from his purse and placed it in the boy's hand. He had thought Mr. Barker was unmarried, but perhaps he was wrong. Either way, knowing all he could about the man was well worth such a small amount of money.

"Now, what woman?"

"She's over there," he replied, pointing down the street.

Aaron followed the boy's finger, and his jaw tightened. Miss Dunston stood with Miss Lockhart outside the tailor's shop.

"Said she's collectin' donations."

The ache in his jaw deepened. "Oh, did she now?" Aaron said through gritted teeth. How dare she break their agreement! She had been the one to propose the thirty-day truce! Once again, he had fallen for her charms. She was far more devious than he had first believed.

"Give me another copper, and I'll tell ya a secret."

Aaron eyed the boy. "Does it have anything to do with that young lady?"

The lad nodded.

Aaron took out two more copper coins and offered them to the boy. Whatever he had to say would be well worth the money. "Tell me what you know."

The boy's eyes lit up at seeing more than he requested. "She said a knight be 'ere that's selfish. And somethin' 'bout Mr. Barker bein' an honorable man. 'More honorable' is what she said."

If Aaron was ruffled before, now he was irate. How dare Miss Dunston talk about him behind his back. And accuse *him* of selfishness! Fuming, he marched across the street toward the tailor's shop. Not only would he confront Miss Dunston about her derogatory description of him, but he would also give her a few choice words to put her in her place!

When he peered into the window, however, his eyes widened in shock. She was at it again! Her hand rested on the clerk's arm, and she was flashing him her seductive smile. Oh, this woman was terrible! Who would conduct themselves in such a brazen manner? Miss Lockhart was nowhere to be found.

Not wishing to cause a scene, Aaron hurried over to a vegetable cart across the street where he could wait for her to emerge without being observed.

"Sir Aaron, is that you?"

Aaron turned toward the female voice to find Miss Miriam Connelly, the daughter of an extremely wealthy shipping merchant, smiling at him. She wore a pale-green dress printed with tiny yellow flowers. Her black hair was pinned up in the latest fashion and topped with a white hat. He would not say she was plain, but she most certainly was not handsome.

Beside her stood who could only be her lady's maid with her black and white livery and white lace mob cap.

He gave her a deep bow. "Miss Connelly, an honor to be sure. Have you had a chance to speak to your father about what we discussed when we last met?" He had approached the young woman three days earlier, using his charms to convince her that the gentlemen's club would be well worth her father's investment.

"He returns tomorrow from York," she replied. "I'll ask him once he's had a chance to rest."

He gave her an innocent smile. "A knight's strength comes not from himself but rather the ladies who aid him." Taking her hand in his, he kissed her knuckles. "A plain man such as myself is in awe of a woman of your striking beauty."

Miss Connelly tittered, a nasally sound that reminded him of his grandmother who always seemed to suffer from a stuffy nose. "Oh, Sir Aaron, you're far from plain." Her pink cheeks did nothing to improve her looks. Such a pity, too. She was an agreeable young lady. "Perhaps you would like to call over for tea."

"I would like nothing more," he said. Catching Miss Dunston leaving the tailor's shop, he bowed once more. "But I'm afraid I cannot today. I have a business engagement that requires my attention. Perhaps another time? Good day to you, Miss Connelly."

He turned back toward the tailor's shop just in time to see Miss Dunston enter the narrow walkway that led to the alley. That girl was a fool! And as stubborn as a mule. What sort of business would she have in such an out-of-the-way place? Did she not know that only lovers and brigands frequented alleyways?

Keeping ten paces behind her, he followed her into the walkway, keeping as quiet as he could. When she turned to the right down the alley, he stopped at the corner and peeked around. It was much darker than he would have thought, and the bright light at the end where a large field lay made it more difficult to see well.

A large stack of crates lay beside the wall, and he scurried to them, watching as she came to a stop in front of a young man Aaron recognized as the tailor's nephew. It took him several moments to remember the lad's name.

Jeffery? Jeffery Venter. Yes, that was his name. And Aaron did not like him.

He strained to hear what they were saying and clenched his hands into fists. He was offering her a donation for the theater? So, the young boy outside the theater had been telling the truth. Miss Dunston had gone back on her word! Well, she would pay—

"What do you think you're doing? Let go of me!"

Rage such as Aaron had never endured filled him. How dare this young villain accost any young lady, let alone Miss Dunston!

With swift steps, Aaron marched over to the pair, and without thought, struck the man in the chin. Jeffery tumbled over and fell onto his back.

"What is wrong with you?" he demanded of the young man. "Don't you understand that she has no interest in you?" What he wanted to do was pull this man from the ground so he could pummel him. Yet he restrained himself.

"S-sir Aaron!" Mr. Venter said as he pulled himself to his feet. "I'm sorry, sir. I didn't mean any harm." He turned to Miss Dunston, his eyes nearly covering his face. "I'm sorry, miss. I didn't mean to upset you. I just thought... I'm sorry. It won't happen again. I swear."

Aaron grasped hold of the front of the boy's shirt. "Miss Dunston is spoken for by me. Just see you don't mistreat her, or any other woman for that matter, with such disdain again."

"I swear to you it won't happen again," Jeffery said. He held out a five-pound note. "For her cause."

Snatching the note from his hand, Aaron waited for him to return to the shop, the door slamming in his wake. He then turned to scold Miss Dunston for her poor judgment in coming into the alley in the first place.

Only, he found he could not. Her lovely blue eyes were rimmed in red, and tears trickled down her cheeks.

"I... I should have not met him alone," she murmured. "I feel so foolish."

Her pain tore at his heart. Before he could stop himself, Aaron wrapped his arms around her. She lay her head against his chest and wept.

"It's over now," he whispered as he stroked her hair. "You're safe."

She lifted her face, and a small smile settled on her lips. "Thank you for saving me, Sir Knight. You truly are a hero."

Memories of how he had earned his title sneaked into his thoughts.

He was no hero but rather a man trying to find his way in life. But oh, she was a lovely creature with her tear-stained cheeks and lovely blonde tresses.

"I've learned a lesson today," she said.

He scrunched his brow. "Is that right? And what did you learn?"

Her face flushed with clear embarrassment. "That although Mr. Venter's actions were inexcusable, meeting him alone in a shadow-filled alley was not such a wise decision."

Aaron released her and took a step back. Would he always have to instruct her? "That may be true, but you've once again missed the point completely. I tried to warn you, Miss Dunston, but you refused to listen to reason. Your flirtatious ways have finally caught up to you. After today, every man in this village will believe he can get a kiss from you in exchange for a five-pound note! It's very unladylike and far beneath you to behave so provocatively."

Miss Dunston placed a hand on her hip and scowled. "*My* flirtatious ways? And what can we say about yours? Why is it you are allowed to use your looks to get what you want, but I—being a woman —cannot?"

Aaron's frustration grew. Were all women this simpleminded? "Men are different from women, Miss Dunston. We're allowed certain privileges because of where we stand in society." Miss Dunston went to speak, but he would not allow her to interrupt. "Nevertheless, this matter is the least of your worries. You've broken the agreement we made by speaking to Mr. Barker. And by calling *me* a selfish fool!"

She gaped at him. "He told you that?"

"So, you don't deny it?" Aaron countered. She lowered her head, and he added, "If you must know, a young boy overheard you. Either way, you cannot be trusted. Since you've broken our agreement, I'll resume my search for investors."

With a jut to her chin, Miss Dunston replied, "Do as you wish. For I'll not give up on my quest. I'll have what I want, Sir Aaron. Just you wait and see!" And with that, she turned away.

"Ha!" he shouted after her. "You know you cannot best me!"

She stopped and turned to glare at him. "What I know is that

you're a stubborn scoundrel, which is why you chose to follow me."
Once again, she turned on her heel.

He hurried after her. "I followed you because I care for you and
don't want to see you hurt."

Miss Dunston turned around, a deep frown marring her lovely
features. "What did you say?"

Aaron's mind raced. He had been so angry that he had spoken from
his heart without thinking. He had suspected that being away from her
had left him wanting to see more of her, but this new realization
stunned him. Looking down at her, however, he knew he truly did care
for her. Perhaps now was the perfect time to express it. Or at least
expand on it. They were alone, which would not happen again, he was
certain.

Yet his pride wriggled its way into his mind. Any feelings he
expressed for her beyond what he had already said she would only use
against him. No, he could not repeat what he had said.

"I said you should take care, or you'll trip, and I don't want to see
you get hurt," he mumbled.

With a shake of her head, Miss Dunston turned back around and
left him standing there alone.

Without her.

And that was a feeling he now despised.

Chapter Eighteen

T he corridor outside Louisa's room was filled with the sounds
of laughter and hurried talk as the students made their way
downstairs for luncheon. Louisa, however, had no appetite,
nor had she since her encounter with Mr. Jeffery Venter four days
earlier. Since Sir Aaron had shown such bravery, such heroics in saving
her from the clutches of a villain.

Finding herself in his arms had made her heart flutter and her legs
grow weak. She felt protected as she listened to the beating of his
heart. Comforted by the sweet whispers as he stroked her hair. She
could have remained there forever.

But then he had to go and ruin it by opening his mouth.

No one in England—nay, on this earth!—was as self-serving and
arrogant as that man! His natural good looks were marred only by the
words he spoke. If she could place a gag in his mouth to be removed
only when she wished him to kiss her, perhaps they would have a
future together. Yet since that was unlikely to occur, they would doubt-
less part ways once she saved the theater. After all, he had no plans to
remain in Chatsworth once their contest was completed.

Now more than ever, Louisa vowed to save the theater if only to best him. He was a self-righteous, egotistical monster who needed to be taught a lesson!

She sighed. If she believed this, why did she still wish to see him again? To be near him? To have him hold her once more?

"Shouldn't you be heading downstairs?" Ruth asked as she peeked through the door. "I imagine Mrs. Shepherd has put together a wonderful luncheon."

"Thank you, but I'm not hungry. Why don't you go without me?"

Ruth clicked her tongue and closed the door behind her. "I may be hungry, but I won't leave you alone. Not when I see something bothering you." She crossed her arms and frowned. "What's wrong?"

Louisa sighed again. "Go on and eat, Ruth. I'll be all right. There is no need to worry about me."

Ruth's frown deepened, and she narrowed her eyes. "You know very well that the hungrier I become, the more my temper flares, Louisa." She raised a menacing fist. "Now, you'd best tell me, or I'll flatten your nose."

Louisa could not help but laugh. Those who did not know Ruth might have trembled at her threats. Yet anyone who was acquainted with her in any way knew that her bark was worse than her bite. And despite her fierceness, she was never hateful. When she wanted something, she got it. That was who Ruth was.

"It's that blasted knight again, isn't it?"

Louisa gave a dejected nod and fell back on her bed to look up at the ceiling.

"I don't want to miss luncheon, Louisa, so speak."

Smoothing her skirts, Louisa exhaled. "I'm sure you remember the first time he said he cared for me, do you not? Well, it seems that I care for him, too. But I'm at a loss as to what to do. He can't be trusted, Ruth."

"And what makes you say that?"

"He broke our agreement!" Louisa said in exasperation. "And don't look at me like that! I know I'm not any better, but at least I have a valid reason for my behavior." She heaved another sigh and then paused. "For goodness' sake! When did I become so melodramatic?"

Ruth fell back onto the bed beside Louisa and said, "Love is an odd thing, isn't it? I find myself thinking about the captain, though I know I should not." She turned her head to look at Louisa. "If I tell you something, do you promise not to repeat what I say?"

Louisa rolled her eyes. The last thing she needed was to listen to one of Ruth's outlandish stories. Then again, perhaps doing so would take Louisa's thoughts off the knight.

"I promise," she replied. "Did you really meet a captain?"

Ruth wore a wicked smile. "Not only did I meet one, but he also kissed me. In Mrs. Rutley's office!"

Turning onto her side, Louisa frowned. "When did a captain of any sort come to the school?"

"Two winters ago, there was a terrible snowstorm. So terrible that travel was nearly impossible. Do you remember?"

Louisa nodded. "I do. Or rather I heard about it. I had gone home for Christmas that year, and we got little snow."

"Yes, very few of the students had remained that year," Ruth replied. "Well, a captain—his name is Luke Bannermann—he sought refuge here at Courtly Manor. We fed him and drank tea together while he was here." Her voice took a dreamy quality. "Oh, Louisa, he was so handsome, so dashing, and he told me the most wonderful stories about his travels. Well, when Mrs. Rutley excused herself for a few moments, I asked him two questions."

"Go on," Louisa said, intrigued. "What did you ask?"

"First, I asked him if he'd be willing to come for me when I finished school."

Louisa grinned. So, that was why Ruth always spoke of seafaring adventures.

"Then, I asked him to kiss me as a way to seal his promise to do so if he agreed."

Louisa covered a gasp with her hand. "And did he?"

"Of course, he did," Ruth replied with a sniff. Then she sighed. "But last winter, I received a letter saying he had to break his promise. He did not explain why, and I've not heard from him since."

"I'm sorry, my friend," Louisa said, taking Ruth's hand. Here she was fretting over Sir Aaron—whom she could see whenever she liked

—when her friend was pining for a man she would likely never see again.

"It's odd," Ruth said as she stared up at the ceiling. "As angry as I am over his abrupt ending to our future, I cannot stop thinking about him. I keep hoping that, one day, he'll return for me, yet I know the chances of that happening are slim indeed." She shook her head. "It's all so confusing."

Ruth had never been one to be so forthcoming with her troubles, at least not with Louisa. What had made the ship's captain change his mind? Had he only used Ruth to get a kiss and later regretted his actions? Or did he find and fall in love with another woman? Poor Ruth.

Well, Louisa was not going to ask those questions aloud. Let Ruth keep what little hope she had.

Ruth pulled herself up to a sitting position and took Louisa's hand. "The reason I shared my story is because love is never easy. I'll still wait for my captain to return, at least until summer. If he doesn't come, I'll leave without him. I can't wait around for him forever, especially since he's already said he'll not be returning for me. But your knight is already here. I suggest you do what you must because he may just leave one day and never return."

The thought of Sir Aaron not being in her life was strangely disconcerting and left her feeling... alone.

"I suppose you're right," Louisa said. "But what about the theater? I've heard he has set up a meeting with Mr. Barker in two days. What if Sir Aaron is able to convince him to sell?"

Ruth pursed her lips and knitted her brows in thought. "We must find a way to stop him. You say he's arrogant, so let's find a way to use that against him."

With a laugh, Louisa stood. "I thought you were hungry."

With a wave of her hand, Ruth also pulled herself from the bed. "It can wait. Your need is greater."

Louisa smiled. "It would be quite easy to play to his sense of self-importance. But how?"

Ruth rubbed her chin, her green eyes gleaming. "He's seeking investors, correct?"

Louisa nodded. "He is."

"Then we'll provide one for him. Lord Artemus!"

"Lord Artemus?" Louisa asked, confused. "Who is he and why would he wish to invest in a gentlemen's club?"

With an aggravated click of her tongue, Ruth replied, "Must I explain everything? Do you not remember our recent history lesson? The lord from Hensworth?" Louisa gave her a blank stare. "The founder of Chatsworth."

"But he's been dead for hundreds of years!"

"Do you honestly believe Sir Conceited knows anything about the history of the area? Or that the Artemus marquessate died out centuries ago?" Ruth replied with a wide grin. "I'd wager he doesn't even read. Follow me. I have an idea."

Grabbing Louisa's hand, Ruth pulled her out into the corridor and downstairs, stopping at Mrs. Rutley's office. "Don't worry," Ruth said as she pushed open the door and headed to the headmistress's desk. "She won't be back for hours."

Louisa nibbled her bottom lip and glanced at the closed door. If Mrs. Rutley or Mrs. Shepherd caught them there without permission, both of them would be in a great deal of trouble. She glanced at her hands. Just because none of the students had been forced to wash dishes as a form of punishment during her time there, that did not mean it could not happen.

"What are you doing?" she asked Ruth, who was hunched over the desk, the sound of a quill scratching parchment. "You can't be writing on behalf of Lord Artemus! Nor his descendent."

Ruth glanced at her with a mild look of annoyance. "Not from Lord Artemus. From Mrs. Rutley. Now be quiet, so I can think."

The minutes that passed felt like hours. Finally, Ruth stood and blew on the page before handing it to Louisa. "You should read it before I seal it."

Taking the letter, Louisa read it over. "This must be the cleverest idea you've ever devised," she said after finishing it. "Sir Aaron is dim-witted enough to believe it!"

Laughing, Ruth took back the letter. "He is a man, after all. Were you aware that they have smaller brains than women? Mrs. Shepherd says the good Lord gave them physical strength and saved the wisdom for us women."

Louisa nodded. She had heard Mrs. Shepherd's thoughts on the subject before, including her belief that if women were allowed to own and run more businesses, they would be so successful that men would die of jealousy.

As Ruth used Mrs. Rutley's stamp to seal the letter, Louisa experienced a small twinge of guilt. What they were doing was wrong, but their cause was good. Plus, Sir Aaron had to be taught a lesson.

To win this war, Louisa had to speak to Mr. Barker before Sir Aaron. Then she would allow the knight to court her.

And she had no doubt that he would ask. After proving her ability to outwit him, how could he not?

Chapter Nineteen

For the third time in the past hour, Aaron reread the letter in his hands. He had written Miss Duston as an attempt to ease her scorn. The young woman was a delicate creature and was easily agitated. Thus, he would have to choose his words with care.

Stopping in the middle, he read aloud.

"Although I cannot admit to any wrongdoing on my part, I do recognize that you believe I have committed an offense of some sort. Therefore, I would ask that you put away any misconceptions you may have about me and allow me to call on you again. After all, my mere presence can help you in your endeavor of seeking wisdom."

He paused. Something about his writing did not sit well with him, yet he could not place a finger on the exact problem.

Then he laughed. How could he be so slow-witted? The way he phrased his request to call on her was no better than a street urchin begging for coins. It would only strengthen her misconception of a woman's place in society!

The door opened, and Scriven entered. "I beg your pardon, sir, but Miss Dunston demands to speak to you."

Aaron placed the letter aside and rose from his seat. "What's this? She *demands*? Where is she now?"

"Forgive me, sir, but they are her words, not mine. She also says"—
he cleared his throat and flushed—"She'll wait *here*, for she's not
worthy to sit in your home."

"And where is 'here' exactly?"

The butler reddened further. "The front door, sir."

A sudden spike of amusement made Aaron grin. "Well, it appears
she's finally found humility. I'd say that's nothing short of a miracle."

"Perhaps others will follow her lead," Scriven mumbled.

Was that sarcasm Aaron heard in the man's tone? No, that was silly.
The butler had never been impertinent in the years in Aaron's employ.

"I'll go see her," Aaron replied.

As he entered the foyer, Aaron slowed his pace to allow himself a
moment to take in the young lady. Her deep-blue dress suited her well,
not only in its color but also in how it clung to her feminine form. Her
hat was adorned with several blue feathers, and black slippers peeked out
from beneath the hem of her skirts. In her hand, she clutched a letter,
and her face expressed a deep sadness that tugged at Aaron's heart.

What was most odd was the sympathetic pat on her arm that came
from Miss Lockhart. The redhead never seemed the consoling type.

"Good afternoon, ladies," Aaron said with a bow.

Miss Dunston started and looked up at him. "Forgive my intrusion,
sir, but Mrs. Rutley wished us to come as soon as we could." She
handed him the letter. "Mrs. Rutley asked me to deliver this letter to
you. I even used my allowance to hire a carriage as part of my
punishment."

Aaron arched a single brow. Punishment? For what?

Well, it was no business of his.

"What is this concerning?"

"I don't know what it says exactly, but I'm here to apologize for my
behavior. I'm afraid I've conducted myself poorly as of late, but I
promise I do know how a lady should act. I'm here to assure you that
I'll not be disrespectful again."

A small smile tugged at his lips. Finally, the woman had seen the
errors of her ways.

Yet her sad expression created a twinge of guilt within him.

Hurting her had been the last thing he wanted to do. But if she became a better woman because of that lesson, it was well worth the humiliation she had to endure.

Sliding a finger beneath the seal, he unfolded the letter.

Sir Aaron,

I have recently learned that Miss Dunston's behavior has been less than exemplary over the past few weeks. I cannot express my embarrassment, for she has received better instruction. My students are trained to serve great men such as yourself and to find any one of them showing such disregard for your station greatly troubles me.

Aaron stifled a grin. Great man? Well, this Mrs. Rutley was far more intelligent than he first suspected if she recognized his exceptional qualities.

Not only do I apologize for what you have been forced to endure, but I also have instructed Miss Dunston to beg your forgiveness. I have learned you are seeking investors to open a gentlemen's club where the Chatsworth Theater is currently located. As a woman, other than my knowledge of running a young ladies' school, I lack the training in the area of business.

I have, however, mentioned your plans to an acquaintance of mine. Lord Philip Artemus of Hensworth has expressed a great deal of interest in this enterprise of yours and is excited at the prospect of doing business with you, a knight. He would be honored to have you call to his castle tomorrow at noon, where the two of you can discuss this wonderful opportunity without the interference of any ambitious females.

· · ·

Aaron nearly jumped for joy. A lord who resided in a castle wished to do business with him? He could not have asked for a more agreeable situation!

"Where is Hensworth?"

"Hensworth?" Miss Dunston asked, her eyes wide. "It's a two-hour journey northeast of Chatsworth by carriage. Why? What is in Hensworth?"

"That is none of your concern," he said curtly. He folded the document and slid it into his inside coat pocket. "So, you've displeased your headmistress, have you?"

"How did you...? Oh. Yes, well, I suppose she said so in her missive. I've been assigned to do hard labor in the kitchen for the remainder of the week, and I'm not to leave the school unless... Well, what does it matter?"

"Unless what?"

She heaved a deep, heavy sigh. "Unless you call on me," she replied with a scowl. "Mrs. Rutley believes I can learn from you. I suppose she's right in that assessment, but that does not mean I have to like it."

Aaron was uncertain if his elation came from the meeting with Lord Artemus or this sudden admittance to the truth. As far as he was concerned, it could be either. Or both.

"So, you admit you were wrong concerning men and what they do? You finally understand a woman's place?"

Miss Dunston gave a sad nod.

"And what about this nonsense with the theater? Are you giving up this ridiculous crusade of yours?"

"Yes, Sir Aaron," she whispered, her lower lip quivering.

A sudden burst of guilt washed over him. Had he gone too far? Indeed he had if she was on the verge of tears.

"Although I disagree with your willingness to solicit donations, I do admire your passion." He had said this in hopes of seeing her smile at least once before she left, but the sad frown remained in place. He searched his mind for the right words. What did women wish to hear? "Through all this, Miss Dunston, you've retained what is most important. Your beauty."

With another heavy sigh, Miss Dunston said, "Thank you. After all, that is all that matters to a woman. I'll bother you no longer."

Scriven opened the door, and Aaron watched the two young ladies walk through the entryway. Without warning, fear rushed through him. If she left as disconcerted as she was, she might never be willing to see him again. He could not have that.

"Miss Dunston," he called after her. "When I return from Hensworth, may I call on you? I do enjoy your company."

"I would love nothing more, sir," she replied. "Thank you again for showing me the correct path a woman should take. Who knows where I would be today if I continued living as I was?"

Was it his imagination or did her eyes have a mischievous glint to them as she said this?

As the carriage pulled away, he took out the letter and read it over again. Something was amiss, but he could not say what. He did not know Mrs. Rutley's writing, but he believed the seal was hers.

What he had wished for was that Miss Dunston would stay away from the theater, and now she would. Yet why did he feel dejected? His victory was not as sweet as he had expected.

Then a new thought occurred to him. He was supposed to meet Mr. Barker at the theater tomorrow at noon—the same time he was to meet this Lord Artemus. Clearly, he could not be in two places at one time, but keeping this engagement with Lord Artemus was far more important. He no longer had to concern himself with Miss Dunston getting in his way now that she was restricted to the school. Once this new investor signed a contract, he could return to make Mr. Barker an offer too good to ignore.

Two hours later, he was on his way to Hensworth, intending to stay at an inn. He wanted to be well rested for his meeting.

And at a castle, of all places!

Yet he could not get his mind off Miss Dunston. Was purchasing the building in which resided the theater worth the trouble it was causing them?

What was this love of which she had spoken before?

He denied the idea of love. But if he did, how would he describe the feelings he felt every time he was near her?

Aaron grimaced at the thin ray of bright sunlight that tried to penetrate his eyelids from the small opening in the curtains. For a moment, he lay wondering where he was. The room was unfamiliar to him.

Oh, yes, he was in Hensworth. And he was at an inn. Or what passed as an inn. The place was more a boarding house than an establishment meant to offer travelers a place to rest their weary bones. Worn furniture, dusty shelves, and several cobwebs in the far corner of the room confirmed the landlady's excuse that she had not had a proper guest in years.

The village of Hensworth had proven to be far smaller than Aaron had expected. But just because a village was small did not mean a wealthy man did not live there. Every place had a history of ebbing and waning in population, and from what he had learned since his arrival the day before, the closing of the mines had sent the families scurrying in search of work.

Unfortunate, that. All parents, especially those willing to put in hard work, deserved to raise a family without fear of losing their only source of income. He knew firsthand how difficult it was to relocate. After all, that was what he had done by moving to Chatsworth. He now had to meet new people, establish new relationships, and accustom himself to the various shopkeepers. At least he had been blessed with a congenial disposition. It would have been much more difficult if his temperament were less pleasant.

After dressing, Aaron went down for breakfast and was met with a plate of undercooked eggs and wrinkled fruit.

"I'm sorry we don't have more, sir," Mrs. Jensen said, wringing her hands. "I don't cook much these days, and when I do, it's only porridge. But I couldn't offer you just that now, could I?" Given that the woman had maybe one tooth in her entire head, it was no wonder her diet was limited to soft foods. Her graying braid wrapped around her head reminded him of wool with its tiny hairs sticking out in every direction.

"Not to worry, Mrs. Jensen," Aaron said as he pushed away the plate. "I'm not all that hungry. But I do appreciate going to such efforts to make my stay here pleasant."

Mrs. Jensen beamed at the kind words. One catches more flies with honey than vinegar, or so went the saying, and Aaron had proven that point time and again. That he was being deceptive did not even enter his mind. Even false courtesy was far better than none.

He stood on the front step to survey the street that ran in front of him, then frowned. It had a proper High Street with lines of buildings, but few offered any goods or services. Most had boarded-up windows and broken or missing signage. What had once been a flourishing village was now nothing more than a shell of itself.

Aaron had gone into the one remaining shop when he arrived the day before, and within it was a hodgepodge of other shops. In the back was a butcher's counter. Shelves along the walls of either side offered anything from buttons to bags of flour. And all at exorbitant prices. But if one had a need, what other options did he have?

"Where is that blasted Claremont?" Aaron murmured. He had instructed the driver to be in front of the inn by nine, but he was nowhere to be seen.

An older man in stained trousers and a ragged shirt came stumbling toward him. The last thing Aaron needed was to be seen speaking to a pauper. What would Lord Artemus think of him then? Yet as he scanned the area, he realized he had no reason to worry. No one else was about.

"We don't get many visitors here," the old man said, his voice sounding as if he were traveling in a carriage over a road covered with boulders. He wiped his nose on the sleeve of his coat and looked Aaron up and down. "Got any coin?"

For a moment, Aaron considered sending the man away. But seeing the deep lines on his worn face and the slope of his back, he could not. What sort of life had this man lived? A very hard one by the looks of it.

Reaching into his pocket, Aaron took out a single coin and placed it into the grimy hand of the old man without looking at it.

His eyes went wide, and he gave Aaron a toothless grin. "Thank you, sir!"

"I'm looking for a castle," he said. "One belonging to Lord Artemus."

The old man chortled. "Is that what they call it these days? A castle?"

Aaron stared at the man. Surely, those of the lower class were educated enough to know what a castle was? "Do you know the place?"

"I do," the old man said, nodding. "You go down the road there till you come to a big birch tree. It was planted by my grandfather over a hundred years ago." He beamed at this, and Aaron tried to school his impatience. "From there, take a right. Artemus's place is not half a mile farther."

Thanking the man, Aaron let out a sigh of relief at his approaching carriage.

"Sorry, sir," Claremont said as he leapt from his perch. "Afraid the wheel wasn't feelin' right, so I wanted to be sure it was safe."

With a dismissive wave of his hand, Aaron relayed the directions to the driver and stepped into the vehicle. Settling onto the bench, he could not wait to return to the comforts of Hearsely Estate.

Today if all went well, Aaron would have a prominent member of society as an investor. Once Lord Artemus agreed, others would follow, he was sure of it. Sometimes seeking investors was like opening a dam. Once the first, well-placed stone was removed, the water flowed through freely.

The carriage came to a stop, and Aaron adjusted his cravat and smoothed his coat. He had to look presentable if he was to approach a man as noteworthy as Lord Artemus. Not that he knew anything about the gentleman, of course, but if he was willing to meet with Aaron, he had to be wealthy, indeed.

He went to exit the vehicle and stopped midstep to stare not at a castle but rather at a small cottage. The roof was covered with a conglomeration of boards and thatch. Moss and lichen allowed only spots of gray stone to peek through. Bubbled glass filled the frames of two tiny windows that had once been painted red.

In front stood a man so ancient that he might have been a passenger on Noah's ark. He was hunched and leaned heavily on a walking stick. Aaron wondered at the wisdom of keeping on a groundskeeper of such an advanced age. Lord Artemus should have offered the man retirement long ago.

But what was it to Aaron? Perhaps the lord pitied the dotard. Aaron certainly did.

"What do you want?" the old man snapped in that clipped way many elderly people spoke. He squinted. "I'm not selling my home no matter how much you offer. You got that?"

"I'm here to speak to Lord Artemus," Aaron said, peering past the cottage. "I was told his castle was nearby, though I don't seem to see it. Is it beyond those trees?"

The old man guffawed. "Castle? There hasn't been a castle here in two hundred years. Uprising and all that. Poorly built and crumbled like everything else around here." The man sighed. "Even the old manor house burnt to the ground years ago. There's nothing more left of the estate than a pile of rubble now. And this cottage."

Aaron frowned. "There was a fire? How long ago did that happen?"

The old man sucked on his lips for a moment before replying. "I'd say it's been about eight years now. This is all that's left of the Artemus estate. And I'd know. I'm the last of them."

Chapter Twenty

"You... you're Abraham, Lord Artemus?" Aaron asked the old man, unable to keep his mouth from falling open.

Squinting up at Aaron as if the sun were in his eyes, the old man chuckled. "Don't know nothing about being a lord, but I'm Abraham Artemus. *Mr.* Abraham Artemus." He stressed the title. "My family once owned everything as far as the eye can see. And more. But they sold it off piece by piece over the years. The title died, too, when my great-grandmother couldn't birth any sons. My great-grandfather..." He paused and crinkled his brow in thought. "No, guess it would've been his father, the man I'm named after, was the last to have an heir. He was named after a lord, though. An ancestor, oh, three centuries or so gone now. The rest of us, well, we've had to make do without the title, but it's not always easy. Especially now that the money's gone, too." He frowned at Aaron. "Who told you there was a castle here? Someone swindle you, did they, young man?"

The old man's laugh made Aaron's hands clench. What a fool he had been! That letter had to have been a forgery. A schoolgirl had tricked him! How had he not seen this coming? It was now so obvious! Somehow, Miss Dunston had learned about the meeting he had scheduled with Mr. Barker. How could Aaron not have recognized the young lady's underhanded attempt to get him to leave Chatsworth? Attempt? This was no attempt. She had been successful in her trickery! After all, why was this meeting scheduled at the exact time and on the very day as the one at the theater?

Well, that recalcitrant schoolgirl had gone too far this time. Not only would he chastise her for her chicanery, but he would also speak to Mrs. Rutley about the girl. Let her headmistress deal with her punishment. If Mrs. Rutley was anything like the headmaster of the school he had attended, the punishment would be a lesson well learned.

"My apologies for bothering you, sir," Aaron said. "It appears I've been misinformed." He looked around at the land that surrounded them. "And as to your bad fortune, may you see a better future ahead."

Mr. Artemus frowned. "Bad fortune? I have a roof over my head, food on my table, and want for nothing. Well, nothing except Gladys, my wife. She died eleven years ago this March."

Aaron glanced longingly at the waiting carriage. He did not have the heart to listen to an old man's recollections of his life. Even an important knight could only bear so many sad tales.

"Ah, I see now," Mr. Artemus said, tapping the side of his nose.

Now it was Aaron's turn to frown. "And what is it you see?"

"You're young. I'd bet my little cottage here that you're hoping to add more to your coffers. Isn't that why you were so quick to come in search of Lord Artemus?"

Aaron did not reply. How could he refute the statement?

"Well, you should watch your step. The Artemuses believed their destiny lay in becoming the most prominent family in all of England. Look where it got them. Greed begets loss in the end."

"Just because your family failed does not mean I shall," Aaron said.

The old man leaned on his cane. "And what constitutes success, do you think? How much land must one man own? How many horses must he stable? How full should his coffers be?" His squint deepened until his eyes were mere slits. "How much is enough?"

"What difference does it make?" Aaron snapped.

Mr. Artemus pointed a gnarled finger at him. "You've been bested by a woman, haven't you?" he asked with a low chuckle. "Don't deny it. It's written all over your face. Ah, lad, just know that it happens to the best of us."

Aaron turned on his heels, the old man's choking laughter following after him like a wolf pursuing a hare.

"Take me straight to the theater in Chatsworth," Aaron hissed at Claremont. He pulled out his pocket watch. It was a quarter past twelve, which meant he would not arrive until three. Half past two if Claremont made haste. "And be quick about it. Don't stop for any reason."

He leapt into the carriage, and the door slammed behind him. His temper flared at Mr. Artemus's continued laughter.

"You've got too much pride," the old man shouted, cackling as the carriage pulled away. "Your fall will be mighty if you don't take care!" Leaning back into the bench, Aaron worked his tight jaw. Much to his annoyance, Mr. Artemus did have a point. Aaron's pride had gotten the best of him. The letter, assumed to be written by Mrs. Rutley, had heaped undue praise on him. That should have been the first warning sign. Why had he not seen it?

By the time he arrived in Chatsworth, with too many hours to allow his thoughts to simmer, Aaron's anger had reached its boiling point. He leapt from the carriage before it stopped and stormed into the theater. Miss Lockhart stood leaning against a wall, and when she caught sight of him, her eyes bulged in her face.

"Sir Aaron," she began, but he spoke over her.

"Is she here?" he hissed.

Miss Lockhart did not respond but instead turned on her heel and fled through the door that led to the auditorium.

Aaron followed after her, doing all he could to keep his rage from erupting. It would do him no good to strangle the woman who had set the fire.

"He's here!" he heard Miss Lockhart shout. "And I've never seen a man so angry!"

After her success in tricking Sir Aaron, Louisa should have been pleased. With him away, she could take his place in meeting with Mr. Barker. The guilt that tried to overtake her for the deception should have been the cause of her displeasure, but it was not.

Unfortunately, because she and Ruth were the oldest of the students, Mrs. Rutley had tasked them to remain at the school while she and Mrs. Shepherd were away. They were not due to return until well after the midday meeting, which only increased Louisa's frustration.

If she did not make that meeting, Sir Aaron would likely stop at the theater the moment he returned. Therefore, it was imperative that she speak to Mr. Barker first.

To make matters worse, Mrs. Rutley had requested that she and Ruth lead a discussion as a way for the newer students to ask questions about staying at the school, yet the silence was deafening.

Leah Gibbons, a mousy girl of fourteen with dark-blonde hair and brown eyes so dark they were nearly black, wrung her hands together.

"Is something bothering you, Leah?" Louisa asked.

"Mrs. Rutley said we can ask questions," Leah said in a voice so quiet that Louisa had to strain to hear it. "I have one, but I'm unsure if it's proper to ask it."

Louisa gave her a warm smile. She remembered what it was like to be the younger student full of worry and frightened she would make a misstep. Yet the only way for her and the others to grow was by learning. Which was what Louisa meant to explain. Yet Ruth spoke first.

"First of all, there is nothing improper when it is just us girls. Ask us anything."

Louisa stifled a groan. Ruth was opening a door that was likely best left closed!

Excited whispers filled the air. "Well," Leah said, her voice at a better volume now, "I heard a rumor—gossip if you will—that one of the former students here was forced to marry a madman who lived in a forest. I think her name was Julia. Is that true?"

Louisa laughed but cut it short when Leah's cheeks turned pink.

"I know it sounds silly," Leah said. "But that is what I heard."

"And who told you this?" Ruth asked.

"Abigail Swanson. The day before she left."

Ruth sighed. "One thing you must learn is that you cannot trust everything you hear. Abigail Swanson enjoys telling completely false tales." She went on to correct the story, or at least a portion of it. Some parts she omitted because of the sacred oath they had made beneath the tree, and Louisa was glad Ruth had remembered that. Leah, nor any of the other girls, did not need to know everything. Ruth only needed to correct the untruth. The rest was none of Leah's concern.

Once Leah was satisfied with the response, another student asked about excursions. Another asked about the London Season. Louisa and Ruth answered every question to the best of their ability, doing what they could to appease them all.

Then Amy Felton asked a question. Of all the new students, Louisa liked Amy the most. Abigail had once attempted to bully her, but a threat from Ruth had put a stop to that.

"Who scratched the initials into the tree?" Amy asked.

To Louisa's relief, Mrs. Rutley returned before she had to answer. The question was far too personal, in her opinion. Plus, now she could leave to see Mr. Barker.

"How is everything?" Mrs. Rutley asked.

"Wonderful," Ruth replied flatly. "We covered a variety of topics to appease their young minds."

Mrs. Rutley smiled. "Don't forget you were one of those young minds once." In her hand was a collection of documents, and a sudden urge to pry rose in Louisa. Yet she pushed it away. The last time she looked into something that was none of her business, she had confused a dog for a young boy. Her days of snooping were behind her.

"We're off to the village," Louisa said to the headmistress. "Is there anything you would like us to bring back with us?"

When Mrs. Rutley replied in the negative, the two young ladies donned their spencers and walked out into the bright afternoon sunlight. Louisa's plan for the day was simple. She planned to speak to Mr. Barker to assure him that she could save the theater. And to convince him that selling to Sir Aaron would be a grave mistake. For him and for the village.

Louisa picked up her step. It was nearly half-past two, two and a half hours past the meeting Sir Aaron had scheduled with Mr. Barker. It was vital that she be there before he realized he had been tricked.

They arrived in the village quicker than they had ever traveled, and soon they entered the theater. A painting of a wall with curtained windows provided the backdrop for two of the performers who were rehearsing their lines. Mr. Barker stood in the center aisle, his hands on his hips.

"Excellent, Miss Susan! Continue with that same emotion throughout the scene. Milford, you must project your voice if you want to be heard. Remember, this isn't your mother's sitting room. Everyone in the entire theater must hear what you're saying."

Miss Susan, a buxom woman with brownish-blonde hair and a dark beauty patch on her cheek, reddened. "Thank you, Mr. Barker. She then turned back to Milford, a man around her same age and at least a head taller than she with dark hair that curled around his ears.

With a nod from Louisa, Ruth returned to the foyer as Louisa approached Mr. Barker.

"Well, hello, Miss Dunston," he said. "This is a welcome surprise."

Louisa returned his warm smile. "How was your visit with your brother?"

Mr. Barker frowned. "It was pleasant enough, I suppose, but he helped me get a better understanding of my predicament. I'm afraid that unless things change quickly, I'll have to sell. There's just too much work to be done."

Louisa pulled the money she had collected from her reticule and handed it to him. "This is for you. I received twenty pounds from the shopkeepers and fifty pounds from the party. I'm sure I can collect significantly more once the Season ends and the wealthier families return. I've also had two others pledge funds once you've made your decision."

She did not mention that ten of those pounds came from her own savings.

"Young lady, what you're doing for me is very kind," Mr. Barker said as he looked at the money in his hand. "And though this will be helpful, I'm afraid it's not nearly enough."

"Not nearly... how much do you need?"

Mr. Barker sighed as he pocketed the money. "There are issues with the back wall. It's leaking, you see. I haven't painted anything but settings for more than twenty years. Most of the seats are worn and uncomfortable. And who knows how long it will be before that stage collapses? There are more repairs than I can count, and we've not sold enough tickets to cover the expenses for the current production. I'll need at least six thousand pounds to get the place back into proper working order."

Louisa nearly choked. Six thousand pounds? Such a number was unfathomable!

His chuckle held little mirth. "I see by your expression that it's far more than you expected. Even if I were to get the donations I need and make the repairs, interest in the theater will continue to decline. London seems far closer today than it was when I first opened, so anyone interested in entertainment can go there. And most men prefer the pub to a good play."

Louisa sighed. "You see?" she insisted. "Women have no place to go and sit with their husbands and feel as if they are at least somewhat equal. Nowhere but here. Please, Mr. Barker, give me a chance to save the theater. I'll do anything to help, just tell me what to do."

He patted her hand and smiled. "That's very kind of you, Miss Dunston, but what you're asking is nearly impossible. I mean no offense, but you're just a girl. I'm not sure what you *can* do."

"I may be considered a girl, Mr. Barker," Louisa said, holding back the indignation that wanted to burst from her tongue. "But I'm far more than that. I'm someone who never gives up because I don't lose. So, unless you wish to hand your theater over to a selfish man who has no one's interest at heart but his own, tell me how I may help."

Mr. Barker studied her for a moment before replying, "You know, I think I believe you. You want to help, do you? Well, how about this? I'll give you tickets to sell for our next production, which begins two weeks from this Friday. Perhaps you can ask for donations as well. If by some miracle, you are able to collect enough money by opening night, I'll do whatever I can to keep the doors open."

"That is a wonderful idea!" Louisa said. "I'll start today."

One of the doors burst open, and Ruth came running down the center aisle.

"He's here! And I've never seen a man so angry!"

Chapter Twenty-One

There stood Miss Dunston beside Mr. Barker. So, the chit was up to her old games, was she? How dare she use her coquettish ways on the poor landlord!

Honor would be restored in Chatsworth this very day if Aaron had anything to do about it!

"Lord Artemus sends his regards," Aaron snarled.

Miss Dunston swallowed visibly. "Oh well, thank you. You know, I really must go—"

He grabbed her by the arm to force her to turn back toward him and glared down at her. "I'm sure you have a few minutes to spare. After all, I've journeyed so far to see you. And we have so much to discuss."

"I really must get back to the production," Mr. Barker said, clearly failing to appreciate the spectacle taking place before him. "Sir Aaron, I'll have time to speak to you momentarily."

Once the man was out of earshot, Aaron rounded on Miss Dunston. "How dare you send me away as you did! Have you no conscience?"

She gave an angry tug at her arm and pulled away. "I have no conscience? And what about yours? This theater means a great deal to me, and you could not care less!"

"Purchasing this building means a great deal to me, and I need no further interference from you. What must I do to put a stop to your meddling? Do you want money? Is that what it is? I'm sure we can come to a reasonable agreement."

"Money?" Miss Dunston asked with a sniff. "My father has plenty of money. Far more than you, I'm sure. No, I want nothing that comes from your coffers. What I want is to save this theater, for that is what is best for the village."

Aaron could not help but laugh at the absurdity of this statement. "I know what's best for this theater. And for the village."

"I'll decide what's best for the theater," Mr. Barker said as he approached them, his face dark with anger.

Forcing a smile to his lips, Aaron said, "Yes, of course, sir. After all, it belongs to you. But when you're ready to sell, I'll be happy to take it off your hands."

Miss Dunston gave one of her dramatic sighs that sent a pleasant pebbling to his skin. "Mr. Barker loves the theater as much as I and knows I can save it from closing."

"As if you know what's best," Aaron began, but Mr. Barker cut off his words.

"May I please speak? Both of you, be silent!" The proprietor turned the ring on his finger. "As I told Miss Dunston, even if the funds were raised tomorrow, there is no guarantee I can remain open in the coming years. But it's well worth the trouble if people return. The problem is ticket sales are low this year. Therefore, I want to recruit both of you to help with selling tickets for this month's production. It's my last chance to bring it back to its former glory."

Aaron stifled a snort. This man expected a hero—a knight!—to sell tickets to a play? How dare he make such a trivial request of him!

Miss Dunston, however, was quick to agree. "Tell me how I may help. I can go house to house if you'd like. This will save them the annoyance of waiting until the last minute and finding no seats available. You will also know how many showings of your play you can offer.

More tickets sold means more nights of performance." She flashed Aaron a mischievous grin. "Whatever you need, I shall do."

"I think that's a marvelous idea," Mr. Barker said.

Aaron stifled a groan. Why would he agree with Miss Dunston? But her innocent smile gave him his answer. It was a lovely smile, after all.

"As I mentioned earlier," Miss Dunston said, "if I sell enough tickets, that money can cover the cost of the production. Any donations you receive beyond that can go to the repairs on the building and the planning of future performances."

Aaron frowned. If Miss Dunston wished to spend her days as a ticket saleswoman, so be it. He had no desire to become an employee of the theater.

Then a thought occurred to him. What if she chose to use her coquettish ways to convince the men of the village to purchase the tickets? Given how lovely she was, she could raise a great deal of money, which would undermine his plans for the gentlemen's club.

Not only that, but something far worse could happen. What if her ways led her to another man catching her eye? Or she, his? Aaron could not have either. She needed someone with sense around her, one willing to protect her at all costs.

"I'll accompany you," he said. "After all, people will be more inclined to purchase from a knight with my standing than some unknown schoolgirl."

Miss Dunston's narrowed eyes made him grin. Even when her temper flared, she was beautiful.

"I don't care how the tickets are sold," Mr. Barker replied. "I just need to get through this production. After that, I'll make a final decision on what to do with the theater. Now, we'll not speak of the future until the tickets are sold, and the play has begun. Is that clear?"

"Mr. Barker," called the brown-haired woman standing midstage, "I have a question about this line."

"I really must get back to rehearsal. But once we're finished, I'll find the tickets." He walked away, leaving Aaron alone with Miss Dunston.

"I'd prefer if you not accompany me, Sir Aaron," she said with a scowl. "Your arrogance has a way of putting people off."

Aaron barked a laugh. "My arrogance? Every wife in the village will run you out after they catch you flirting with their husbands!" He took a small step toward her, ignoring the gaping look she gave him. "It's about time you set aside this act of innocence, Miss Dunston. You of all people should know that your flirtatious ways will one day get you into trouble. You've fooled many men, myself included, but it's time to put a stop to such unbecoming mannerisms."

Rather than angering her, however, she smiled. "Including you," she whispered as she walked her fingers up his chest and winked. "It's clear you enjoy my... what did you call it? Oh yes, my flirtatious ways. I don't understand why they annoy you so. Perhaps you're jealous?"

"Jealous of your flirting?" he asked with a snort.

Miss Dunston shook her head. "Of the men who receive it. I'd even go so far as to say you wish I limited my flirting to just you."

Aaron could only gape in disbelief. Never had he encountered such pomposity from anyone before! Yet, could he dispute her accusation? Indeed, he could.

"You spout nonsense, Miss Dunston. I can assure you of that."

"I see. So, this is all to keep me... innocent?" She batted her eyelashes, and not for the first time, his breath caught in his throat.

Forcing air back into his lungs, he said, "Before we begin this endeavor, we must discuss you sending me to Hensworth. When are you expected back at the school?"

"I have a few hours," she replied. "Why?"

"Let's go to the park. We can talk privately there. I believe it's in our best interest that we work together, but to do so, we must decide the rules. Now, I can wait here and collect the tickets if you would like to run some errands."

She nodded, turned, but then stopped. "My mind tells me I mustn't trust you, Sir Aaron. That I should not allow you to have all the tickets." She knitted her brow and tilted her head. "Yet my heart says that after all we've endured together thus far, you'll not deceive me."

Aaron raised his brows. "So, what will you do?"

Without replying, she turned and walked away, leaving Aaron

standing there in bewilderment. Her heart told her to trust him? Did that mean she cared for him as he did her?

Yet how far did his caring go?

In the short time they had been acquainted, he found her smile, her laugh, her words pleasing. When he was not in her company, he felt alone and looked forward to seeing her again.

He could not help but chuckle to himself. She was a clever young woman indeed, sending him off on a wild goose chase as she had. Yet, he would never say as much to her. He would not want her thinking she could get away with such treatment at every turn.

Regardless, he did care for her, and although he was not ready just yet to admit it, he might even admire her.

Chapter Twenty-Two

A chorus of birds welcoming the warm spring weather accompanied Louisa and Ruth as they walked down the path through Yeats Park. Their destination was the privacy of the bench where Louisa had spied on Sir Aaron and Lady Mathison.

"I'll be nearby," Ruth said as they approached Lover's Nest. "Will you be all right on your own?"

Louisa smiled. "Yes, thank you. I really should apologize for sending him to Hensworth. That was mean-spirited on my part."

Ruth grinned at her. "Mean-spirited? I don't believe so. Deceiving? Most definitely." She walked to a nearby bench where she could do her duty as chaperone but would not encroach on their privacy.

The park was empty, which was best as far as Louisa was concerned. The last thing she needed was an audience listening in on her business. Some people were far too nosy for their own good! Why anyone would be interested in what she had to say to Sir Aaron was beyond her. It was not as if what they would overhear would help them or someone else in any way. Eavesdropping had its place, but not every discussion needed to be overheard. She was glad she had learned that lesson.

As she waited for Sir Aaron to arrive, Louisa considered how she would broach the subject of how she had deceived him. He had every right to be displeased. If Sir Aaron had sent her on such a wild goose chase, she would have returned ready to pummel him.

When she caught sight of the knight sauntering down the path, her breath caught. He truly was a well-formed man, imposing and pleasing to the eye. Too bad he lacked decency.

You should talk, Louisa Dunston! At least he has not been as underhanded as you!

"I placed the tickets in my carriage," he said, sitting beside her on the bench. "We can discuss them later. For now, I'd like to speak about Hensworth."

Louisa sighed. "Yes, well, for what I did—"

He raised a hand to forestall her, and she closed her mouth. When he laid his arm across the back of the bench, a sense of being protected washed over her.

"I must admit that I was livid when I learned that the castle was nothing more than a rundown cottage. And when I learned that Lord Artemus was not a lord at all but rather the remnant of a titled family, my ire doubled. I swore to give you a proper scolding when I returned and see you suffer as you made me suffer."

Louisa nodded, her throat constricted with guilt. "I'm truly sorry," she whispered. "I was so caught up in what I wanted that I did not consider what my deception would do to you."

Sir Aaron nodded. "That is why I curbed my anger after seeing you at the theater. I realized I could not hurt you. Even when I felt justified."

Louisa could not stop her eyebrows from rising in surprise. The kindness in his words came from a genuine place. His heart.

"I don't care who it is, Miss Dunston, be he a fool of a man such as Jeffery Venter—or myself, for that matter—I don't wish to see you hurt. *That* would anger me. For you are a woman who should be cherished."

His words were like a sweet melody unto her heart, and she had to grasp hold of his arm when her head became light.

Although his declaration pleased her, a question came to mind.

Was she truly a woman to be cherished? She ached to reveal the secret she had told no one, not even her Sisters. What would he do, what would any of them do, if they knew the truth? She was unwilling to take the chance that he would abandon her. The risk of losing him now that they had found one another was too high.

"Well, I believe you're a hero, Sir Knight. A man who must be honored." She frowned. Why did he wince at her words?

He'll tell you once he's ready, she reminded herself.

"What are we to do from here?" she asked. "I'm tired of the battles we've been having. Perhaps it's time we end this feud."

Sir Aaron sighed. "I agree. We only spite ourselves with these games we're playing." He let out a soft chuckle. "And I'd prefer not to go on any more impromptu journeys to deserted villages."

Louisa smiled. "Then this is what I propose. Each of us has a different objective in mind for the theater. Yet there is no reason we cannot work together. Therefore, from this moment on, let's put aside our differences. No more quarreling. No more devious acts. The cost of repairing the roof is far higher than I anticipated. And then there are the other costs, such as painting the walls and replacing the flooring and seating, all of which require even more money. I must focus on the theater, not arguing with you. Therefore, for now, I suggest we concentrate on selling tickets and table our respective plans until later. What say you?"

For a moment he remained quiet, and Louisa wondered if he would reject her offer. Then, to her surprise, he smiled. "I must admit, spending time with you is a pleasant thought. And it will keep other men at bay."

Her breath caught at this. Was he jealous?

"We'll do this together as you propose," he continued. "And regardless of the decision Mr. Barker makes, at least the theater will not be empty for its upcoming—and perhaps final—production." He stuck out a hand. "We businessmen shake hands as a sign of agreement."

Louisa eyed his hand skeptically. "Are you certain you wish to do business with a woman?"

This time when he laughed, her heart gave a pleasant flutter, for it was not filled with contempt nor was it degrading as it had been in the past. Instead, it was filled with what she could only define as happiness.

"Since you and I have become acquainted, I've reconsidered my stance on conducting business with women. You, Miss Dunston, are a sharp young lady who can achieve anything you set out to do. So yes, in this matter, we are equals."

Confidence filled her heart. and she shook his hand. "Thank you. It's pleasant to be recognized for more than my outward appearance."

"Trust me," Sir Aaron said with a wide grin. "You're more than just a beautiful woman. I'd say you have many wonderful qualities I find appealing. So many that if I listed them all today, we would be here all night."

Louisa's head swam, and she hoped she would not faint. "I must admit that your list would be exceptionally long as well."

Silence settled around them for several moments as they looked at one another. Was it possible for time to stop just for them?

Sadly, the spell broke when he cleared his throat and said, "I really should be going."

He stood and offered a hand to help her up from the bench. As she stood before him, she contemplated this new path they had begun. They were now business partners, but she could not ignore the romantic attraction that had budded between them.

Gazing into his deep-blue eyes, Louisa wished he would kiss her. That he would give her a gift that she could savor until they met again. This time, however, she restrained herself. Not for the sake of protecting herself but rather because she wished to protect him. For the first time in her life, she felt like more than a simple schoolgirl who used her feminine wiles to get men to do her bidding. Now, she felt like a woman of worth.

He offered her an arm, and she took it. They strolled through the park, Ruth silently falling in behind them. When they reached the exit, Sir Aaron said, "We really should devise a plan for how we'll sell these tickets. Have you any ideas?"

Louisa smiled. How wonderful that he asked her opinion rather than dictating his plans to her!

"Mrs. Rutley has an extensive list of acquaintances. I can write to many of them and request a meeting. There, we can offer them the tickets and discuss the possibility of donations. We'll explain that Mr. Barker will decide how those funds are used but that he has mentioned renovations and repairs to the building in which the theater sits. If someone seems disinterested in that plan, you can then bring up what you hope to see happen with the building." She looked up at him. "What do you think?"

"I think it a wonderful idea," he said, coming to a stop in front of his carriage. "I'll call over to you on Wednesday at midday." He glanced around. "Would you like a ride back to the school?"

"Thank you, but no. I'll walk. It allows me to exercise as well as to contemplate our next steps."

After Sir Aaron's carriage pulled away, Louisa and Ruth made their way back to the school. The days ahead would be interesting, to say the least. But spending time with Sir Aaron while working toward her goal delighted her.

Yet a small amount of worry tugged at the back of her mind. What was going to happen once the tickets were sold, and the production was successful? Would their conflicting objectives create a rift so great that no amount of romance could bridge it?

Chapter Twenty-Three

Mrs. Agnes Rutley had enjoyed only a handful of significant friendships. Acquaintances, she had many. But true friends she kept to a select few because too many people were untrustworthy. She would trust Mrs. Shepherd with her life. None held the same status in Agnes's life. Except perhaps Henry, Lord Walcott.

Lord Walcott's friendship began more than twenty years earlier. And most unconventionally. It was born out of an argument—or rather with her chastising him—which quickly evolved into an unmatched camaraderie. They became so close that they set aside the need for formal address.

The late-afternoon sun poured through the large window of her office as she sat behind her desk, listening to Henry expressing his frustration with a lazy maid—or so he believed—as if he had taken over his title yesterday. Why did he not simply give the girl the sack and hire a replacement? Or have Deacan, his butler, do it if he found the task distasteful. After all, was that not why the man received one of the highest earnings of any other butler in the area?

Despite her ready suggestion, Agnes offered no counsel on the matter. Over the years, she had learned that once Henry verbalized his frustration, he either found a solution to the problem or realized it had not been as bad as he first believed. If he did not, then she would speak her mind. But it was always better to allow men to work out things for themselves. Few were willing to take a woman's suggestions to heart, anyway.

And indeed, it was not long before he decided to give the girl a sharp talking-to and allow her one more chance to show her capabilities.

"I hear she's providing for five siblings after the death of her parents," he explained. "I cannot be the cause of the family losing their home." Henry really was a good man.

The conversation soon turned to his visit to the village. "Barker appears to be struggling with what to do with the theater. Were you aware that our newest resident wishes to purchase the building and turn it into a gentlemen's club?"

Agnes smiled. "I'm well aware. But as you know, Louisa Dunston is on a quest to see it remains a theater. What's more, she and Sir Aaron have joined forces to sell tickets together for the next play." She went on to explain what Louisa had told her the previous day after her encounter with the knight. "I think it will do them both good. Sir Aaron is trying to find his place in this world just as much as Louisa is."

Henry crossed an ankle over the opposite knee. "Agnes, you do realize this man is high in the instep and doesn't even realize his knighthood does little more than lift him from the dregs of society."

"Oh, I see. So, I'm a dreg, am I?"

"I didn't mean to say—"

Agnes held up a hand. "I know what you meant, Henry. But you're being too hard on the young man. It's not as if he came from a family of servants. He's received a good education despite his lack of title, and he seems to have a good head on his shoulders. I would not cast him aside just yet."

"Be that as it may, I hear he enjoys charming others to get what he wants. More so young women who are easily enchanted by such tactics." Henry let out a sigh. "It's one thing to be polite, but just because he's handsome does not mean he should use his good looks to turn the heads of the young ladies of our village. This is not London."

"No, it's not. And Louisa has made me well aware of his methods."

Henry chuckled. "Then why would you allow him to call on her? Or to collaborate as they are? She's an impressionable young lady. Are you not concerned he'll use that against her?"

"Louisa has been forthright about her frustration with Sir Aaron," Agnes replied. "But you'll be surprised to learn she is not all that different from him. I think they will be good for each other."

Henry's brows knitted. "You think two vain people can be compatible?"

"Of course," Agnes said with a laugh. She adored Henry, especially when he gave her that bewildered look he wore now. Not in a romantic sense, for they could never be more than friends. "Why would I not?"

With a heavy sigh, Henry said, "I think it best that you say no more." This was a clear signal that he knew he had already lost any argument that might arise about the subject.

"May they call on you to help them?" Agnes asked. "Surely, you would be willing to purchase a ticket?"

"Why me?"

Agnes smiled. "They must begin somewhere. Why not with you? After all, you're the most giving aristocrat in Chatsworth."

Henry sighed. "Oh, very well. They may call tomorrow at one. But there is another matter we must discuss. Something much more serious."

Intrigued, Agnes asked, "And what is that?"

Henry shifted in his seat, placing both feet on the floor. "Lord Ezra's returned to Chatsworth. And he's even more cantankerous now that he's been cast from the family by his nephew. We both know why he's here and what he's willing to do."

Agnes nodded. She had already received this news from another source. She and Lord Ezra Colburn, uncle to the Duke of Elmhurst, had once shared in a short courtship. When she called off the courtship, he became angry. And vindictive.

Julia Wallace, a former student and now the Duchess of Elmhurst, had taken an interest in his nephew, and Lord Ezra had become enraged. He was certain Agnes had been behind the union, although he could not have known how close to the truth he was. Therefore, he had doubled his promise to see Agnes destroyed, and she feared he would not hesitate to make good on that threat.

Yet her worries were not for what she might lose, but rather the effect it would have on those around her.

"I cannot stop this storm from coming," she said with determination. "I'll face it no matter how strong it is." She shrugged. "If he wins, I'll be happy knowing I fought him to the best of my abilities. But I won't take it lying down, Henry. You know that."

"I was afraid you would say that," Henry said. "But perhaps you should leave for a few months. Wait for his temper to cool. Tell everyone you've fallen ill and need time away. Then hire an interim headmistress to take your place. Lord Ezra has never been a patient man. He'll soon grow bored and leave. Once he's moved on to torment some other poor soul, you can return."

Agnes gave her friend a warm smile. "I appreciate your advice, Henry. I truly do. But we both know it's time Lord Ezra and I ended this feud. It's gone on for far too long, and I don't want to see anyone else get hurt."

With a deep growl, Henry sat forward in his chair. "Are you listening to yourself, Agnes? He'll stop at nothing to get what he wants. And don't forget you're not the only one who would receive the brunt of his anger. Think of Mrs. Shepherd."

With a sigh, Agnes stood. "Mrs. Shepherd has no need to worry. I'll make sure of that. What happened—"

A soft knock on the door had her stop what she was going to say. "Yes," she called.

The very woman of whom they were speaking entered the room. Mrs. Shepherd bobbed a quick curtsy. "I'm sorry, Mrs. Rutley. I didn't want to disturb you, but Mr. Barker's here to speak to you."

Agnes frowned. "Now why would he be calling at this late hour?" she murmured. Aloud she said, "See him to the drawing room. And have a tea tray sent up."

Mrs. Shepherd gave her a worried look. "I... I think you should see him now."

Henry rose and buttoned his coat. "It's getting late. I'll call again another day, and we can take up this conversation again."

After bidding her friend farewell, Agnes asked Mrs. Shepherd to bring in Mr. Barker. There was no sense in going to the drawing room. She preferred her office when discussing business. If that was why he was there.

A moment later, Mr. Barker entered the room. In his hand, he held the stem of a single red rose.

"Mr. Barker," Agnes said, coming from around the desk to meet him in the middle of the room. Mrs. Shepherd left the room, closing the door behind her. "Please, have a seat. To what do I owe the pleasure?"

His face turned an alarming puce, and Agnes wondered if he was on the verge of having some sort of fit. "Th-this is for you, Mrs. Rutley."

An awkward sensation washed over her. "Oh? Well, thank you. That was kind of you." Taking the rose, she placed it on the desk.

Mr. Barker fidgeted with the ring on his finger, and Agnes waited for him to explain his sudden call, but all he did was stand and grin at her.

"Was there a reason for your call, Mr. Barker?"

As if coming out of a trance, he nodded. "It's taken me mustering every ounce of courage to come here today," he said.

Agnes withheld her groan from what she feared would come. She had no time for a man's infatuation. Especially from one for whom she had little interest. Although Mr. Barker was unaware, Agnes had known for some time about his infatuation with her. How else would one explain his sudden inability to speak properly when she spoke to him? Or why his hands were clammy whenever he offered them to her?

"I recently learned from Miss Dunston that you've mentioned me on several occasions. In fact, she says you spoke very highly of me. That I'm an honorable man, perhaps even more so than a particular knight who recently arrived in Chatsworth."

Agnes sighed. She had no interest in Mr. Barker. Or any man, for that matter. Her life was the school and its students. She had no time for romantic entanglements. The challenge now was to convey this without hurting the man in the process. She did like him, just not in the way he hoped.

"Miss Dunston speaks the truth. You are a kind man who is much more respectable than most. Yet I'm afraid I'm far too busy to have any other interests outside of instructing my students. I do hope you understand."

"Oh. Well, yes. I suppose I do." His voice had a melancholy ring to it.

"Mr. Barker, think of my school as your theater. You must dedicate all your time to seeing that everything goes according to plan. I must do the same."

He gave her a half-smile. "Well, yes. I suppose you're right. I'm sorry to have bothered you."

"But you're never a bother, Mr. Barker," Agnes said. "Your gift has made my day even better than it was. Therefore, thank you, my friend."

His posture straightened. "Yes. Yes, we are friends, aren't we? I like that. Thank you, Mrs. Rutley."

Agnes walked him to the door and wished him a good evening. When she went to return to her office, however, she found Louisa standing on the fifth step of the stairs.

"Louisa, I would like to speak to you, please."

Louisa descended the last steps and came to a stop in front of Agnes. "Yes, Mrs. Rutley?"

"Mr. Barker has this strange notion that I have a romantic interest in him. Do you happen to know why?"

With raised brows, Louisa replied, "Everyone knows he does."

"Everyone? And who is everyone?"

"All the students," Louisa said. "I hoped to use that knowledge to help save the theater. I didn't mean any harm." She sighed well enough to have taken the stage. "Doing so was not fair to him, was it?"

Taking Louisa's hands in hers, Agnes saw the sorrow in the girl's eyes. "It's never fair to manipulate anyone's feelings for personal gain. Or any gain, for that matter. Mr. Barker has been the subject of embarrassment more often than you realize. Not because of anything he has done but rather because he's an easy target for gossipmongers. He's less likely to come to his own defense. But that does not mean he's not worthy of the respect of others. He provides an important service to the community—a source of entertainment. Don't allow your goal for the theater to blind you to recognize what you do may hurt someone."

"Blind me?" Louisa said indignantly. "I can assure you, Mrs. Rutley, it has done no such thing. If anything, Sir Aaron is to blame. But as I said before, I truly believe there is hope for him."

"I'm sure you set an example for him as we discussed?" Agnes said. "There have been no outlandish games since we last spoke?"

"None." Louisa dropped her gaze. "I may have crossed a line or two, Mrs. Rutley, but not as much as he did."

Agnes was unable to help herself. She laughed. "I suggest you think on that statement some more. You'll be spending a great deal of time with Sir Aaron beginning tomorrow. Oh, and I must write to your father. They should be back home by now."

Seeing the girl off, Agnes returned to her office. She would write to Mr. Dunston. Before she sat to write, however, she removed a letter from her desk drawer that had arrived the day before.

She had never met the Baron of Lenten, but she knew two things about him. One was the threat Louisa had heard the man make against Agnes, and the other was the fact he was involved somehow with Lord Ezra.

Her eyes skimmed over the request to call to the school. This was just the beginning of the storm she could not avoid. She would honor his request, but for now, the letter she needed to write to Louisa's father was much more pressing. And no harm would come to delay the storm for another day.

Chapter Twenty-Four

Puffs of clouds dotted an otherwise clear sky as Louisa stood waiting with Ruth for the arrival of Sir Aaron. After speaking to Mrs. Rutley the previous evening, Louisa had spent a great deal of time contemplating the advice she had received.

What her headmistress said was true. She, Louisa, had not used her marvelous education to demonstrate proper etiquette. How was the knight to learn by her example if she did not do her best? Bombarding Mr. Barker as she had was inappropriate and rash, neither of which depicted ladylike behavior.

Well, she was determined never to do such a thing again.

Today, she and Sir Aaron were to begin their shared quest of selling tickets to the upcoming play. Louisa had never been in this position before. In a way, they would become peddlers of sorts, and that sent a shiver of excitement down her spine. They would begin at Foxly Manor, the home of Lord Walcott, and from there, several others Sir Aaron had arranged. Louisa had written personally to six other households and hoped for favorable replies soon.

"We're no better than London street urchins hawking their wares," Ruth mumbled at Louisa's side. "I thought those days were behind me."

Louisa turned a shocked look on her friend. "London? I thought your family was from Rochester."

Ruth tucked a strand of red hair behind an ear. "They were, but we took up residence in London. Why must I be the one to chaperone, Louisa? Listening to the two of you argue is going to drive me mad. I wish Mrs. Garvey had not left." The last was said so quietly that Louisa was sure it was not meant to be heard.

Mrs. Garvey was one of the hired chaperones no longer employed by Mrs. Rutley. Louisa was glad the woman had found a permanent position. If that woman were sitting beside her rather than Ruth, who knew how much Louisa and Sir Aaron would complete today?

Mrs. Garvey would have been on them like a fly on a middle heap. At least Ruth would allow them some bit of privacy. To discuss their strategies for selling tickets, of course. If they shared in a kiss or two... well, that would be a bonus.

Louisa laughed at Ruth's mumblings. "I've told you. Our days of arguing are over. We're now working together on a common goal. Otherwise, how will we be successful?"

Ruth's only response was that irritating arch of a single eyebrow.

Sir Aaron's dark carriage came trundling up the drive, and when he alighted, Louisa could only stare. Had he taken extra care with his hair? Had his coat received an extra brushing? Not that he was disheveled in the past, but somehow, he seemed more... dashing.

"Ladies," he said, giving them a bow. "Miss Dunston, were you able to secure an audience with any of the more prominent families who are still in residence?"

Louisa nodded. "Lord Walcott will see us this morning. I'm still waiting for replies from the others. But I have no reason to believe they will refuse."

Sir Aaron smiled. "Very good. To Foxly Manor." This was to the driver. "Shall we?" He offered a hand to help her into the carriage, which she took with a mixture of reluctance and excitement. Reluctance because she worried what his touch would do to her, and excitement for the same reason.

As she moved past him, the strong scent of lavender and citrus nearly sent her stumbling up the step. My, but he smelled so wonderful!

"Are you all right?" he asked.

She swallowed hard. "Yes. I'm afraid my skirts got in the way."

As they settled onto the bench, Louisa studied the man across from her. Why was he smiling at her in that devilish way? And why did she feel as if his eyes could see into her soul? Was he wondering if they would kiss today?

Stop that! she told herself. Today had a specific purpose, and it had nothing to do with how he smelled or whether they would do something they should not. She was now a businesswoman and, therefore, had to set an example. That meant not falling for his charms.

No matter how much she wanted to do so.

The problem was she had no idea how any woman could resist him. Her mind drifted to the kisses they had shared, and a wave of heat washed over her. This was going to be far more difficult than she first believed.

"Your face is flushed, Miss Louisa. Are you ill?"

Louisa started. "Pardon? Oh no, I'm well." She really did have to keep her mind on why they were together today. "I was considering how to broach the subject of the tickets to Lord Walcott. I've known him far longer than you have, so I should be the one to present our plan."

Sir Aaron laughed. "So, you would like me to remain silent? Yes, I'm sure you'd be pleased if I allowed you to do all the talking at every meeting."

Louisa gaped at him. How dare he question her motives! Then again, those who make accusations are more likely to be guilty of the offense of which they are accusing others.

Before she could comment, however, he slapped his knee and barked a laugh. "Your temper flares faster than lightning strikes, Miss Dunston. Forgive me, I was only teasing. You're right. You should be the one to address him first."

This man could send her emotions bobbing up and down like a ship on a stormy sea! And although he had sent her confidence soaring, she had to make sure they worked together. "After we speak to Lord Walcott, I say you should be the one to speak to the next gentleman. We can take it in turns. Is that fair?"

"I believe that is a wonderful idea," he replied. "And I say we take it a step further. When you are tasked to present, you'll also introduce your plan for the theater. If you're unable to convince the person that your idea is of value, I'll bring up my idea for a gentlemen's club. The same works the other way around."

She considered this. It was a good plan. "I agree."

As the vehicle continued down the road, Louisa reflected on their strange relationship thus far. What began as a mutual dislike had slowly evolved into something far different. They had grown to care for one another. This quest for the theater was a reasonable way to strengthen the bond that was forming between them. Perhaps they would even fall in love.

When he had saved Louisa from Mr. Venter in the alley, Sir Aaron had confessed that he cared for her. Choosing to keep her thoughts to herself did not mean that she cared for him less, but she was not ready for such a proclamation. Not just yet.

Once they arrived at Foxly Manor, a stiff, middle-aged butler with a ring of gray hair circling an otherwise bald pate led them to the parlor. The room was tastefully decorated. Feathery bronze fern leaves dotted with tiny red rosebuds papered the wall. Red and bronze fabric covered two chairs and a couch, as well as the patterned Indian rug that lay beneath the low table between them.

"Sir Aaron, Miss Dunston, and Miss Lockhart, my lord," the butler announced before moving aside to allow the trio to enter the room.

Lord Walcott set the book he had been reading on a side table and rose from his chair. "Good morning and welcome to Foxly Manor. Please sit."

"Thank you for agreeing to see us, my lord," Louisa said as she sat beside Ruth on the couch. "I know your time is important."

The earl chuckled. "Yes well, I'll always make room in my schedule for one of Mrs. Rutley's students."

Louisa could not help herself. She shot Sir Aaron a grin as he sat in the chair beside Lord Walcott.

"I understand you're selling tickets to one of the productions at the theater."

Louisa opened her mouth to give him the speech she had prepared, but another voice spoke first.

"I am, my lord," Sir Aaron replied, much to Louisa's irritation. "Barker fears attendance will be less than satisfactory, and I wanted to do what I can to help. After all, no gentleman can allow any man to suffer, especially one who provides the community with such a wonderful form of entertainment."

Louisa sighed. The knight had conducted himself as a gentleman for all of half an hour. And not only was he rude, but he also grinned at her like an impudent child who had pushed past everyone to reach the front of the crowd. But upon seeing the smile Lord Walcott wore and the twinkle in his eye, she remained quiet.

"Is that so?" the earl asked as if this was news to him. "Do you know what I find interesting? The fact you've offered to help save the theater when you're hoping to purchase the building to put in a gentlemen's club."

Mrs. Rutley had once said that life provides opportunities to everyone, but women must seize them the moment they became available. Otherwise, men would tread all over every woman to steal that moment of good fortune from her hands.

And now was one of those moments.

"That *is* quite interesting," Louisa said as if the information were new to her. "One might even venture a guess that it is quite—how shall I say it—a parody? Yes, it appears to be precisely that."

Sir Aaron's eyes narrowed, and Louisa gave him a wink that made him chuckle.

The butler returned with a tea tray, and after serving, he left the room.

"I cannot say with any certainty what Barker's intentions are with the theater," the knight said as he picked up his teacup. "Regardless, I'm bound by a promise to do what I can to help. Not only as a knight but also as a gentleman. You'll soon learn that I'm a man of my word, my lord."

Lord Walcott crossed one leg over the other. "I admire your resolve, Sir Aaron, but as I said before when you approached me, I cannot in good conscience invest in this plan of yours."

Louisa beamed. Until he turned that gaze on her.

"Although I respect your hope in keeping the theater as it is, I believe your fight may be futile."

Louisa's heart sank. The earl was a wise man, one well respected by the entire village. If he thought there was no hope, there likely was none.

Yet he surprised her with his next statement. "But if Barker decides to keep it, I'll promise one hundred pounds toward any renovations."

Unable to help herself, Louisa gaped at him. One hundred pounds? That was a goodly amount of money. Far more than she could have ever hoped to receive!

"Now, as to the tickets. I would like to purchase two. What are the dates of the performances?"

As Sir Aaron gave Lord Walcott his options, Louisa sighed. By showing restraint, she had emerged the victor. She would have to keep that in mind for the future.

After giving Sir Aaron the required money for the tickets, Lord Walcott stood, a clear dismissal. At the front door, he said, "Oh, I nearly forgot. Mr. Gilbert Lofting, a dear friend of mine, would like you to call. I hope you don't mind that I took the liberty of scheduling a meeting for two o'clock."

"Not at all, my lord," Louisa said.

After receiving directions to Mr. Lofting's house, they bid the earl farewell and made their way to the waiting carriage. Ruth stepped into the vehicle first, and when Louisa went to follow suit, Sir Aaron took hold of her arm.

"I have a feeling I upset you in there. Please understand that I tend to open my mouth without thinking. I hope you'll be willing to over-look a moment of poor judgment and allow me the chance to prove I can be a proper gentleman."

Louisa smiled. "I do understand, sir. I have areas of my life on which I'm working, as well. Therefore, yes, I'll offer you such a chance if you promise to be patient with me."

"There is one other thing," he said with a wink.

"If you accuse me of flirting with Lord Walcott," she said in mock indignation, "I may just strike you. So choose your words carefully."

He chuckled. "No, it's not that. I would like to congratulate you."

"Congratulate me?" she asked. "Whatever for?"

"For stealing his attention away from me. You emerged victorious, and I failed. Well done, Miss Dunston. Enjoy your victory."

Her heart warmed at such a compliment. "Thank you. I shall."

"I certainly hope so, for I'm about to show you what winning truly looks like." He added another wink.

Arching a single eyebrow, Louisa said, "Are you offering a challenge, Sir Knight? If so, I accept!"

Sir Aaron extended an arm toward the carriage door. "Then we must make haste, for our battlefield awaits."

Chapter Twenty-Five

T he estate of Mr. Gilbert Lofton was surrounded by dense forest and consisted of a large, two-story house and a garden that would have rivaled that of any nobleman. As a shipping merchant, Mr. Lofton had built a fortune providing the means to import teas, dyes, and rugs from the Orient.

Although most importers relied on the East India Company for their shipping needs, a handful of smaller shippers found buyers willing to pay a handsome fee *not* to be forced to make agreements with such an unscrupulous organization. Paying the outrageous taxes required for their goods crippled too many enterprises, and Mr. Lofton was one of those offering a way to receive what they needed for a fraction of the price.

The road they took was less traveled, and the carriage shifted precariously over the many ruts and depressions created by the harsh winter.

"If Claremont does not slow down—" Aaron began to say.

Then two things happened at once. The carriage made a sharp jolt to the right before coming to an abrupt stop. And Miss Dunston landed right into Aaron's arms.

With his back pressed against the window of the leaning carriage,

Aaron's heart pounded in his chest as he inhaled the sweet fragrance of lilacs. Her feminine form pressed against him, his hands gripping her waist as he searched her blue eyes.

The sudden urge to confess his feelings for her erupted in him. To tell her that although he had once believed that romantic notions were for lesser men, he now possessed them. That he wanted to kiss her cheeks, her ears, her forehead, those pouty lips. That he had an over-whelming desire to hold her and never release her.

Somehow, he knew that if he were to do any of those things, he would be left whispering all his secrets to her. Including revealing that he was not the hero she believed him to be. And that could not happen.

"Are you all right?" he asked.

Miss Louisa gave a small nod. "I... I believe so."

With great reluctance, he released his hold on her, and to his surprise, she frowned. He placed the back of his hand on her cheek, unable to stop a sigh from escaping his lips. Oh, but what soft skin she had!

"I'm glad," he said. "The thought of you being hurt... well, it bothers me."

"Sir? I'm so sorry, sir!" Claremont called in a panicked voice as the vehicle door swung open. "Is anyone hurt? Can I help?"

A burst of mischievousness ran through Aaron. "I would see to Miss Lockhart. I believe Miss Dunston is in good hands." He winked at her, and she laughed. And what a sweet laugh she had!

Aaron climbed from the vehicle, and at once his feet sank into mud. "I just purchased these boots," he grumbled. He traipsed around the carriage, noting the way it leaned to one side. "Is it a wheel?"

Claremont nodded. "I'm afraid so, sir. The moment I felt it seize, I stopped. Otherwise, the carriage would've tumbled over completely."

"You did the right thing," Aaron said. He studied the wheel but knew nothing about the maintenance of a carriage wheel. Yet he was a knight and therefore had to act as if he did. Having the women believe he was less of a man would be unbearable. "It appears this wheel is slightly bigger than the others. Perhaps that is the cause of our prob-lem. I'll have to have it replaced."

Miss Dunston alighted from the carriage, careful to step on stones so her shoes did not get mud on them. Although she was smiling, Miss Lockhart was not.

"The wheel is not a different size," Miss Lockhart said, "but rather the axletree has not been oiled properly. And it appears one of the lugs is missing." She straightened up and dusted her hands. "I'll return to Chatsworth and bring back Duncan. He'll know what to do."

Duncan Prudy was the village blacksmith. No one called him Mr. Prudy, for that had been how his father was addressed, and Duncan never got on with his father. Once Mr. Prudy was gone, no one thought twice about calling Duncan other than by his Christian name.

Or so Aaron had been told by one of the street vendors the week before.

Aaron cleared his throat. "As I said, the axletree. Claremont, escort Miss Lockhart since this is our fault."

Claremont gave Aaron an indignant look. "My fault? But sir..." Aaron glared, and the driver added, "Yes well, my apologies, sir. Come, Miss Lockhart. I'll see you get there safely."

When the pair was gone, Aaron returned his attention to Miss Dunston, who stood shaking her head. "What now? Will you complain about my misfortune?"

"Not at all," she replied with a sniff. "I'm surprised you're able to go through the door of your carriage given how big your head gets."

Aaron could not believe what he was hearing. "Are you saying I'm prideful?"

"Of course. Once again, you've been bested by a woman, and as always, you're incapable of dealing with it."

"Bested?" he asked with a laugh. "By Miss Lockhart? She gave nothing more than a speculative guess."

"Speculative guess says you. Yet we both know she outwitted you in an area restricted to men."

The rustling of leaves made them both spin around as a red fox burst from the underbrush to the left and ran past them to disappear into the forest on the other side of the road. Whether they had startled him, or he simply had somewhere else to go, Aaron was uncertain. But he enjoyed watching the lithe movements of the creature.

"Your sister, Lady Mathison," Miss Dunston said. "You mentioned that she hopes her husband succumbs to illness because he's a cruel man."

"Yes? What of it?"

"Do you think Lord Mathison is the only man who treats his wife in such a terrible way? I would venture to say that many ladies live a similar life."

Aaron frowned. "I don't understand your point."

"My point is simple, Sir Aaron," Miss Dunston said. "Not everything is a competition of wit or strength. Yet women are reminded every time they fail, much like your sister has endured. Surely, there are times when we deserve at least a crumb of recognition. Like Miss Lockhart understanding the problem with the carriage wheel."

Aaron searched for a proper argument but found none. An image of Horatia came to mind. She had once confided a secret to him.

"I reminded Reuben that I could help him. After all, Uncle George taught me about the stake he owned in that copper mine. But he laughed and left me standing alone, feeling ashamed. I know I'm no expert, but I learned a great deal that summer."

Hearing that his sister was being treated so callously had angered Aaron. To him, such men were lower than dogs. Yet had he not viewed women in much the same way? And what was worse, he had mocked Miss Dunston's attempts at learning how to conduct business or scolding her for interfering in what should have been left to men.

"You're right, Miss Dunston," he said with a heavy sigh. "I must admit, you've shown me that my judgment of women is somewhat... skewed."

She arched an eyebrow. "Somewhat?"

"Well, perhaps a shred more than somewhat," he replied with a small chuckle. "But not by much. But no, you were correct. Women should be recognized for their accomplishments, especially those who go beyond the playing of an instrument or how well she can handle a needle." He grinned. "But only by small amounts. We wouldn't want their heads to become so large that they're unable to get in and out of carriages."

Miss Dunston laughed. "Perhaps I could learn how to restrain my pride."

At that moment, Aaron realized he wanted nothing more in life than to hear this woman laugh. To listen to her speak. Her very being made him feel... worthy for the first time in his life.

And he enjoyed their banter. "I could teach you how to restrain your pride... as much as you could teach a roomful of women how not to flirt."

With a gasp of mock indignation, she slapped his arm. "Don't go on some tirade with me, Sir Aaron Kirkwood! Though, perhaps we could both learn from each other."

"Learn what exactly?" he asked.

She shrugged. "Perhaps we can open our own university. Of sorts. I can teach women how not to flirt, and you can teach men how to rein in their arrogance. Are those not our strongest abilities?"

Aaron could not stop himself from roaring with laughter. How had he not noticed her humor before today? And as he gazed down at her, he realized he had not looked past her beauty. "Miss Dunston, you're as lovely as you are wise. I believe we can work well together using our... strengths."

"Are you asking me?" she whispered as he took hold of her waist.

A strange nervousness filled Aaron, a feeling to which he was unaccustomed. Yet he pushed it aside. He had something more important to do this day.

"We do tend to argue—"

She snorted. "Tend to?" He gave her a mocking glare, to which she responded with her lips pressed together and her eyes wide with expectation.

"As I was saying, we do tend to argue, and that is because one of us is stubborn—"

She shook her head. "I'm willing to look past your stubbornness, Sir Aaron."

"Will you not be quiet for a moment to allow me to say what I wish to say?"

Again, she pressed her lips together, this time nodding her agreement.

"Good. Now, I think we can both look past our faults." Gone was the playfulness, replaced by a cloud of sobriety. "I wish to court you, Miss Dunston. If you'll have me."

He had expected a quick response, a sure affirmation, but he was met with a deafening silence. Did she not wish to court? Was *her* pride so great?

Miss Dunston dropped her gaze. "When you saved me that day in the alley, you said you cared for me. I must know if you truly do."

"I do," he replied without hesitation. "I do care for you. Perhaps even more than I care for myself."

A moment later, she fell against his chest, causing him to draw in a deep breath. Although she had not given a verbal response, he found it unnecessary. Allowing him to hold her had been her answer.

The distant sound of voices ended their embrace. From down the road, he could make out Miss Lockhart walking with Claremont and a man on horseback beside them.

"We can discuss this more later," Miss Dunston whispered. Then she grinned up at him. "And I'll write to my parents to tell them the good news."

Soon, the blacksmith was repairing the wheel, affixing a new lug, and oiling the axletree. It appeared Miss Lockhart had been correct in her assessment of the problem.

Aaron glanced at Miss Dunston. Although he was pleased with their newfound courtship, he could not help but worry about the days ahead. He had no doubt who would emerge victorious in the war for the theater. He made a solemn vow to be gentle when she lost. His victory could be what drove them apart once more.

Chapter Twenty-Six

Three days after the carriage mishap, Louisa found herself standing beside Sir Aaron outside Hawthorn Manor, the home of Mr. Lush. The two-story, gray-and-brown brick abode might have been impressive in its younger days, but it had a rundown feeling to it. Once lush gardens were now overgrown, and more than one of the dozen windows had been replaced by brick.

Given the expected payment for window taxes, it was no surprise. Many property owners either could not afford the fees or simply refused to pay them. Either way, removing windows meant paying less in taxes. The poorest removed every single window, leaving them wallowing in darkness. The cost of candles was beyond many families, some reading and sewing by firelight or rush lights once the sun had set.

Sir Aaron leaned close and whispered, "It's my understanding that Mr. Lush enjoys a drink. Or four. That should make it easier to convince him that my idea for the theater is the better choice."

Louisa laughed. Yesterday, she managed to sell eight tickets whilst Sir Aaron received not even a maybe. "I wish you luck," she whispered back as they walked to the portico. "But I've a feeling it will be I who emerges victorious once again."

They grinned at each other, and Ruth's groan did not escape Louisa's ear. She glanced over her shoulder at her friend. Ruth's smile looked more like a scowl, making Louisa laugh again. Ruth had been quite vocal about how going from house to house was tedious. The last thing she wanted was to be seen as some sort of humanitarian. Or so she said. Louisa knew her grumbling was more an act than truth.

A cast tin bell hung from a hook beside the door, a frayed cord hanging from its clapper. The clang that came from it was more melodious—and much louder—than Louisa had expected.

The door opened to a butler whose livery had seen better days. He had wire gray hair and sallow skin, as if he had not seen the sun in decades.

"Sir Aaron Kirkwood and Miss Dunston to see Mr. Lush," Sir Aaron said.

"This way, please," the butler said, his voice quivering.

The trio stepped inside. The small foyer was gloomy with dark-stained walls and a low ceiling. A portrait of a stern-looking man hung from the wall above a side table. A yellowing vase held a bouquet of dried flowers. Above them, a medieval wooden chandelier held six candles, dried wax hanging from their stubs.

A deafening battle cry filled the air as a matching pair of boys around eight years of age burst into the room, both with the same untamed red hair and faces full of freckles. The pursuer threw his arms around his prey and sent them both sprawling to the floor in a jumble of arms and legs and grunts and growls. Then they stopped to stare at the butler. With matching grins, they pounced, wrapping their arms around the poor man's legs.

"Bring us cake or off to the dungeon with you!" one of the boys cried.

"Oh, for heaven's sake," a man's voice shouted from one of the rooms off the main corridor. A tall man with a protruding stomach entered the foyer. With round cheeks and a red nose, his echo resounded in the room. "Percy, Peter, release poor Drummond at once!"

The boys hurried to their feet and clasped their hands behind their backs. "Sorry, Father," they said in unison.

"I'm afraid the twins take after their mother," Mr. Lush said with a smile. "Who is no doubt napping again."

"I'm doing no such thing!" a female voice said from atop the narrow staircase that led up to the second floor. She was no taller than the twins with dark hair and a warm smile. "Boys, to your room this instant. Mrs. Collins has been looking everywhere for you. If you shirk your lessons one more day, I'll see you go without supper for the next two days!" She pointed up the stairs. "Go!"

Panic filled their faces. "Yes, Mother." And they took the stairs two at a time.

"Drummond, will you please bring us a tray in the drawing room?"

"Yes, madam," the butler said before bowing and hurrying away.

"My wife, Patience Lush," Mr. Lush said. He held out a hand for Sir Aaron to shake. "Sir Aaron. A pleasure as always."

"May I present Miss Louisa Dunston and Miss Lockhart," Sir Aaron said.

"The pleasure is all mine," Mr. Lush said as he took first Louisa's and then Ruth's hands and kissed above their knuckles.

Mrs. Lush smiled. "It's so very nice to meet you. Won't you come in and sit?" She cast a glare on her husband. "Men may enjoy standing around for hours on end, but I, for one, prefer to engage in conversation while seated like civilized people."

Louisa and Ruth followed Mrs. Lush into the drawing room, which was tastefully decorated with mahogany-framed Georgian furniture. Louisa sat between Ruth and Sir Aaron on a beige-and-red-striped fabric couch. The fabric of the couch on which the Lushes sat across from them was beige. And threadbare.

Two chairs, both covered in red that matched the striped fabric, sat together at one end and a large fireplace at the other. Gilt-framed paintings of fruits on tables and flowers in vases hung from beige walls. A portrait of the Lush family hung above the fireplace, Mr. and Mrs. Lush resplendent in blue and their twin sons appearing far more angelic than they had upon Louisa's arrival.

"Thank you again for inviting us to your home," Sir Aaron said. "It's a magnificent estate. One of the finest I've seen yet." He flashed a toothy smile.

Mr. Lush beamed. "We've put a great deal of effort into our home, have we not, my dear?"

His wife gave a derisive sniff. "If it weren't for my insistence, no improvements would be made at all. At least I've been allowed to redecorate our bedchambers."

Louisa was ready to engage in their game. "I couldn't agree with Sir Aaron more. Your home reminds me of one belonging to a prominent man my family visited in London. He and Father spent a great deal of time at the theater. They would spend hours discussing the plots of the latest plays they had attended." She added a reminiscent tone to her voice.

"Speaking of the theater," Mr. Lush said. "Rumor has it that Barker is considering closing the one in Chatsworth and selling the building."

Sir Aaron nodded. "He may, yes. Which is why I'm here."

For several minutes, he explained his plans for the building. Louisa remained quiet. Her turn would come soon enough.

Over the last few days, Sir Aaron had kept his promise to teach her the finer points of business, focusing more on the art of negotiations. Louisa found it all far more fascinating than she would have believed and had used some of the tactics herself.

The butler entered in the middle of Sir Aaron's speech, and Mrs. Lush poured the tea. Sir Aaron had not even paused to take a breath.

Mrs. Lush was frowning by the time Sir Aaron finished. "Surely, you're not in support of this gentlemen's club, Miss Dunston?"

Smoothing her skirts, Louisa gave the woman a practiced smile. "I, too, see a bright future for the theater, but my vision is a bit different. I want a place where both men and women can congregate and enjoy a few hours of leisure time together." She glanced at Sir Aaron. "I hope to sell enough tickets and solicit enough funds for the theater to see continued success. As a theater."

Mr. Lush's teacup clinked in its saucer as he set it down. "A most noble idea, young lady. But I'm afraid I must agree with Sir Aaron. Chatsworth needs a gentlemen's club. The population of the village is growing every year. Tea houses are appearing all over the country, not to mention the various dressmakers and millineries. Goodness, women have far more shops available to them than men do already. Plus, if a club is not built now, it's only a matter of time before it is. They are becoming more popular every year."

"An insightful point, sir," Sir Aaron said. "And you could not be more correct. We men are being forced out of the very towns we've built."

Louisa had to bite her tongue to keep a retort from bursting from her lips, but the smile on Mrs. Lush's lips gave her hope.

"Don't listen to my husband, my dear. Regardless of what he wants, I would like to purchase twenty tickets."

Mr. Lush nearly leapt from his seat. "Twenty? Dear Lord, Patience! What will you do with twenty tickets?"

Unperturbed, Mrs. Lush raised her teacup, a tiny smile on her lips. "We ladies need a place as much as you gentlemen do. I see no reason we cannot share the same place." Louisa stifled a giggle at the woman's firm nod.

As if giving up on the argument, Mr. Lush sighed and changed the subject. "Have you had the opportunity to join in a good hunt yet, Sir Aaron?"

As the men discussed the topic of fox hunting, Louisa glanced at the knight. She had enjoyed the two of them working together, even if their goals differed as they did. The man she had thought her sworn enemy was not the man for whom she had come to care. To what extent, she was still unsure, but it was there all the same.

After a while, Mrs. Lush set down her empty cup and stood, sending both men leaping to their feet. "I'll get you some money for our tickets," she said, either missing her husband rolling his eyes or choosing to ignore him.

"If Barker does sell to you," Mr. Lush said, "I wish to invest. But I do have one question."

Sir Aaron smiled. "Of course. Do you wish to know the identity of the other investors?"

Mr. Lush shook his head. "I'd like to hear more about you, Sir Aaron. Is it true you saved Princess Sophia from being terrorized by five highwaymen? Were you not afraid?"

Louisa frowned. Rather than the usual prideful grin he displayed, a sadness crossed his features. "Yes well, it was something like that."

Before Mr. Lush could ask him to expound, Mrs. Lush returned.

"Here we are," the woman said in a jolly tone. "And a small donation for your cause." She leaned in closer and added in a whisper, "We women must band together, do we not?"

Louisa stared dumbfounded at the twenty pounds the woman placed in her hand. "Thank you very much, Mrs. Lush. That's very generous of you."

Once the trio was in the carriage and heading back to Courtly Manor, Louisa was pleased with yet another victory. Sir Aaron, however, kept his gaze on something outside the window.

"You don't seem very happy, Sir Aaron," Louisa said. "I would have thought you would be ecstatic. After all, you managed to secure another investor."

"I am happy," he replied, but his tone said otherwise. Then he sighed. "I'm just tired is all." He turned to look at her. "Let's do something besides sell tickets tomorrow."

"Like what?" Louisa asked, her heart palpating at the idea of spending time with him in a more personal capacity.

"I'm not sure just yet, but be ready by eleven, all the same."

She raised her eyebrows. "And what should I wear, do you think?"

"Clothing appropriate for any sort of outing," Sir Aaron replied. "That way you're prepared for anything."

Chapter Twenty-Seven

For so long, Aaron had equated happiness with that feeling of achievement each time he purchased a new business or agreed to another form of trade. The more shops, hotels, land, and ships he possessed, the more others recognized his abilities as a businessman, and the happier he would be. To him, the contentment he so coveted would only be achieved when his empire was complete. When he saw himself as successful—nay, when everyone else saw his success! —only then would his destiny be fulfilled.

Now, however, the dulcet tones of Miss Dunston's laughter as she held her new puppy had him questioning this logic. There she was, a simple schoolgirl who wanted no recognition, no public acknowledgment for what she was trying to accomplish. All it took was the gift of a small dog to make her smile. And that smile strangely brought him a sense of joy. It was as if pleasing her had a greater effect than gaining ownership of any building or signing any contract.

Had he chosen the wrong aspirations in life? Could true happiness come from pleasing the lovely young woman who sat across from him? Was he destined to do all he could to see that the twinkle remained in her eye?

Yet that made no sense. How could he delight in witnessing such joy in another person? Why did he feel so fulfilled knowing he was the cause?

And what did this sudden insight mean for his future?

For their future?

Her hint that she would marry him had not escaped his notice. Granted, they had been discussing a mutual attachment to the dog, but her meaning had been clear. Had the subject come up in conversation even three weeks earlier, it would have had him doubling over in fits of laughter. Now however, he found the notion welcoming.

There was no doubt that he had strong feelings for Miss Dunston and that she reciprocated them. Yet were they merely smitten with one another? Could what they had come to share carry them into marriage?

Well, he had no reason to concern himself with such an important decision at present. One did not simply jump into marriage without giving it a great deal of thought beforehand. For now, he would simply enjoy her company.

When they arrived at Hearsely Manor, Aaron said, "Would you like one of the stable hands to take the dog?"

Miss Dunston shook her head. "No. I'd like to keep him with me for now."

"Very well." He looked up at the clear, blue sky. "It's a lovely day. What do you say to a stroll around the gardens?"

"Oh yes, let's," she replied, her cheeks a delightful pink.

As they strolled, Aaron glanced sideways at Miss Dunston several times before motioning to the puppy and saying, "He will need to walk on his own soon. Unless you mean to carry him into adulthood."

"Funny you should say that," Miss Lockhart said from behind them. "I was thinking the same thing."

Miss Dunston laughed. "That's quite enough. Both of you. I'm just advising Patch on what he should expect, living with you, Sir Aaron. It won't be easy for him."

"Oh? And what should he expect?" Aaron asked, amused.

She stopped to place the puppy on the grass. "That you're a kind man. Stubborn, yes, and perhaps a bit vain, but kind all the same."

Aaron placed a hand to his chest and gave a mocking gasp. "Why,

Miss Dunston, you've paid me a compliment. Have you fallen ill?" He placed a hand on her forehead the way his governess had when he was young. "No, you have no fever. Surely you haven't consumed a bottle of wine without my knowledge! Have you a flask hidden somewhere on your person?"

Her laughter once again sent a warmth coursing through his veins. He offered her his arm, and she accepted it. "Don't worry," he said, smiling down at Miss Dunston. "I'll take good care of him until..." He paused. He had nearly said *until you come to live here*, but it was far too early to make such an assumption. "Until you're able to take over that responsibility."

She glanced over her shoulder. Aaron followed her gaze to where Miss Lockhart had stopped beside a large lilac tree. "Yes, I'll likely have to collect him soon," Miss Dunston said with a sigh. "Then I'll return home and prepare for a life I don't want."

For a moment, Aaron felt awkward. They had been courting only a few days. Despite his recent revelation of his feelings for her, he prayed she did not expect him to propose marriage.

To his relief, it was she who changed the subject. "What was it like to meet the King?"

They came to a stop near a hedgerow, Patch waddling across the grass to sniff beneath the closest hedge.

"Trust me, I could almost ask the same of you. The ceremony took a matter of moments, and I was not invited to stay afterward. Not even to share in a cup of tea."

Miss Dunston laughed. "Were you frightened when you fought the highwaymen?"

His heart began to race. Perhaps it was time for him to tell her the truth. Yet, what if she became disappointed when she learned that rather than a gang of highwaymen, or even one, the man he staved off was a drunkard who had no designs on hurting the Princess at all? Would she be so offended at his lie that she no longer wanted to see him again?

The thought of losing her was too much to bear. Therefore, he changed the subject this time. "Will your father allow you to keep a dog?"

She shook her head. "I don't think he'll care if I have one or not. I'd be surprised if he notices Patch, let alone that I've returned home."

Although Miss Dunston had explained that her father favored her sisters, Aaron could not shake the feeling that there was more to the separation of father and daughter than she had revealed. Whenever she mentioned her father, there was a pain in her eyes that caused his heart to clench.

"Perhaps Patch will help you and your father to grow close again," Aaron said. "Maybe he'll be a bridge that allows you to cross whatever rift that now separates you."

Rather than responding, Miss Dunston shook her head and hurried over to where the puppy was wriggling beneath the hedge. "Oh, just look at him! He's already getting dirty."

Aaron snorted. "If you think he's using my bath, Miss Dunston, you're sorely mistaken."

She frowned at him. "If we're courting, would it not be better if you were less formal?"

He cleared his throat. "I suppose so. Miss Louisa. But the question still stands."

She grinned and then picked up the dog. "My confidence in this arrangement is waning. If you're unwilling to share your bath, then I imagine you'll not offer him your bed, either. Where will he sleep?"

"I hadn't considered that," Aaron said. "I'll have Paul mind him at night. He's one of the stable boys. I realize some men allow dogs to sleep inside the house, but I find the idea rather unsavory. Animals are meant for the outdoors. That is why God gave them fur."

"Is that so?" Miss Louisa asked. "Then why do not men sleep outside?"

Aaron found her mischievous grin delightful. "Because unlike animals, we have no fur."

She laughed. "But are men not as much animals as dogs are?"

"I'm offended that you believe so, Miss Louisa," he replied, although his words held no heat whatsoever.

As they continued their stroll, Patch once again in Miss Louisa's arms, Aaron was relieved that the subject of the dog's living conditions, nor marriage, returned. The former was hardly worth discussing, and the latter... well, he preferred not to have to consider it. Not yet, anyway.

When he returned the two young ladies to the school, Patch accompanied them. He and Miss Louisa agreed to continue their ticket sales and fund collecting the following day.

"I'm not all that sure he'll be safe in the stable," Miss Louisa said as she petted the dog's head. "I'll find somewhere better for him to sleep."

Aaron stifled a groan. He would not give in and thus needed to put his foot down. No matter how Miss Louisa's blue eyes begged him.

"That truly is the best place for him," he said. "Now, I must go. Until tomorrow." He bowed and walked away.

An hour later after returning to Hearsely Estate, Aaron sat hunched over a ledger in his study. Concentrating on his work was proving nearly impossible. His mind kept drifting to Miss Louisa.

Why did her father not show the same affection he had for her sisters? Typically, the youngest child received the most attention, but that was not the case with her family. What made her so different that the man who should love her the most would have such disregard for her?

Her relationship with her father, however, was not his only concern. What sort of future lay ahead for an unworthy knight and a lovely young lady about to leave school? And what would become of their courtship once a decision was made about the theater? Had he made a mistake in asking her to court when he had not even considered marriage?

What began as a way to curtail any deceptive behavior had become something far different from what he would have expected, something far better. In the short time they had spent together, Aaron had changed. He was not a different person, not completely, but he had seen small alterations, all of them good. He was now considering that women should be allowed certain privileges they currently did not have. With certain limitations, of course. There was no need to turn the world on its ear for the sake of allowing women to go through life willy-nilly.

Yet allowing them to read whatever they chose would not bring too much chaos to the status quo. Even if they chose books on the sciences or business, he saw no reason they could not be allowed to read them. But no matter how much of a hold Miss Louisa had taken on him, he could not in good conscience be swayed in all matters. After all, men needed to retain some sense of dignity in this life.

A tiny whimper made him glance down where Patch rested on a small blanket beside his desk. Upon arriving, he had gone to hand the pup to the stable boy, but an image of Miss Louisa came to mind. With a sigh, he carried the dog inside the house with him. "Don't tell Miss Louisa that I'm allowing you to stay in the house," he said, waving a finger at the puppy as if he would understand what it meant. "She'll think I'm weak and will wish to take advantage."

Patch gave a tiny bark but immediately returned his head to where it rested on his front paws. Yes, he would make a wonderful addition to the household.

It was just too bad the puppy's future was as undetermined as that of Aaron.

Chapter Twenty-Eight

T he weather was warm and not a single cloud marred the
otherwise deep-blue sky as Louisa walked beside Ruth on
their way to Chatsworth. Ruth intended to visit the newly
opened pawnbroker.

"I used to frequent the London shops," Ruth had said. "They will
allow anyone to use anything as collateral for a loan, even clothes and
teacups. And when someone is unable to pay off the loan, the proprietor sells the goods in his shop. It's brilliant, really. He earns money
while also helping others."

Why Ruth would need a teacup or clothes that had been previously
worn, Louisa could not fathom. Not that her friend had much, but she
did not lack anything, either.

Accompanying Ruth to the village was always a quiet affair, allowing
Louisa's mind to wander. After all, her friend was not one for chatter,
which meant the majority of their journey was typically done in silence.

Louisa and Sir Aaron had spent three days over the past week out
and about selling tickets and collecting money for their individual
causes. Some men grumbled they would not attend the play that was to
take place in ten days, although they purchased tickets all the same.

Louisa continued to receive small donations, typically from women, yet Sir Aaron was seeing far more interest. Just two days earlier, they had called over to the home of Mr. Harold Green, who owned a string of apothecaries throughout southern England, making him a wealthy man indeed.

During their time at the man's home, five boys ran past the drawing room, whooping and wailing as they waved wooden swords in their hands.

Their father ran a shaky hand through his thin, graying hair and said, "A gentlemen's club would be a wonderful place where men can go for a bit of rest and relaxation. I've no idea how I have managed to survive as long as I have without such a place."

"Let's meet again," Sir Aaron had said, much to Louisa's annoyance. "Then we can discuss the particulars of my plan. I'd very much appreciate your input."

It was not until they turned down the dark alleyway that Louisa realized where Ruth was taking her. Rake Street.

The true name was Drake Street, but it had been dubbed Rake Street by the residents of Chatsworth due to the gaming hell located there. As long as one had money he was willing to bet, anyone was welcome. It was one place where commoners could be found in the same room with those of the nobility. Even if they likely did not share the same table.

They stopped in front of a shop with three large golden balls hung above the door. On the door was a sign that read, "*James Trout, Proprietor.*" Through the window, Louisa could see two men with long beards and wrinkled clothes. They did not appear poor but rather... rough. That was the only word that came to her mind when trying to describe them.

"Ruth, wait," Louisa said as she took hold of her friend's arm. "Are you sure this is a good idea? The people inside look no better than those entering the gaming hell we just passed. Perhaps we should go somewhere else."

"Oh, don't worry about those two," Ruth said. "If they try anything, I'll just fight them."

"That is what I'm afraid of," Louisa whispered before following Ruth into the shop.

Louisa stopped to assess the place. Ruth had been right. Pawnbrokers would take anything as collateral. Along the left wall ran a long counter, behind which were numerous shelves filled with a vast collection of items—teacups, plates, remnants of bolts of cloth, silk handkerchiefs, anything a person from any walk of life might own. How many of those items had been pawned and never retrieved because the money that was loaned for them was lost at the gaming tables? She suspected it was far too many.

Thankfully, the two unkempt men exited only moments later. "You see?" Ruth said, glancing over her shoulder. "We're safe here."

The proprietor was around forty with dark hair speckled with silver. His coat, unlike his previous patrons, was freshly pressed and brushed. "This is not a millinery," he said as he looked Louisa and Ruth up and down. "And I don't have any dresses at the moment if that's what you're after."

"I'm looking for any knives you might have," Ruth said.

"Knives?" the man repeated. "What do you need knives for?"

Ruth gave an indignant sniff. "I don't know. To cut my food. What does it matter to you? Will you show me what you have or not?"

Louisa could not help but gape. Why was Ruth being so abrupt with the man? Surely, he would throw them out!

Yet he did not. Instead, he chuckled and said, "There's no need to be saucy. I just got some in yesterday. Hold on, I'll be right back."

Once the man was gone, Louisa turned on Ruth. "Why are you being so hateful to him?"

"Hateful? This is how one conducts business with these types. And because I'm a woman, he'll try to overcharge me. I want him to know who he's dealing with straightaway, that way he doesn't take advantage of me."

"They'll do that?" Louisa asked, shocked.

Ruth snorted. "Men live for it."

"But in the shops we usually frequent, the men are always pleasant. I've never been overcharged."

"There are exceptions, of course. And they have a particular reason for their actions."

Louisa frowned. "Such as what?"

With a wide grin, Ruth replied, "They believe that if they're pleasant, they have a chance with you."

Louisa's frown deepened. "A chance for what exactly?"

"That you'll give them one of the kisses you offered Sir Aaron," Ruth said with a grin. "Rumors do spread, you know."

Louisa's cheeks heated with embarrassment. "Ruth! At least show some decorum!" This made her friend laugh all the louder. "Oh, enough of this silliness, please!"

The proprietor returned and set five knives of varying sizes and shapes on the counter.

"Mr. Trout, is it?" Ruth asked. He responded with a nod. "Is it true that you'll buy anything?"

"Not everything but anything that I can resell at a profit. Though I can't seem to think of anything that I haven't been able to resell yet. Have you a horse? A bit of jewelry? Whatever it is, I'll see what I can do. If you're looking to make a purchase, I can see if we have a price on which we can agree."

Ruth picked up a steel-handled blade. "I'm interested in purchasing this knife, but I don't like the quality of it. In fact, I think you should just give it away."

To Louisa's surprise, Mr. Trout laughed. "An excellent way to begin negotiations, miss, but that knife'll get a crown anywhere."

"Oh, I don't doubt that," Ruth replied. "But we're here, not anywhere else. If you can get a crown for this, then I suggest you get it from someone else. I'll offer you three pence."

"Three pence? Are you mad?" he sputtered, although his indignation seemed more a part of the show than true outrage.

Louisa enjoyed watching as the two bartered back and forth. Finally, Mr. Trout raised his hands in defeat. "Fine. Two shillings, but I'll not go any lower. I gave the man a bob for it in the first place! At least allow me to double my money."

Ruth grinned. "Agreed." She stuck out her hand, and Mr. Trout shook it.

Despite her friend's obvious sense of pride, Louisa wanted to die from embarrassment. Not only had Ruth entered such a shop, but she also had bartered for a knife, of all things. She may as well have been caught kissing a man at a party!

Mr. Trout wrapped the knife in a scrap of burlap, and Ruth placed it in the bag she wore on her wrist, one end sticking out from the top.

"And what about that spyglass?" she asked, pointing at one of the shelves. "Let me see that."

Mr. Trout smiled. "That just arrived yesterday. A real captain, he was." He walked over to collect the item.

"Another unbelievable story," Ruth whispered, making Louisa choke back a giggle.

The proprietor placed the spyglass on the counter. It was retractable and cased in bronze.

"It comes with a wooden box, too," Mr. Trout said. "Why don't you take a look at it?"

Ruth picked up the telescope and slowly turned in it in her hand. With her fascination with the sea, Louisa understood her desire to purchase it.

"Where did you get this?" Ruth asked in a voice far harsher than Louisa would have expected.

The proprietor, who was resentful at Ruth's tone, raised himself to his full height, which was not all that tall. "It's like I told you. A captain brought it to me yesterday. Didn't even want to pawn it. Said he had no use for it anymore and wanted to sell it outright."

"Ruth?" Louisa asked. "What is wrong?"

Ruth's face had gone a bright red. Whether from anger or sadness was unclear.

Not looking up from the spyglass, Ruth asked, "Did he say what he was doing in Chatsworth?"

Mr. Trout blew out his breath. "All he said was that he was here to sign some sort of agreement, then he'd be going away for a few weeks before returning. I think he's planning to settle here." He motioned to the telescope. "Eight pounds."

"Fine," Ruth replied without bartering. "Get the box."

Louisa tried to say something, but Ruth waved her away. Once the transaction was completed, she followed her friend outside. Ruth's strides were long, and her eyes were filled with rage.

"What is it?" Louisa asked as they turned onto High Street. "What's gotten you so upset? Does this spyglass remind you of him?" She spoke of the captain who had broken Ruth's heart.

Ruth came to a sudden stop and withdrew the ornate wooden box. "It reminds me of him because it is his. Look at the name inscribed on the case."

Louisa's eyes widened. "*Captain Bannermann,*" she whispered as she read the inscription, "*may your ship never dock.*" Ruth slid the cover back onto the box, and Louisa jumped. "But what is he doing here? And why did he not call on you?"

"Because he's a selfish man," Ruth spat. "One who makes promises only to break hearts. I don't care why he's returned, and I hope he never calls on me. I never want to see him again!"

As they resumed their walk, this time at a more reasonable pace, Louisa glanced at her friend. Clearly, Ruth *did* care about the captain's return. Louisa just prayed that whatever had happened, the man did not hurt Ruth again.

Chapter Twenty-Nine

T he manor house belonging to Mr. Marcus Connelly, a wealthy shipping merchant, was a resplendent three-story home of gray stone offset by red-trimmed window frames and surrounded by rose bushes. Tiny spring leaves peeked from the nibs of the stems, promising a new season of lovely blossoms.

Inside was as splendid as the exterior, with drapes made of the finest fabrics, carefully crafted furniture, and lovely tapestries. Every piece of furniture had been crafted by the best furniture makers in England.

Aaron sat in the drawing room in a George I wing chair covered in crimson fabric. Other pieces in the room came from Chippendale, Hepplewhite, or Sheraton. No expense had been spared in the home's decor, which said much about Mr. Connelly's coffers.

Two days earlier, Aaron had received an invitation to call on Mr. Connelly. Having Miss Louisa accompany him could prove disastrous, for he had used Mr. Connelly's daughter to garner this appointment. Therefore, he had accepted and gone alone but not without a twinge of guilt. All he could hope was that she did not learn of it. Not only would he have to explain how the invitation came about—after all, he had flirted with Miss Miriam to convince her to intercede for him—

but also that he had broken their agreement to work together. Neither explanation appealed to him.

But he had a mission—to hold the deed to the theater. And in the art of war, and more so in business, exceptions had to be made.

After all, some rules were meant to be broken.

Across from him sat his host, a man of fifty with curly red hair common among the Scottish. And a stark contrast to his daughter's black tresses. Aaron was relieved he had not seen that young lady since his arrival. And he prayed he would not. Had this meeting come up two weeks ago, he would have thought differently, but now, the idea of toying with her made him strangely uncomfortable.

"Even the day I returned from York," Mr. Connelly was saying, "I was beset upon by a barrage of questions from Mary."

He spoke of his wife, but how the woman ever got a word in edgewise was a mystery to Aaron. The husband had spoken without ceasing since Aaron's arrival, and he wondered if the man ever took a breath.

"Don't women understand that we men already suffer enough in this world without their input?"

Aaron went to respond, but Mr. Connelly did not give him the opportunity.

"So, I retreated to my study with a bottle of brandy, but even there I've no respite. Drat it all! I don't want to use that room as a sanctuary as well as work. And with four daughters, every other room is occupied with one project or another. The parlor has the best light, so Priscilla uses it for her painting. The library is Constance's refuge as she spends every minute of every day reading. The pianoforte was moved into the ballroom for Miriam to practice her playing and Martha her singing. If I hadn't put my foot down, Mary would have found a use for my study as well! If you're able to build this gentlemen's club as you propose, my life will be much more bearable, for I'll finally have a place where I can be a man."

When the man stopped to take a breath, Aaron used that opportunity to speak. "That is precisely why I wish to purchase the theater— to give us men the chance to escape the women who consume so much of our time and space. I couldn't agree with you more, Mr. Connelly. We need a place to call our own."

In the past, this argument had little effect on Aaron. He had no woman in his life who took up his time and space, so the words held little meaning for him. Now, however, an image of Miss Louisa came to mind. The thought of not being in her company, of leaving her alone, sent a wave of sadness washing over him. A man did not treat the woman for whom he cared with such disregard.

What is your rationale, then, for building a place she cannot enter? he wondered.

It was the same as it always had been. His destiny. Right or wrong, the gentlemen's club was the best place to begin the journey toward the life he was meant to lead.

"And we shall, Sir Aaron," Mr. Connelly said as he set down his teacup. "When my Miriam marries, her husband will no doubt want somewhere to go. She's like her mother with all her questions and nonstop chatter."

Aaron smiled. Louisa had an inquisitive nature as well. In the beginning, her badgering had frustrated him, but that was forever changed. Now he enjoyed their discussions, their banter.

"It does not help that she's plain-looking."

It took every ounce of restraint for Aaron not to react. Did he just hear the man say his daughter was plain? What father described his daughter thus? Granted, Miss Miriam was not beautiful, but neither was she homely. She would make some man happy, one day. It just would not be him.

"Now, don't play innocent with me," Mr. Connelly said. "A wise man is able to admit when his daughter is lacking. And Miriam is just that." His lowered brows gave him a calculating look. "By the way, she's requested that you take a stroll around the gardens with her. She's waiting for you in the parlor. Will you do this for me? One good turn and all."

Aaron's mind raced. He did not want to betray Miss Louisa's trust. After all, they were courting now. Neither did he want to give Miss Miriam the wrong impression. Not anymore. Yet if this stroll resulted in another investor, could he refuse?

No, he could not. Mr. Connelly's investment was far too important. Aaron stood. "I'd like nothing more than the chance for good company," he said, putting out his hand. "We have an agreement, then, pertaining to the club?"

Mr. Connelly rose and shook his hand. "We do. We can discuss the particulars once Barker agrees to sell. And enjoy my daughter's company." His eyes twinkled as he said this last.

Miss Miriam wore a dark-blue gown with yellow and green embroidered flowers on the bosom and around the bottom hem of the skirts. In her lap was an embroidery hoop, her hands working the needle deftly. Behind her stood a woman in livery, likely her lady's maid. So, she had expected him to accept the offer to accompany her. That did not bode well for him.

"Sir Aaron," she said as if surprised by his sudden appearance, although her eyes said she had expected him to come to her. She set aside her embroidery and dropped into a low curtsy. "How wonderful to see you again."

"And you, as well," he replied with a bow.

"Well, I'll leave you to it," Mr. Connelly said. "And Miriam, don't bombard him with questions. Allow a man to speak and be thankful he's taken time from his busy schedule to share in your company."

Miss Miriam dropped her gaze. "Yes, Father."

For some strange reason Aaron could not explain, he felt pity for this young lady. How many women had he made feel as dejected as this father did? The disgust he had for himself did not sit well in his stomach.

"Shall we?" he asked, forcing a smile as he offered his arm.

With her lady's maid following behind, Aaron allowed Miss Miriam to lead him out to the rear gardens of the house. Several gardeners tilled the soil in preparation for spring planting, none even glancing in their direction as they began their stroll down the cobbled footpath. Perhaps he should tell her about Miss Louisa, so there was no misunderstanding.

"Did Father agree to join you in your business venture?" Miss Miriam asked.

Aaron nodded. "He did."

"I'm very happy for you. I made sure to speak highly of you, just as you asked."

That tiny tug of guilt began to gnaw at Aaron. "Thank you. I greatly appreciate what you did. More than you can know."

The path split in two directions to encircle a grassy area with a bird bath in the middle. To the far right sat a bench, and she led him there.

"I hope you don't mind if we sit," she said, giving him a demure smile. "I woke up earlier than usual to prepare for your visit. I hope I can compare to the ladies of London."

Aaron wanted nothing more than to leave. But he had brought this all upon himself and therefore had to remain. "Your dress is lovely. You really shouldn't have gone to such trouble for my arrival. I'm just a simple man."

"Oh, no," she whispered. "You're far from simple. When we spoke beside the vendor's cart that day, your kind words remained with me." Her blush covered her entire face. "Sir Aaron, no man as handsome as you has ever taken an interest in me before."

Swallowing back a groan, Aaron said, "Miss Miriam, although I do find your company enjoyable, I'm afraid we cannot take it beyond that."

Grief filled her features, and she lowered her head once again. "Plain," she said beneath her breath. "It's because I'm plain, is it not?" She looked up at him, tears glistening in her brown eyes. "Don't lie to me, please, for Father has said that I'll never be a great beauty."

"Not at all," he said soothingly. "Your appearance has nothing to do with our future—or lack thereof. You see, I'm already courting another woman."

"Oh, I see," Miss Miriam said. "And is she beautiful?"

Aaron nodded. "She is."

"And have you known her long?"

"I have," Aaron replied. "For some time now."

A frown crossed her lips. "Yet you flirted with me and gave me hope that you might be interested in me?"

"It's not—"

She raised a hand to forestall him. "Don't worry, Sir Aaron. You're not the first gentleman to use me to get to my father. Or rather my father's wealth." She sighed heavily. "I had hoped this time would be different, but alas, I've been fooled yet again."

For years, Aaron had relied on his handsome features and charm to get what he wanted, but not once had he considered how his actions affected others. Until now.

"I'm truly sorry."

Her laugh had a cynical note to it. "Sorry? Men like you are never truly sorry for what they do. You'll always step on the heart of some poor, unsuspecting woman to get what you want. I pity this poor creature you've managed to capture, for she'll be mourning her crushed heart as much as I mourn mine. No, I don't wish to hear your lies any longer. Please, just go. I'd prefer to be left alone."

With shame clinging to him, Aaron stood and considered apologizing again. Yet her look told him doing so would be in vain. Therefore, he dipped his head and left.

Soon, his carriage was trundling toward Chatsworth. What should have been a moment of revelry had become one of revulsion. Revulsion for himself. Revulsion for the choices he had made in his life. Yet something she had said was untrue. Miss Louisa should never be pitied, for Aaron had become a better man.

Yet what he had done to Miss Miriam had been wrong, and he prayed Miss Louisa did not learn of it. For he was unsure if he would be able to explain himself without driving her further away.

Chapter Thirty

The opening night of the play was scheduled in two days. It was then that Louisa would learn of its fate. Not only had she sold every ticket given to her, but she had also gathered both donations and promises of donations—all carefully noted with names and their prospective amounts in a small notepad she carried in her reticule. That money was allotted for repairs and renovations to the building in which the theater was located if Mr. Barker so chose.

Before she could give Mr. Barker the list and the money, Louisa had another task to accomplish. Amy was finding the adjustment to her new life away from home difficult and had been given special permission to skip her lessons for the day so Louisa could help ease her discomfort.

"If I were to get ahead on my studies, perhaps work late into the night to complete my work or to read more, do you believe it may be possible to leave the school early? Perhaps by a year or more?" This was just one of a multitude of questions Amy had asked since leaving the school. The girl was unhappy with her lot, but she refused to say why.

Louisa remembered her first year at Mrs. Rutley's School for Young Women. Because of her circumstances, she found being away from home exciting and pleasing. But that was not the case for all the students. Those who came from a close-knit family struggled the most. Was that why Amy was unhappy? Because she missed her family? If only the girl would confess what was troubling her, Louisa would be better able to help her!

"I'm afraid it doesn't work that way, Amy. Whether you like it or not, Courtly Manor will be your home for the next four years."

When Amy frowned, Louisa turned to look at the girl. "What is wrong, Amy? Why do you want to leave so badly? I can't help you if you don't confide in me."

Amy's round cheeks reddened, and she twisted a strand of blonde hair around a finger. Looking first left and then right, she whispered, "If I tell you something, you cannot repeat it."

Louisa smiled. "I swear to you that I will not. No, what is troubling you?"

Tears welled in the girl's blue eyes. "It's my mother."

A carriage trundled past them, its wheel turning up a fine cloud of dust. Once the sound of the horse's hooves faded in the distance, Amy still had not offered any more information.

"Is she ill?" Louisa prodded.

Amy shook her head. "No."

Louisa stifled an annoyed sigh. The girl was not making this easy! "Do you miss her? Is that why you want to return home so soon?"

Amy shook her head again.

"Well?" Louisa asked, her patience running thin. "I cannot offer advice if you keep your troubles to yourself. I know sharing worries can be difficult, but you can trust me." She pushed out her lower lip for effect. "Or is it that you don't trust me? I thought we were friends, but maybe I was wrong."

"Oh, no!" Amy said, her eyes widening. "I do trust you. It's just that... well... Oh, this is so difficult!" She sighed. "Mother has this friend, you see. I was able to keep them apart before, but with me here, I no longer can."

Louisa frowned. What an odd reaction. A young child being jealous of a parent spending time with someone other than her was one thing, but a girl of fourteen? Quite odd indeed.

"You cannot have her all to yourself," Louisa said. "Sometimes women need someone to whom they can confide, someone to share things they cannot share with their children. You should not be upset when your mother wishes to spend time with a friend. This friend, she will never replace—"

"He," Amy corrected.

The sudden realization of the situation made Louisa come to an abrupt halt. "Oh, I see. So, this friend is... well, more than a friend?"

Amy sighed, and the two resumed their walk. "Father is away often. When Lord Tutton first called, I thought it odd. Yet, who was I to wonder? There was always a reasonable excuse—a document to deliver or an inquiry to make. Then one day I overheard them talking in the parlor. I'll not repeat what they said, but there was no mistaking the intimacy behind their words. After that, I made sure I appeared whenever they were alone. I was in search of a book I had left behind, or I ran out of thread for my needlework. Whatever excuse I could come up with, I used. If she left the house, I invited myself." She dropped her gaze. "I acted the petulant child at times, but I had no choice. I couldn't allow her to go off on her own. What if they had plans to meet?"

"Are they aware you know about the... situation?" Louisa asked.

"No," Amy replied. "I've not told her I know."

Louisa placed a calming hand on Amy's arm. "I'm truly sorry," she said, her heart heavy for the poor girl. "The only advice I can offer is this. When she comes to visit, speak to her about your concerns. Only when our problems are aired, can we address them. Either confront her or let it go. But if you choose the latter, you must also accept that nothing will change. I'm not saying she'll stop seeing this gentleman, but that is not for you to decide."

"Do you speak so openly with your parents?" Amy asked with surprise.

Louisa went to nod but stopped. That was untrue. Yet explaining her situation would only put an added burden on the girl, and she could not do that. This was about Amy. "It's complicated," she replied.

When they arrived at the village proper and were heading toward the theater, a well-dressed young man with wild blond hair and protruding teeth stopped and grinned at Louisa.

"Well, hello, Miss Dunston," he said.

It took a moment for Louisa to recognize him. She had met Mr. Rupert Scarsdale at the party Lord Walcott had hosted the previous month.

"Mr. Scarsdale," she said, bobbing a quick curtsy. "It's a pleasure to see you again."

He beamed at her. "Not as much as it is for me. I was planning on writing to you today."

"Is that so?" Louisa asked. "How fortunate that we've run into one another, then. Now you can simply tell me directly what you meant to write."

Mr. Scarsdale drew in a deep breath. "After we spoke at Lord Walcott's party, I spent a great deal of thought to what you said."

"You mean about the theater?"

He gave an exasperated shake of his head. "Miss Dunston, at the risk of being too bold, it was clear that you took an interest in me. 'Any lady would be honored to have me call on her.' That was what you said. Therefore, I would like permission to do just that."

By the time he finished, his face was red to his ears, but his smile was broad. Yet if she and Sir Aaron were courting, any sort of encouragement on her part would be unkind.

"I appreciate your offer, Mr. Scarsdale," she said, choosing her words carefully. "If it were not for Sir Aaron, I would consider—"

"You'd consider?" Mr. Scarsdale interrupted with a contemptuous laugh. "That is a far cry from what you proposed that night." He lowered his voice, a sneer crossing his lips. "Don't play innocent with me. You flirted with me in hopes of getting a donation for the theater. No matter if you were spoken for or not, you had no intention of allowing me to call on you, did you?"

Louisa went to argue, but she found she could not do so. Everything he said of her was true.

"As I thought," he said, the contempt coating his tone. "Good day to you."

Guilt tore at Louisa. How many men had she treated as callously?

Too many. And long before this quest to save the theater. Doing so always uplifted her and made her feel important and worthy. But it had come at a high cost.

"Don't let his lies upset you," Amy offered. "He's clearly an irritable man. Look at it as a narrow escape from what could have been a terrible situation."

Louisa sighed. "But he did not lie. Everything he said was true. My behavior has been unbecoming, and even more so as of late. Sometimes my flirting brings me shame, but I've always been able to justify my actions in one way or another."

"I don't understand," Amy said, frowning. "Why act in a way that makes you feel shame?"

Louisa went to respond but grabbed Amy by the arm and pulled her into the doorway of the nearest shop.

"What is it?" Amy asked.

Louisa put her finger to her lips and peeked around the corner. Lord Ezra Colburn, the very man who had threatened to ruin the school, who seemed to despise Mrs. Rutley more than anyone else on this earth, was speaking to the proprietor of the theater.

Now, what does he want with Mr. Barker? Too bad they were too far away to make out what they were saying.

The two men shook hands, and Lord Ezra stepped into a waiting carriage. Louisa waited until the carriage was gone before emerging from their hiding place and hurrying to the theater.

Mr. Barker was sweeping the foyer when they entered. "Ah, Miss Dunston, what a pleasant surprise. And Miss Felton if I recall? I have a good mind for names."

"Yes, sir," Amy replied.

A wave of guilt washed over Louisa for the lies she had told this man concerning Mrs. Rutley's attraction to him. Now, with Lord Ezra causing who knew what sorts of problems, it was about time she was truthful.

"I owe you an apology, Mr. Barker," Louisa said, a sourness rising in her stomach.

"Do you?" Mr. Barker asked, clearly taken aback.

"Indeed, I do. It concerns my headmistress. I'm afraid I haven't been exactly forthright with you about what she feels for you." She could feel heat rise in her cheeks as she went on to explain. Confessing her wrongdoing was not as easy as she thought it would be. Then again, perhaps discomfort was her penance for her dishonesty.

When she was finished, Mr. Barker smiled. "There is no need to apologize, Miss Dunston. Mrs. Rutley and I are friends. I have a great deal of respect for her, and that is what matters."

"You're a kind man, Mr. Barker."

He snorted and waved a hand at her. "It's all in the past now. So, how many tickets did you sell? I assume that's why you're here."

Louisa gave him a proud smile. "All of them. I've also collected money and have a list of those willing to donate if you choose to keep the theater open."

Mr. Barker gaped as she handed him the money and the list. "You should feel proud of yourself, Miss Dunston. I'll never be able to thank you for giving me this opportunity."

"You're more than welcome," Louisa replied. "Though, I must ask. Have you decided what you plan to do?"

He chuckled and returned to his sweeping. "Lord Ezra just asked me that very question, and I'll tell you what I told him. After the performance on Friday, I want you and Sir Aaron to each present your plan to those who are in attendance. You'll explain how much it will cost to implement said plan, and we'll put it to a vote. Let's allow the people to decide."

Louisa smiled. "I would be honored to do so, Mr. Barker," she said. "And don't worry. Come Friday, we'll be celebrating our victory!"

As she and Amy walked back to the school, Louisa imagined herself giving her speech and the applause and adulation that would follow. Yet the victory she so desired no longer held the appeal it once had, for it meant Sir Aaron would lose.

But they would be able to work past such a problem.

Would they not?

Chapter Thirty-One

Sir Aaron had invited Louisa on an outing as a way to celebrate all they had accomplished. Although Louisa ought to have been enjoying the passing scenery and enjoying their time together, she found herself wishing she had not accepted. What if all they had built together came crashing down because of a vote? This problem should have been at the forefront of her mind, but instead, she shoved it into a trunk and slammed down the lid to keep from considering it.

To make matters worse, she had written to her father about Sir Aaron. He had replied, saying he would collect her Monday morning. What he did not include was his approval.

He cares nothing for you, she told herself. Finding her own husband only made his job that much easier. Now he could wash his hands of her once and for all.

And after the performance tomorrow, it likely would not matter.

The carriage began ascending a sharp incline, slowing their pace. She considered asking Sir Aaron where they were going, but his demeanor appeared to reflect how she felt. Sad.

Yet it was not her father nor the decision concerning the theater that bothered her. Rather it was herself. She had concealed far too much from the man for whom she had come to care. And although she would tell him, now was not an appropriate time.

The carriage slowed to a stop, and Louisa alighted, Ruth following after. They had stopped just before the crest of a tall, lush-green hill. Louisa's wide-brimmed hat shaded her from the warm rays of the sun that hung in a deep-blue sky, and she stopped to draw in a deep breath, savoring the freshness of the air.

Sir Aaron offered his arm. "If you don't mind, I'd like to complete our journey to the top on foot."

She followed his gaze up the slope, which led to a rocky peak.

"I think I'll remain here," Ruth said, crossing her arms with a scowl and leaning against the carriage. "I'm not up for climbing mountains."

Louisa, however, snaked her arm through his and grinned. "Well, I'm up for the challenge."

The climb was far more difficult than she first thought. Soon, she was panting, and her calves were straining with the effort.

"Tomorrow, we learn the fate of the theater," he said. "How do you feel?"

Louisa sighed. "I'm excited and yet also worried. But if I've given my best proposal, all I can do is leave it up to the attendees to decide. And you? What are your thoughts on the matter?"

The knight shook his head but offered no explanation. Instead, he said, "Lord Walcott mentioned this place to me. From what he says, it should be well worth the trouble."

She gave a winded laugh. "Well, I certainly hope so. I doubt I've worked so hard to go anywhere since I was a girl."

Yet when they reached the crest, they were both left speechless. They were rewarded with the most fantastic view Louisa had ever seen. Below them lay the village of Chatsworth, the sun's rays highlighting it as if it were a scene on a stage. Stone walls and hedgerows indicated the divisions between properties. Houses and estates speckled the lush green fields. Tiny white dots marked herds of sheep.

"It's so beautiful," she breathed. "I don't think I've seen anything so lovely in my life."

"I have," he said.

She turned to find him looking at her, and a flush coursed through her body.

"You're so beautiful, Miss Louisa," he whispered. Hearing her name on his tongue warmed her soul. "Working together these past weeks has made me see you're more than simply beautiful." Her heart fluttered as he took her hands in his. "But I cannot allow this to go any further without confessing something to you."

"What is it? You may tell me whatever you wish. Nothing will change what I feel for you."

"I've no doubt that is true." He shifted his feet and dropped his gaze. Something was wrong, although she could not fathom what it could be. He was no rogue and certainly had no illegitimate children. What was he keeping from her?

"I'm not the hero you believe me to be."

Louisa shook her head. "But you saved the Princess."

"Perhaps, but not in the way everyone believes."

Louisa nodded. "What do you mean?"

"I was in London, on Regent Street, when Her Majesty stepped from a carriage. A harmless old drunk was, let's say... enthusiastic when he saw her. So much so that he rushed toward the vehicle. I did nothing more than hold him back, but the story grew within seconds. Regent Street became a faraway forest, and the drunkard became a band of thieves. My holding back the man became a battle with swords. The more the story was told, the grander it became."

He shrugged. "Two weeks later, I was summoned to the palace where the King himself offered me a knighthood. If I deny the part I played, the Princess is deemed a liar. After all, she made no attempt to rectify the events. But if I accept, it makes me a liar. I chose the latter to save Her Majesty from embarrassment, but even that would be untrue. I enjoyed the attention I received for my heroic act. Or rather as my factious act."

A soft breeze blew past them, and for a moment, all was quiet. Although Louisa wished to console him, she sensed he had more to say.

"I'm no hero. Nor am I a great businessman. I admit I have some ability, but not to the degree I have led everyone to believe. For all my shortcomings, I have but one hope—that you're not disappointed because of the lie I've perpetuated. Because I love you, Miss Louisa, and would like nothing more than for you to be my wife."

If Sir Aaron had not been holding Louisa by the hands, she would have tumbled down the steep incline. He loved her! Oh, he had misrepresented himself, certainly, but the fault was not all his own. And what harm came from rumors that augmented a man's honor? It was not as if he created the tale himself.

He loved her!

If he was willing to bare his soul at the expense of his integrity, she could reveal that which she held closest to her heart. Something she had told no one, not even her closest and dearest friends.

"Do you recall when I told you about my sisters?" she began.

Sir Aaron nodded. "I do. You have three if I remember correctly, and your father favors them over you."

"Yes, and that is true, but it is not the full truth. My father not caring about me has nothing to do with me being the youngest as I've intimated before. Nor does it have anything to do with my parents believing they've already found their places in society because of the men my sisters married. I am the problem."

She dropped her gaze, finding it hard to look him in the face. Her heart pounded in her chest so hard that she thought it would burst through her sternum. If she spoke the words, they would only become truer. Was that what she wanted?

"I'm not sure I can say it. For if I do, you'll want nothing to do with me. Just like my father."

He placed a finger beneath her chin, lifted her face to look at him, and smiled. "There is nothing you can say that will drive me away. What could you have done that was so bad?"

A lone tear rolled down her cheek. "Since I was young, I spent a great deal of time spying on others—as you know from my eavesdropping on your conversation at the park. Just before I was sent to Courtly Manor, I overheard a conversation between my parents." She gave a deep sigh. "I should have put a stop to my spying then, but what I heard only pushed me to do more. I'm delaying, I know. And I'm sorry. It's not easy to say."

"Trust me," he said. "It cannot be worse than my secret."

She shook her head. "I learned my mother had an affair."

"But you cannot blame yourself for her wrongdoings," Sir Aaron said.

Louisa gave a choking sob. "But you don't understand. I'm the result of that affair!" Tears poured down her face as she continued. "It's the reason I'm always flirting. I have used my beauty as a means of protection from the hurt I have inside. To enamor a potential suitor so that if he were to learn the truth, if he finds me attractive enough, perhaps he'll look past this terrible fault of mine."

Louisa looked up into his warm blue eyes and was surprised to find no judgment in them. "We're very much the same, you and I," she continued. "And like you, I want to put the past behind me. For I love you, too, and would like nothing better than to become your wife. If you'll still have me now that you know the truth about my birth."

His strong arms wrapping around her was his response. He held her, whispering words of love as she wept. And when she looked up at him, he did not hesitate to press his lips to hers.

"I don't care about who you used to be or how you came into this world. I'm just thankful that you did. Otherwise, I would be alone."

Her heart beat with love as she said, "I don't care who tries to harm me, be he a drunkard or a highwayman, for I know you will always protect me."

They held each other for what seemed an eternity until they stood, hand in hand, looking upon the village of Chatsworth once again.

"My destiny lies in that village," Sir Aaron said. "But once we're married, we'll likely move to another place. But no matter where we go, we'll always be at one another's side, growing an estate that we can one day leave to our children. That is the destiny that lays ahead of us."

Although the idea of traveling the country appealed to Louisa, doubt tugged at her. Was her destiny nothing more than to help her soon-to-be-husband acquire wealth? Surely, life had more in store for her than that?

Chapter Thirty-Two

Sitting in the drawing room of his Chatsworth home, Sir Aaron Kirkwood, Most Noble Order of the Garter, had never felt better. His journey to fulfilling his destiny would begin this evening with the decision of the fate of the theater. Just one stepping stone toward making a true name for himself rather than carrying the burden of a lie as he had done for far too long.

Yet his mind was not on what was to take place after the play. Instead, it was on the conversation he and Miss Louisa had shared the previous day. Had he known they would share their deepest, darkest secrets, would he have offered that outing? Likely not. Now that it was done, however, he was glad they had.

To finally reveal the lie behind his knighthood had been a relief. Her acceptance had been like air to a person drowning. Never had he expected anyone, but more especially the woman he loved, to accept him despite the falsehood his life was.

And to hear the story of how Miss Louisa came into this world made his heart ache. The fact she was the result of an affair might make others turn their backs on her, but he did not care. He loved her. That was all that mattered. When her father arrived on Monday, Aaron would meet his future father-in-law.

Yet one twinge of regret tugged at Aaron. He had failed to reveal another secret to Miss Louisa, for doing so would cause her undue worry. A letter had arrived three days earlier. Lord Ezra Colburn sought an audience. Yet the man was not to come alone. Lord Lenten would be in his company.

After his insults when Aaron and Miss Louisa had helped with his dog, Aaron would have preferred to never see the baron again—or Lord Ezra for that matter—but curiosity kept him from refusing the call.

"Lord Ezra and Lord Lenten," Scriven announced before moving aside to allow the two gentlemen to enter the room.

The temperature plummeted with the entrance of Lord Ezra. His black attire matched his dark hair and eyes. And his presence.

Lord Lenten's entrance warmed the air only faintly. His blue coat was as impeccable as his carefully combed blond hair.

Aaron waved away the butler and turned to bow to his guests. "My lords, welcome to Hearsely Estate." He motioned toward the seating area in front of the fireplace. "Sit, please. Would you like a drink? I have the finest brandy or a nice port. But I highly recommend—"

"Before we enjoy your hospitality," Lord Ezra interrupted, "my friend has something to say." He turned to his companion. "Go on, Lenten."

Lord Lenten slid a finger beneath his cravat. Red tinged his features, and he shot Lord Ezra a glare Aaron was certain he was not supposed to see. "The day we encountered one another on the road, when you gave aid to my dog... well, my actions were less than appreciative. In fact, they were downright deplorable. As I'm reminded of often." He shot Lord Ezra a harsh glance again before adding, "Therefore, I wish to apologize for my rudeness."

Aaron narrowed his eyes. Why was a baron asking forgiveness of a knight? Then again, human dignity called for moments of humility. "I accept your apology, my lord. But I do have a question. Why threaten Mrs. Rutley and her school?"

Lord Ezra clapped his friend on the back. "I'm afraid the fault is mine, Kirkwood. Mrs. Rutley and I have a history, a long and somewhat difficult friendship if you will. It seems that when I have a few brandies in me, I tend to express a certain... frustration with the woman. Oh, don't get me wrong. Mrs. Rutley and I have mended our differences, or at least enough to be cordial to one another, but I must harbor some deep-seated animosity toward her if I'm less than complimentary when I'm inebriated. My friend here was only repeating what he heard from me in those alcohol-ridden moments. The truth is, I only wish her and her students nothing but the best."

Aaron gave the gentleman a half-smile. "Then you have no grievances toward the woman or her school?"

Lord Ezra's eyes narrowed. "Grievances? No. But I'll dedicate the rest of my life to destroying her." The room fell silent before the man barked a harsh laugh. "Of course not. How absurd would that be?"

Aaron gave a relieved chuckle. The man was right. A nobleman seeking vengeance against the headmistress of a girl's school was preposterous. "I'm glad to have the chance to hear your side of the rumors. After Lord Lenten's comments and what I've heard... Well, it does not matter."

"The gossip among the women of Chatsworth runs strong," Lord Ezra said with a snort. "Though, I must admit there are men who can be just as bad. Now, how about that drink? I'll take a brandy. Lenten?"

Aaron joined the two men in their laughter. Clearly, Lord Ezra held no ill will toward anyone. Or at least not toward Mrs. Rutley. Yet this begged the question as to why he had called. The uncle to a duke would not have made such a formal request of a mere knight only to have a friend offer an apology.

Pouring them each a glass of amber liquid, Aaron joined them in the seating area, taking the couch while the two lords each took a chair.

"I sense there is more to this call than an opportunity for an apology, my lord."

"You see, Lenten?" Lord Ezra said with a chuckle. "I told you this young man is perceptive."

The compliment made Aaron smile. He recognized the not-so-subtle use of flattery. After all, he had used it himself often enough.

"You're correct, Kirkwood," Lord Ezra replied. "We have another reason to be here today. Mr. Neil Barker."

Aaron shifted in his seat. "And what have we to discuss about the proprietor of a theater?"

"My family has resided in Chatsworth for several generations," Lord Ezra explained. "I've dreamed of seeing the village grow, so honorable men such as yourself will want to live here and invest in all the area has to offer. I'll not lie. I'm interested in purchasing most, if not all, of the land within the village proper."

Aaron took a sip of his brandy. What did such a move mean for such a quaint place? Clearly, he knew far too little about the man who sat before him.

"It has come to my attention that Barker has plans to sell the building in which the theater now resides. I once frequented the place and enjoyed the performances there. But its time has passed. The residents no longer have as much of an interest in watching the paltry plays they put on there. London is not all that far to travel to see a decent production. I went to Barker with a more than reasonable offer, but he refused it. Or rather, he said that you would have the first claim to it if he decided to sell."

Aaron smiled. "That is true. In fact, tonight after the play ends, Miss Dunston and I plan to speak to those in attendance. He plans to put his decision to a vote. If I win, which I believe I shall, I hope to make it into a gentlemen's club. With proper investors, of course."

Lord Lenten's brows rose. "What a marvelous idea! What better way to draw more people to our humble hamlet!"

Lord Ezra waved a hand to silence Lord Lenten and said to Aaron, "I try to be as accommodating as I can when it comes to investment, which is the reason for my call today. Let's forget about asking a dozen or more men to put up the funds. Instead, let's keep it between the three of us."

Aaron frowned. "I'm sorry, what do you mean exactly?"

"What do I mean?" Lord Ezra repeated. "I mean that you'll join me in turning Chatsworth into a proper municipality. But we shan't stop there! Once I have the theater, I'll purchase the building beside it. My hope is to expand the village one building at a time. The last thing we want is to watch our little town turn into the next Spelling." He stood and waved his arms in very much the same way a showman would present his next act. "Yes, we'll create a city so great, everyone of distinction will want to live here. And your name will be written all over it!"

Aaron had only heard of Spelling. From his understanding, it was a nearby village that had died out after many of the mines, once providing the residents an income, were forced to close.

"You're new here, Kirkwood. But if I'm to guess, I'd say you're here to make a name for yourself. Am I correct in saying so?"

Aaron could not help but nod.

"Then join me! Join us!"

As much as Lord Ezra's speech had moved him, Aaron was conflicted. He had promised Miss Louisa not to proposition any other investors until after tonight's decision. Even the offer itself did not feel quite right. Yet, this is what he wanted, was it not? Perhaps his worry was causing him to overthink. "As welcoming as your offer is, I cannot commit to it just yet. I've promised Miss Dunston she would have an opportunity to present her plans for saving the theater, and I cannot go back on my word."

Lord Ezra blew out a heavy breath. "Spoken like a true man of honor. But have you considered what will happen to you if she's able to get enough votes to win this contest, for better lack of a word?"

Aaron frowned. "I doubt she'll win. I've been able to secure far more money from my investors than she has collected donations. Even so, not giving her the chance to at least try does not sit well with me."

"Yet have you considered how devastating the humiliation will be when she loses," Lord Ezra said. "Ah, well, the decision is yours. But understand this. If she fails, I'll make an offer this very evening with or without you." He turned to Lord Lenten. "Let's go. I have work to complete, and I'm sure Kirkwood will need some time to consider his decision. We'll see ourselves out."

Panic filled Aaron as the two lords headed toward the door. Chatsworth would indeed grow in the coming years, and he could be an important part of that growth. Now was when he could secure his destiny, but his chance was walking out the door.

"Lord Ezra, wait."

Both men stopped and turned around. "Yes?" Lord Ezra asked.

An image of Miss Louisa came to mind of when they had agreed to work together. They had even shaken hands. Yet she had also confessed that the cost of replacing the roof alone was far more than she had expected. The truth was, with the other repairs needed, she simply would not be able to raise enough funds. The idea of her being humiliated tonight by Lord Ezra did not sit well with him. There was no longer any choice. He had to make a decision.

Aaron approached the two lords, his hand extended. "You have a deal."

When Lord Ezra took the proffered hand, a coldness Aaron had never encountered before in his life radiated up his arm.

"A wise decision," Lord Ezra said. "I'll inform Barker this evening that we've joined forces. Afterward, we'll celebrate our victory." He placed a hand on Aaron's shoulder. "By working with me, you'll find that you're destined for great things."

Once the gentlemen were gone, Aaron returned to his seat. With each passing moment, the elation he had felt began to wane. This was what he had always wanted—to make a name for himself. Yet doing so would hurt Miss Louisa.

Given time, she would come to see this was the right decision for everyone concerned. What they needed to focus on now was his desire to make her his wife, for that single act would affect both their lives forever.

Chapter Thirty-Three

R uth had nearly squealed with joy when Mrs. Rutley offered to attend the theater with Louisa rather than requesting that she play chaperone. She had commented more than once that she had better things to do than minding two people who had obviously been made for one another. This suited Louisa just fine. As much as she appreciated her friend's willingness to be at her side as of late, Louisa was glad to attend a production with someone who enjoyed such activities as Mrs. Rutley did. And Sir Aaron, of course.

The foyer of the theater was so full that many of the attendees had to stand outside as they waited for the play to begin.

From the auditorium came the sounds of the small orchestra tuning their instruments and adding to the buzz of voices.

"I don't see Sir Aaron," Louisa said, craning her neck to look over the heads of those who filled the room.

She recognized most of the attendees. Lord Walcott stood speaking to Lady Reynolds and her daughter. Miss Constance was a younger version of her mother with her golden blonde hair, heart-shaped face, and haughty expression. Both wore the same flowing white gown with silver threading throughout the bodice and long, white lace gloves.

Mr. and Mrs. Lush stood beside a nearby column, Mrs. Lush tapping her foot in a way that said she had run out of that which came from her name—Patience. Louisa thought of their twins and the poor soul left to look after them while their parents enjoyed time away. Governess to those children was a position she hoped never to be forced to endure!

"I hope he arrives before the play begins," Louisa murmured.

"He still has a few minutes," Mrs. Rutley replied. "I'm sure he'll be here soon enough."

"Why, Mrs. Rutley, what are you doing here?"

Louisa turned to find Lord Ezra Colburn pushing through the crowd. And he was not alone. The cruel man who owned the dog she and Sir Aaron had helped was at his side.

"It's a theater," Mrs. Rutley replied dryly. "I imagine you can guess my reason for being here."

Louisa could not help but grin. No one frightened Mrs. Rutley, and Louise drew courage from that fact.

Lord Ezra gave a mirthless laugh, annoyance twisting his features. "I'm sure you're acquainted with Lord Lenten?"

"I hope you received my letter, Mrs. Rutley," the blond man said.

"And what makes you think I have not?"

"Because I haven't received a reply," Lord Lenten replied.

Mrs. Rutley gave a wry chuckle. "I'll respond in due time, my lord, and not a moment before."

"See that you do," Lord Lenten snapped. Then he looked at Louisa. "I wish you luck in your endeavor this evening, Miss Dunston," he said, and then the two men walked away.

"How does he know what I hope to do?" Louisa asked, frowning. "And why did Lord Lenten write to you?"

Mrs. Rutley raised an eyebrow. "That is my business and not yours, Louisa. And what does it matter if he knows? It's not as if you haven't told everyone in the village about your plans."

Louisa bit at her lip in frustration. Something was amiss, but she could not place what it was. Those two men were up to no good, that much was evident. Did they hope to embarrass Mrs. Rutley somehow tonight?

As she grappled with this conundrum, Sir Aaron came hurrying toward her. "Miss Louisa," he said before stopping to add a quick bow to Mrs. Rutley. He was panting. "Forgive my tardiness."

"You're right on time," Louisa whispered as she assessed the man she had come to love. His neatly brushed hair, perfect lips, and carefully tied cravat sparked that now-familiar flame inside her. She could not wait for him to kiss her again once all this madness was over! "I'm so pleased you're here."

Sir Aaron pursed his lips. "We must speak about the theater—"

But his words were cut short when Mr. Barker announced, "May I have your attention, please?"

"Let's talk after the performance," Louisa whispered as Mr. Barker continued with his introduction.

Sir Aaron gave her a reluctant nod, and she frowned when he hurried away. Where was he off to?

"So, with that in mind," Mr. Barker was saying, "I would like to thank each and every one of you for joining me in this, the first production of another wonderful season here at the theater."

Liveried ushers opened the pair of double doors with white-gloved hands. Others collected tickets and led attendees to their assigned seats until not a single chair was left vacant. Louisa and Mrs. Rutley sat in the back row, but given the size of the theater, they were close enough to see the stage quite well.

Beside her sat the hatter, Mr. Locke. His usually mussed silver hair had been combed and his coat pressed for the occasion.

The stage curtain opened, and the backdrop of Chatsworth was the same as when Louisa had stopped by while the actors had been rehearsing their lines. A blue sky and white fluffy clouds had been added since.

The audience quieted as a half-dozen actors took to the stage. Some carried baskets of flowers, one carried a pitchfork, and another a broom. Music rose from the orchestra pit as an older man and a young woman entered the stage from the right, wearing aprons covered in what appeared to be flour and chatting together, although Louisa could not make out the words.

"Now, child, run along and tell that blacksmith's son that he'd better pay his debt, or I'll see him thrown into prison."

The woman nodded. "Yes, Father, I shall."

To the left of the stage, a young man wielded a hammer, striking a piece of iron, the clanging reverberating through the theater. When he noticed the approach of the young woman, he set aside the hammer and crossed his massive arms over his wide chest.

"Hello, Miss Susan," he said. "I suppose your father wants his money."

To Louisa's surprise, Miss Susan replied, "Oh, Timothy, why have you not paid him? You know Father already disapproves of you. You're only making matters worse with your refusal."

The man grinned. "I'll risk facing his temper if it means having another chance to see you again."

Louisa sighed. She had seen this very play two years earlier and had enjoyed it then. But now that she was in love, it brought her the greatest joy. The story was simple. The couple had fallen in love, but both sets of parents disapproved. In the end, they would marry.

Just as Louisa would, once Mr. Barker accepted the offer to bring in the funds to restore the theater to its earlier glory.

Throughout the performance, the audience laughed in the appropriate parts, women sniffled during the sad parts, but everyone applauded once the play came to an end. The actors took to the stage, bowing and blowing kisses to the attendees. Everyone stood, the applause now deafening.

Louisa glanced at Mrs. Rutley. Although the headmistress clapped, she wore an extremely worried expression.

"Are you all right?" she asked in a loud whisper to be heard over the din.

"Oh yes, I'm well," Mrs. Rutley replied. "I was just thinking, is all."

When Mr. Barker took the stage, the applause subsided, and the attendees returned to their seats. "Friends, I've a very special announcement to make."

Louisa adjusted her posture, readying herself to rise and walk down the center aisle to make her speech once her name was called. She had spent the past two days rehearsing exactly what she would say and felt more than ready. By the time she finished, people would be throwing money onto the stage to see the theater remained.

"As many of you have likely heard by now, the fate of our little theater has hung in the balance. But tonight, I can assure you that this is no longer the case."

"Does he mean to keep it?" Louisa whispered.

Mrs. Rutley shrugged. "I don't know."

"Rather than make this wonderful announcement myself, I would like to ask Sir Aaron Kirkwood to explain what is going to transpire."

Louisa frowned. They had agreed that she would speak first. Why had they changed the plans? As Sir Aaron took the stage, worry formed in the pit of her stomach. But when Lord Ezra and Lord Lenten joined him, she thought she would be ill right there!

"Thank you, Mr. Barker," Sir Aaron said. He had a voice made for the stage, and if she had not been so annoyed, Louisa would have reveled in it. "Friends, for many years, this theater has served the community well. But times are changing. Rather than see this lovely building fall to ruin, we—Lord Ezra Colburn, Ashton, Lord Lenten, and I—have devised a plan. How will we preserve the integrity of this theater while also giving the community a place they can enjoy? By converting it into a gentleman's club."

The response from the crowd was a mesh of jubilation and anger, depending on who was reacting. Louisa was most certainly of the latter. Not only had he betrayed her, but he had also betrayed every woman and every man not of the upper class. He had taken a place that was open to everyone and excluded the majority of those who lived in the area! How could she not have seen this coming?

Mrs. Rutley placed a hand on Louisa's arm, but Louisa pulled away. "Shall we leave?" the headmistress asked.

Louisa snorted. "Not before I've spoken to Sir Aaron. And he had better have an explanation for this treasonous behavior, or so help me!"

As people ventured into the foyer, Louisa found an opening in the crowd and pushed her way toward the stage. Mr. Lush was shaking Sir Aaron's hand when she stomped up the stairs.

Upon seeing her, Sir Aaron said something to his companions and waved her to stage right.

"Miss Louisa, I hope you understand—"

"How dare you!" she hissed, wishing the pain in her chest would subside. "We had an agreement! I was to be given a chance to present my case, and you took that away from me!" Angry tears blurred her vision, but she blinked them back.

"I did it to save you the embarrassment of losing," Sir Aaron said. "You would never be able to raise the amount needed to see this place fully restored."

She gaped at him. His words were like nettles to her heart. "Are you saying that you've never believed me capable of succeeding?"

He shook his head. "I admire what you set out to do, that is the truth. But what you wanted was a task far too difficult to complete." He placed his hands on her arms. "Don't you see? Tonight, we've begun the journey toward our destiny together! Lord Ezra means to change Chatsworth forever. Years from now, they will have written plays and have performances about how we turned the village into something far better."

Unable to stop it, a single tear rolled down Louisa's cheek. "And where will this play be held?" she asked.

Sir Aaron looked as if she had struck him in the stomach. "I—"

"You speak of our destiny as if I'm a part of it, but nothing has changed. Your interests lie only in yours. Mine is of no consequence. Good-bye, Sir Aaron." She turned and walked away.

"Miss Louisa, wait!" he called after her. "You're being impractical. This is not about me or you but rather the future of Chatsworth."

Wiping her eyes, Louisa turned to face him once more. "You're right. I've not been considering the future. But I am now, and you're not in it."

Ignoring his plea that she remain, she walked into the foyer in search of Mrs. Rutley. Both she and Mr. Barker were speaking beside a potted plant, the man playing with the ring on his finger. Then she caught sight of Lord Ezra and Lord Lenten and changed course.

Upon seeing her, Lord Ezra lifted his glass of wine. "A pleasant evening, wouldn't you say, Miss Dunston? And it's all thanks to Sir Aaron."

"You're a scoundrel," Louisa said, not caring a whit for who was listening. "Both of you."

Lord Lenten shrugged. "I've been called worse."

But it was Lord Ezra's next words that caused her ire to reach heights she had never known existed.

"Chatsworth is changing," he said. "Soon, we'll own every farm, shop... and school in the area."

Readying a proper rebuke, Louisa opened her mouth, but Mrs. Rutley took hold of her arm. "Come, Louisa. There is no need to entertain the likes of these men."

With her chin lifted, Louisa followed her headmistress out the front doors and into the cool night air. What began as an evening filled with promise had quickly transformed into a night of despair. She had thought her destiny was with Sir Aaron. A life of happiness and love. And perhaps they would write about him one day. But her name would never be mentioned.

Chapter Thirty-Four

For two days, Louisa refused to get out of bed. She lacked the strength to do more than to rise to relieve herself and return to the sanctuary of her covers. Sir Aaron had called over Saturday morning, but she had refused to see him. There was no reason to do so. Whatever words he wished to say to justify his sedition would only fall on deaf ears. He had broken one promise too many, one more meaningful than all the others, and she could not forgive him.

Despite her stalwart decision to remove him from her life, she was unable to erase him from her thoughts. She missed his smile, his laugh. Being in his company. How could her life progress without him?

She thought about the day they had first met at the tobacconist's shop. That had been their first standoff, followed by another at the very theater she was trying so hard to save. He knew exactly what to say and do to exasperate her and took every advantage to do so.

Despite the difficult start, however, their relationship grew into something she would never have imagined. He had saved her from the tailor's nephew, Jeffery Venter. They had worked together to remove the thorn from the dog's paw. They were perfect for one another.

Until they were not.

The truth was that Louisa's destiny lay in a different direction from his. Sir Aaron wanted to conquer trade and commerce and anything to do with business, and he would do whatever he could to get what he wanted. Even if it meant trampling her in the process. A woman's heart can be won with words covered in sweet cream. Yet it can be lost in a matter of seconds when one adds actions drizzled in vinegar. And Sir Aaron's vinegar-filled actions had done just that.

Louisa ignored the light tap on the door. She did not want to speak to anyone. All she wanted to do was remain where she was and wallow in her sorrow. Alone.

The knock repeated, and the door opened to Mrs. Rutley. "I can't have you lolling around in bed all day, Louisa," she said, her tone kind but firm as she sat on the edge of the bed. "It's not good for you."

Louisa sighed. Even raising her eyes to look at her headmistress took effort, such was her despondency. "I thought I'd be introducing the man who wished to marry me to my parents tomorrow. Now, I'll be returning home without the prospect of marriage." A fresh supply of tears welled in her eyes. "Oh, Mrs. Rutley, is there not a tonic or herb I can take to relieve this pain that's taken over my soul?"

Mrs. Rutley smiled and brushed back a strand of Louisa's hair from her forehead. "You can always go and speak to Sir Aaron."

Louisa let out a half-laugh. "And listen to his excuses to justify his actions? He betrayed me, and nothing he says can change that." Why should it be she who suffered when he was the one who caused the pain?

"You've lost the theater and Sir Aaron in one fell swoop, Louisa," Mrs. Rutley said. "Does the loss of one hurt more than the other?"

Anger bubbled hot in Louisa. Was her headmistress blind? "The loss of him, of course! The theater means nothing."

"Is that so?" Mrs. Rutley asked. "Then why were you so set yesterday to save it?"

Louisa sat up in bed, frowning. What a silly question. "Because Chatsworth needs a place where both men and women can be equals. I've explained this before."

Her headmistress sighed. "I don't doubt your motives, but I would venture a guess that you had a greater interest in defeating Sir Aaron than in saving the theater. Now, don't give me that look, Louisa. You cannot deny that the game the two of you played was a greater motivator than the prize."

"If this was a game," Louisa replied with a sniff, "he did nothing short of cheating."

"I'm sure he did not cheat, Louisa."

Pushing back the covers, Louisa leapt to her feet. "I'm suffering a broken heart, Mrs. Rutley, but it appears you've taken his side over mine."

Mrs. Rutley heaved a sigh. "Louisa, if you had won, what do you imagine would have happened?"

Louisa shrugged. "I'd be happy, of course." She narrowed her eyes. "What is it you're saying? That I should be happy whether I win or lose? That may be true in theory, but we both know that losing only leaves the winner feeling smug and the loser disconsolate."

"Did you not once say that Sir Aaron told you he never believed you could win?"

"He did," Louisa replied with a nod.

Mrs. Rutley smiled. "But I would guess you thought the same of him."

Louisa bit at her lip. "I was so certain I would win, yes, but that does not change what he did. At least I would have won without cheating."

"Did he?" Mrs. Rutley asked. "And what about you? Were you honorable in your actions?" She patted Louisa's hand. "You have every right to feel hurt by what he did, but you were no different. You two are more alike than you're willing to admit." She rose from the bed. "Now, I want you to wash and dress and downstairs for breakfast."

Her jaw hanging open, Louisa watched her headmistress close the door behind her as she left the room. How dare Mrs. Rutley accuse her of being like Sir Aaron! They were nothing alike. She, Louisa, was a thoughtful and caring young lady who wanted to do what was best for the village and its populous. Sir Aaron, on the other hand, was a self-possessed, arrogant scoundrel whose only purpose in life was to make others admire him for empty actions and hollow promises!

After using the water from her pitcher to wash her face and seeing to her morning ablutions, Louisa donned a teal-blue dress, brushed her hair, and made her way downstairs. She was not hungry, so she forewent breakfast and went outside, where she found Ruth and Amy with their heads together beside the great oak tree.

"What are you two doing?" Louisa asked as she approached.

Amy clasped her hands together and bounced on the balls of her feet. "Ruth has invited me to sail to faraway lands with her once I've completed my schooling! Isn't that wonderful?"

Louisa glanced at Ruth. Did she still believe this captain of hers would return? But expressing her doubts would not only disappoint Amy but Ruth, as well.

"Well," Ruth said, "will you go speak to him or not?"

"No," Louisa replied. "There is no reason. Tomorrow my parents will come, and I'll return home. I'm sure they'll have me married off by winter." She shrugged. "That is my destiny."

"You can go with Ruth," Amy said.

Louisa snorted. "That life is not for me."

She paused. What had she always wanted in life? Adventure and exploration. Was that not what Ruth also wanted? Then why did Louisa judge Ruth's dreams as foolish? In fact, what gave Louisa the right to judge that which another wanted with such disdain?

Good Lord, she thought, panic filling her. *I'm acting no better than Abigail Swanson!*

Abigail was an extremely obnoxious and disliked student who had left the school the previous month, much to everyone's pleasure. No one wanted to be anything like her, yet here was Louisa being as judgmental.

Her stomach knotted. Mrs. Rutley had spoken the truth. She and Sir Aaron were far more similar than she cared to admit.

No, that was untrue. Sir Aaron had betrayed her, and that was inexcusable. She had handed her heart to him on a silver platter, and a day later, he stepped on it as if it were nothing more than an insect. And why? All so he could claim victory! He had not changed in the slightest. To him, nothing mattered but what he wanted. Not even her.

Louisa gave Ruth a sad look. "The story you told me about the captain?" she said. "I now understand the hurt it caused you. And why you want nothing more to do with him. It's not worth the pain and struggle, is it?"

Ruth sighed. It sounded almost... resigned. "He was the only man for me. I couldn't even imagine marrying any of these other boring men."

With a nod, Louisa returned to her bedroom, her heart heavier than ever. With the covers pulled up to her chin, she considered Ruth's words. There was no other man for Louisa, for she still loved Sir Aaron. As much as he had hurt her, she wondered if she had enough forgiveness inside her.

Burrowing deeper into the blankets, she wondered if he had any remorse for what he did, for her regret was drowning her.

Chapter Thirty-Five

Sir Aaron Kirkwood, Most Noble Order of the Garter, had never felt more alone. The joy that came with securing the theater had dissipated as quickly as water droplets on a hot frying pan. Had it been worth his trouble if it also meant losing Miss Louisa?

What began as a competition between two people quickly grew into an association that he enjoyed far more than he would have ever imagined. He never considered love a necessity but now it was as important to him as the air he breathed. The trouble was, he had lost her.

He had secured their shared destiny. Why could she not see that what he had done helped them both? Yet it was too late to explain his reasoning to her. This morning, her parents would be coming to collect her, and he would never see her again. The idea of making one last attempt intrigued him, but doing so would be in vain. He had never been one for wasting time, for it was far too precious.

Moving aside the ledgers on his desk, Aaron picked up his teacup.

"You've become awfully quiet, Kirkwood," Lord Walcott said from his chair across from Aaron. "Is all well with you?"

Lord Wolcott had arrived earlier to discuss a proposition for an enterprise in the production of wool. The odd thing was that Aaron could not recall making such an agreement. Perhaps the stress had made him forget.

"Up until two days ago, my future was bright," Aaron said, leaning back in his chair. "Miss Dunston is unhappy with me for purchasing the theater." He shook his head. "Does she not see that her plan was destined to fail?"

Crossing a leg over the opposite knee, Lord Walcott smiled. "I had no idea you could see the future. Tell me, will this season's crops see a decent harvest?"

Aaron clenched his jaw in annoyance. He was in no mood for this man's heckling. "Of course, I don't know the future. But I needn't know the future to recognize she could not win."

Lord Walcott shrugged. "Perhaps, but we'll never know now for certain, shall we?"

"I saved her from the embarrassment of losing," Aaron snapped. "If it hadn't been for Lord Ezra, I would never have seen that flaw in our little contest. All I know is that my decision was made as a way to secure our destiny together, and she wants to throw it all away."

"Destiny, is it?" Lord Walcott said with a small chuckle. "Is that not the name that's been given to you? The Knight of Destiny."

Aaron nodded. "Which only reinforces the fact what I did was fitting."

"It appears to me that you've been blessed with the wrong name."

"What do you mean?" Aaron asked, frowning.

Lord Walcott took a sip of his tea. "I'd have named you the Knight Who Thinks Only of Himself."

Indignant, Aaron slammed a fist on the desktop. "How dare you!"

"How dare I what?" the earl asked, his tone remaining conversational. "Speak the truth? I pride myself in being truthful, Kirkwood, and I stand by what I've said. You thought not of Miss Dunston but rather of yourself. All that has mattered to you since the beginning of this farce is what this victory would do for you. Not once did you consider what it would do for—or to—the young lady. Go on, prove I'm lying."

Guilt tugged at the back of Aaron's mind, but he pushed it aside. "It's not that simple. A man must provide for his wife. I only meant to begin with the theater and expand from there. If she cannot see that—or you, for that matter—there is nothing I can do."

Lord Walcott uncrossed his knees and placed the teacup on the desktop. When he rose, he clasped his hands in front of him. "People already speak your name, Kirkwood. And I've no doubt that whatever scheme you and Blackwood have devised will have the entire village talking. Perhaps your name will become synonymous with the founders of Chatsworth because of the wonderful changes you bring."

Aaron gave a relieved sigh. Finally, the earl reorganized the sense in his decision! Why had the man not simply said so?

"But in the future, when you return home at night, Miss Dunston will not be there. Your bed and your heart will be empty. And with each building you purchase, each parcel of farmland that is tilled, your coffers will grow. But so will your loneliness."

Aaron's heart began to race. Not from anger but rather from fright. Being alone had always been his worst fear.

"You really should consider what you're giving up, Kirkwood, for most of us experience only one love in our lives. No matter how successful you are, no matter how full your coffers become, none of it compares to sharing your life with someone you love. You speak of your destiny? Well, I've just explained it to you, and it looks bleak, indeed." He stood and buttoned his coat. "I have a meeting at one, so I'll take my leave. Consider my counsel, Kirkwood. I'll see myself out. Good day to you." And with that, he left the room.

For a moment, Aaron considered calling after Lord Walcott, to tell him he was wrong. Yet he could not, for the evidence presented proved him right.

Yet had the man in Hensworth, Mr. Abraham Artemus, not said very much the same thing?

Rising from his chair, he made his way to the library to stand in front of the Sword of Destiny. The weapon that had changed the destiny of England. That brought an end to the War of the Roses. Aaron had wanted nothing more than to be equal to—if not greater than—his ancestor who had carried this sword. To carve his own destiny.

With careful hands, he opened the glass case and took the heavy broadsword in hand. He took a step back and held it up in front of him. The blade had tiny nicks but light still bounced off the polished steel.

"I had hoped to wield you in triumph," he muttered aloud.

Images of his arrival in Chatsworth flashed in his mind. Odd as it was, the sword wrapped in a heavy blanket and resting beside him had him believing it could lead him to his destiny.

He had been as lost then as he was now. All he had to hold on to was a dream. To become the man he was meant to be. For so long, he believed that was a shrewd businessman who would build a name for himself. But as Lord Walcott had said, even if he realized that dream, he would still return to an empty home.

He had found his calling in life, and if he did not hurry, it would disappear.

Sliding the sword into its leather scabbard, he settled the weapon on his shoulder and marched out into the corridor.

Scriven was speaking to one of the maids when Aaron approached. "What can I do for you, sir?" the butler asked.

"Have my horse saddled at once."

With a quick nod, Scriven waved away the maid, who bobbed a quick curtsy and hurried off to do whatever the butler bade of her.

Aaron headed outside, where a warm sun greeted him. As he waited for his horse, he began to pace, the pebbles of the drive crunching under his boots.

"Is everything all right, sir?" the butler asked, a worried frown on his face.

Aaron laughed. "It will be. I've come to realize something, Scriven."

"Oh?" the butler asked. His eyes darted to the sheathed broadsword.

"Indeed. I've been a very selfish man. Arrogant. But starting now, I plan to change my ways."

"Excellent, sir," Scriven said, reddening, likely embarrassed that his master was confiding in him.

Masking enthusiasm was not an easy task, but Aaron would not apologize. When the stable hand brought his horse, Aaron buckled the sword to his waist and mounted.

"Are you going to war, sir?" Scriven asked.

Aaron smiled. "No. I'm going to change my destiny."

Chapter Thirty-Six

It was with a heavy heart that Louisa hugged Amy good-bye. After promising to write, Louisa picked up her portmanteau, which was far heavier since her arrival, and made her way downstairs. Today was her last day at Mrs. Rutley's School for Young Women, and although she was ready to take this important next step into the world, she could not help but feel a sense of melancholy.

"Four years, Mrs. Rutley," Louisa said as she approached the school mistress and Ruth, who stood together talking in the foyer. "It feels as if it were only yesterday that I arrived, yet here I am leaving for good."

Louisa recalled her first day here. Worry for what the future would hold had riddled her. What would it be like living somewhere other than home? Would she make any friends amongst the students? And what sort of headmistress would Mrs. Rutley be?

It had not taken her long to realize that her parents had made the best decision for her; she had made many friends and gained an entirely new family. A family who valued her even more than those who had raised her.

"It has been a wonderful four years," Mrs. Rutley said. "You'll be sorely missed, Louisa."

Before Louisa could respond, Ruth threw her arms around her.

"You'll mind yourself, won't you? If you need anything, you can always call on me. No matter if I'm in the middle of the ocean or docked on land, I'll do all I can to come."

Tears filled Louisa's eyes. "Thank you," she whispered, astonished —and pleased—by this outward show of affection from her otherwise reserved friend.

Ruth pushed her away. "Good-bye," she said before bounding up the stairs. But Louisa did not miss the glistening of tears in her eyes.

"Well, Mrs. Rutley, my parents should be here within the hour. They have always been a stickler for punctuality."

The headmistress smiled. "Why don't we wait outside? It's a lovely day, far too lovely to be indoors. Plus, there is something you must see."

With an encouraging nod from Mrs. Rutley, Louisa opened the front door and stepped out onto the portico. The day truly was lovely. The air was unseasonably warm, and not a single cloud marred the otherwise clear sky. The scent of budding flowers and fresh-cut grass wafted past her.

But none of that held her attention once her gaze fell upon the figure that stood facing the great oak tree.

Sir Aaron.

She set the bag on the ground beside her and walked toward the knight. He turned as she approached. Why was he carrying the sword that had hung from the wall in his library?

"We must speak before you leave," he said.

Despite her anger with him, Louisa could not deny the warmth that filled her just being in his presence. He was so handsome, so dashing, that she could barely breathe.

He does not truly care for you, Louisa Dunston. If he did, he would not have deceived you.

"I'm here," she managed to say, pleased her voice did not betray her nervousness. "Say what you will."

"You could have won," he said matter-of-factly. "You could have won, and the theater would have remained if I would have given you a chance to state your case. But I allowed my pride to get in the way. I was unfair to you, and for that, I'm sorry."

Louisa sighed. "I, too, was so focused on getting my way, I failed to consider your goals. I made every excuse to justify breaking the rules upon which we had agreed. I acted like a petulant child. Therefore, I also offer an apology."

They stood staring at one another, the only sound the distant cry of a crow. Louisa bit at her lip, wishing the right words would enter her mind. Before she could gather her thoughts, however, Sir Aaron set the sword across his palms.

"The Sword of Destiny," he said as he lifted it, so it hung between them. "Do you remember when I told you the story behind it?"

Louisa nodded. "Indeed. Your ancestor wielded it in the War of the Roses. And according to legend, whoever wields it is led to his destiny. But why have you brought it here?"

"I thought it had led me to Chatsworth so I could purchase the theater, that I had no other reason for being here. But I was wrong. It led me to something far more important, someone more notable. It led me to you."

Her heart skipped a beat as he unsheathed the weapon and dropped the scabbard on the ground beside him. Sunlight glinted off the blade, making it all the more majestic. "I've wanted to make a name for myself by being associated with as many businesses, as many enterprises, as I could muster. Unfortunately, I was willing to do whatever it took to see my destiny fulfilled. Even betraying the woman I love. A friend gave me some wonderful advice. I can own every shop in Chatsworth, every building within ten miles. But because I aimed only for that life, I was also destined to remain alone. But that is not the kind of life I want for myself. What is wealth without having someone with whom to share it? Someone for whom I've come to care a great deal. That sort of life is empty, indeed."

For a moment, Louisa could only stare at him. Was that not what she had come to see as well? "I couldn't agree more," she said. "Now that the theater is gone, and despite my love for you, I've no idea what I want for my life."

Sir Aaron walked around to stand behind her. With the sword in one hand, he raised the sword in front of her. "Hold it," he said.

"Will it not be too heavy?"

"Not if I help you carry its weight."

Trembling, she wrapped a hand around the leather-bound hilt.

"It's said that whoever wields this sword will be led to his—or her—destiny. Now that we wield it together, let's see where it leads us."

With one swift downward motion, he buried the sword into the soft earth, his hands covering hers.

"I'm not a knight of old who changes the destiny of England. Only the man who loves you."

His warm breath sent pleasant shivers down her spine and heat to her stomach. She leaned her head back and said, "All I want is for us to share our love for one another."

As she looked over her shoulder, their lips met in a swift but passionate kiss. "Then let's make this journey together," he whispered as he pulled her back against him.

Walking hand in hand, they returned to the school where they waited in the drawing room for the arrival of Louisa's parents.

An hour later, when her father entered, he asked, "Mrs. Rutley, why is there a sword in your front garden?"

Chapter Thirty-Seven

Sitting across from her father on the couch in the school's drawing room, Louisa traced a nervous finger along a printed vine on her skirt. Her mother sat beside her, as quiet as she, while Sir Aaron and her father discussed their various enterprises. She had forewarned her parents that Sir Aaron would be asking for her hand in marriage, but the subject had yet to arise. Now she worried it never would. Why did men spend so much time focused on business?

"It sounds like your future is well mapped, Sir Aaron," her father said with a smile usually reserved for his best clients.

Sir Aaron cleared his throat. "I believe so, Mr. Dunston. And I'm glad you've raised this topic. You see, Miss Louisa and I have become close over these past months."

Her father laughed. "So I've heard." He looked at Louisa. "I never knew you had such an interest in the theater."

Louisa's cheeks heated. "I do enjoy a good play from time to time, yes. But that was not why I fought so hard to keep our little theater open." She paused. Why should she bother to explain? It was not as if her father had ever shown any interest in anything she said or did.

Now, however, he gave her an expectant look, one she had seen him give her sister Patricia when she was younger and wanted to show him her latest painting. Or Georgia when she had trained her favorite mare to bow. Or even Anne, who possessed a singing voice that even the angels would praise.

Louisa's nervousness increased, but she took a calming breath and said, "I wanted a place where men and women could both be welcomed. Where we could all enjoy time together. And the theater was one such place. I did not want to see it destroyed only to be replaced by an establishment into which women were not allowed to enter. We're already restricted from entering gambling halls and pubs. Not that I want to enter one, Father," she added when her father's brows rose.

"So, let me get this straight," her father said. "You found a problem you felt needed to be addressed and took steps to rectify it?"

"Yes."

He pursed his lips in thought before giving a nod and returning his attention to Sir Aaron. "I'm aware you wish to marry my daughter. You've proven to me that you have good sense and are a capable man. I see no reason to deny your request."

Sir Aaron's smile nearly broke his face in two. "I thank you, sir. I promise to take good care of her."

Her father stood. "I'm sure you will. Now, we really should be on our way. We have a long journey. The sooner we begin, the sooner we'll be home." His expression gave no indication if he was pleased or relieved by the decision he had made.

As they walked toward the front door, Louisa took hold of her father's arm. "Before we go, may I speak with you, Father?"

Her father's brow knitted. "What is it? We've no time to dawdle. I have a meeting on Thursday I cannot reschedule."

"It will only take a moment, I promise."

With a resigned sigh, he nodded and followed Louisa to the far corner of the foyer. "Now, what is it?"

"I'm not at fault for who I am, Father." She had not meant her words to be so direct, but they had erupted of their own volition.

"What do you mean?" he asked with a frown.

"I know..." Louisa blinked back tears. "I know why you favor my sisters over me. Don't deny it, Father. I've seen how you look at me."

His dropped gaze was a confirmation of her fears. "I know about Mother's... indiscretion and that I'm the result of it."

"How—?"

Louisa gripped her skirts as she said, "Does it matter? What I want to know is why you hate me."

He lifted his head, shock filling his features and red rimming his eyes. "I don't hate you, Louisa."

Louisa's heart pounded in her chest. "But you don't love me, either."

Her father sighed. "I know I've treated you differently, and that was unfair of me. And before you say it has something to do with how you were born, let me say this. You are like your mother in so many ways. She was... is an inquisitive soul who wants to know everything. I, on the other hand, have always had my nose in my ledgers and spend all my time with clients. I spent far too much time away from home, which left your mother alone. Loneliness can make people do things they would not otherwise do. I believed I had forgiven her for her indiscretion. Until you were born."

Tears trickled down Louisa's face, and she did nothing to stop them. Her chest hurt, and she wished she had not broached the subject. Now she could do nothing to take back that single piece of hope that she was not the cause of his disregard. Now it had been confirmed.

He placed comforting hands on her shoulders, and she looked up at him. "None of this is your fault, Louisa. I was the fool, not you. I wasted too many years placing my anger where it did not belong. And because of that, I never got to know you." He placed his hands on either side of her face. "My daughter. And for that, I'm regretful."

As if a dam breaking, the tears now flowed. Louisa threw her arms around her father's waist as he gathered her close. "I'm so sorry, Louisa. Can you ever forgive me?"

"I already have," Louisa said, her voice muffled in his coat. "For you've always been—and will always remain—my father. And for that, I'm thankful."

When they joined Louisa's mother and Sir Aaron outside, they did so arm in arm. Louisa's father helped her mother into the carriage, leaving Louisa a moment alone with Sir Aaron.

"I'll write to you tomorrow," he said. "And every day after until you're returned to me."

She waited for him to mount his horse, the sword returned to his waist. "I cannot wait. And you'll take care of Patch, won't you?"

"I shall. And I'll even allow him to continue sleeping in my study."

This made them both laugh.

Once Sir Aaron was gone, Louisa turned to her parents, who waited in the carriage. "May I say good-bye to my friends?"

"Yes," her father replied. "But don't be long." This time his words were not a sharp command.

Louisa nodded and walked over to the great oak tree where the last two remaining people waited.

"Ruth," Louisa said as she stood before her friend, "I did not expect to see you again."

Ruth smiled. "I wanted to give you my congratulations. You've done well for yourself. I'll miss you."

Louisa smiled. "You're my Sister, and I'm thankful for every moment we shared together."

"Every moment?" Ruth asked, her eyes twinkling with their usual mischief.

"Indeed. Every moment. Even those that were less pleasant."

Ruth grinned and hugged Louisa. "We'll see one another again soon enough. I'm sure of it." Then she returned to the school, leaving Louisa and her headmistress alone.

For a moment, Louisa was unsure what to say. How did one thank a woman who had been a surrogate mother as well as a friend? Who had taken in a nosy girl and would now send her off as a proper young lady?

"Mrs. Rutley, I don't have the words to thank you for everything you've done for me."

Her headmistress smiled and wrapped her arms around Louisa. "Sometimes there is no need for words."

Louisa could only nod, for no truer statement had ever been said.

"Now," Mrs. Rutley said when the embrace ended, "your parents are waiting. It's time for you to begin the next stage of your life."

Wiping her eyes, Louisa joined her parents, and soon the carriage moved forward. From the portico, Mrs. Shepherd and Ruth waved, and as the vehicle moved past the oak tree, her headmistress did so as well.

Mrs. Rutley had been correct, for the woman's smile had said everything that needed to be said. And Louisa would never forget that message for as long as she lived.

Chapter Thirty-Eight

Pleasant Grove, Bexley, Northampton, 1809

L ady Louisa Kirkwood gave her two-year-old son a quick kiss on his chubby cheek before handing him over to Mrs. Poplar, the nanny. A middle-aged widow with silver-streaked chestnut hair and a plump, matronly air about her, the woman had been a blessed addition to the staff.

"Be sure Timothy doesn't get in the way," Louisa said. "I had to chase after him three times already today when he was nearly trampled by one of the footmen."

"I'll see he's well taken care of," the nanny said. She lifted the boy, so his legs were hanging. "And you, young sir, will be far too busy to get in anyone's way. How about we chase butterflies? Would you like that?"

"Buttafly!" Timothy cried, clapping his hands together with the eagerness of one his age ready for exploration.

A sudden yelp made everyone turn to see a white spotted dog leap out of the way.

"Patch," Louisa snapped. "Come! Now!"

With his tail wagging behind him, the Dalmatian dashed past the several pairs of legs as the footmen hauled various trunks and carpet-bags to the waiting carriages. He stopped beside Louisa and planted his behind on the ground, staring up at her with his tongue hanging out.

Louisa fished a biscuit from her pocket and offered it to him. "Good boy," she said as she scratched him behind the ears.

"He's so well behaved," Mrs. Poplar said, the lines in the corners of her eyes more pronounced with her smile. "You've trained him well."

Louisa laughed. "Not I. If it had been left to me, I would have spoiled him, and he would have never been trained. Sir Aaron is the one deserving of the praise. He was the one who asked Mrs. Pentham to create these treats as a way to reward Patch for good behavior. Without them—and Sir Aaron's firmness—I'm not sure the results would have been the same."

She gave her son one last kiss, forcing herself to ignore the arms that reached for her. "You go with Mrs. Poplar," she said, tapping the tip of his nose. "I must speak to your father, but I'll see you very soon, my love. Will you catch me a butterfly?"

Timothy nodded. "I bring you buttafly, Mama!" He wriggled in the way that said he wanted to walk, and Mrs. Poplar lowered him to the floor but kept hold of his hand. "C'mon, Pash. We gonna go cash buttaflies."

"Patch," Mrs. Poplar corrected. "Now you try. Pat-ch."

The boy crinkled his nose. "Pat-ch. Pash!"

The nanny sighed. "We'll get it right next time."

Louisa smiled as she watched the boy and dog, followed by Mrs. Poplar, head toward the back garden. When Timothy was born, Patch had taken on the role of protector and companion. Whenever he was not by Aaron or Louisa's side, he could be found in Timothy's room, his head resting on his paws as if guarding the boy's sleep. Or at his side, as he was now, off on some sort of adventure like two best friends.

Louisa soon made her way down the corridor toward the study in search of her husband.

As she passed the library, something caught her eye. She came to a stop, took two steps back, and looked into the room. Even after three years of marriage, Louisa's breath still caught whenever she looked at her husband, especially when he was unaware she was watching. When he smiled, as he did now while he stood staring at the wall, her heart fluttered as wildly as it had when they first met.

"What are you doing?" she asked after having her fill of his handsomeness.

Aaron extended an arm, and he pulled her close, her back to him. "The Sword of Destiny," he said as he tightened his embrace. They gazed up at the glass-encased weapon mounted upon the wall just as it had been when Aaron resided at Hearsely Estate. It had been one of the first items of importance to find a place in their new home. "I'll always regard it with awe. Though not as much as I do my wife." He kissed the top of her head. "I remember the day we placed our hands upon its hilt and made our promise. And although I believe that sword has been a part of what guides us, I understand something far greater leads us to our destiny."

Louisa sighed and leaned the back of her head against his chest. "Oh? And what is that?"

He turned her around to face him, his arms still wrapped around her. "Our love for one another."

Smiling up at him, she said, "I couldn't agree more. And that love will accompany us to Paris. And wherever else we find ourselves in the years to come."

They stood quiet for several moments, each in his or her own thoughts. Then Aaron said, "I still cannot believe someone swooped in and pulled Mr. Barker's theater right out from under us. How much more could they have offered than Colburn?"

She glanced up at him. "What is stranger still is how Mr. Barker refused to say who his benefactor was. No matter how many times we asked, he replied that it was no business of ours. I'm pleased that he kept the theater but allowed the building next door to become a gentleman's club."

Aaron laughed. "If he would have mentioned he owned that place in the beginning, we would have never had the chance to compete against one another."

"Yes, but we also would never have combined forces and fallen in love, either."

"And now look where we are," he said with a sigh. "Off to Paris and into our future."

During her first year of marriage, Louisa discovered she had an affinity for writing. Franny Burney, one of England's most celebrated female novelists, received a copy of one of Louisa's stories, though Louisa had no idea from whom. Mrs. Burney was so impressed that she offered to lend her expertise.

Because Louisa wished her next story to take place in Paris, Mrs. Burney suggested she go to that city and become immersed in its culture, which meant she was off on her first true adventure. At first, Louisa was uncertain if Aaron would agree, but when he learned her reason for wanting to go, he readily assented.

"This will give me the chance to offer some fine French wines at our clubs." He had opened three more gentlemen's clubs during the years since their wedding. "If I can schedule meetings with the best wineries, perhaps they can offer me better prices."

Louisa raised an eyebrow. "And what about the tea shops?" she demanded. "Will you ignore them?"

"Of course," he replied, although there was a playfulness to his tone. "Oh, very well. If I must, I can also see about finding us a French baker who can make those lovely little cakes you so enjoy."

"I?" she demanded. "You mean the ones *you* enjoy? It was not my hand Mrs. Pentham slapped to keep you from sneaking one in the middle of the night."

This had them both laughing. Aaron had indeed been caught by the cook as he searched her kitchen, but only once. Yet Louisa had teased him about it ever since.

Louisa sighed contentedly. Their entire life lay before them, and it promised to be full of adventure. There was even talk of one day visiting America. But for now, like every other day since they had spoken their marriage vows, Louisa enjoyed being held by the man she loved.

For it was love that had brought them together. The same love that showed how precious life could be.

The very love that drew them together now in a kiss that said nothing—not even a disagreement about the use of a particular building—could tear apart a young woman and her knight.

Epilogue

Courtly Manor, 1825

Lady Louisa Kirkwood wiped at her eyes. "And that, my friends, is how I fell in love with the Knight of Destiny."

"Did you ever learn who saved the theater?" Diana asked.

Louisa shook her head. "Mr. Barker never revealed his benefactor. I stopped by to see him on my way here. I hadn't realized he passed away. But the theater is still running. When I spoke to the current director, I was surprised to learn that Mr. Barker hasn't owned the building for twenty years. In all this time, I believed someone had simply given him the money. Now I learn that someone purchased the building and allowed him to continue running the theater. And what's more, in lieu of rent, the owner is paid a percentage of the profits! Now, who would make such an agreement?"

Mrs. Rutley's cough had everyone turning in concern.

"Are you all right?" Louisa asked. "Can I get you some water? Or a warm washcloth?"

Waving a hand, Mrs. Rutley said, "No. I'll be fine. But you can hand me that box."

On the nearby nightstand sat a small chest-shaped box, and Louisa handed it to her headmistress. Mrs. Rutley opened it and retrieved an object and placed it in Louisa's hand.

A ring. But not any ring. The very one Mr. Barker once wore. The symbol of who owned the theater.

Louisa gasped. "You? You purchased the theater?"

Mrs. Rutley smiled. "Of course, with the help of Lord Walcott. And there is more."

Louisa reached into the box and removed what she recognized as one of the tickets she and Aaron had sold. "Why did you keep this?" she asked.

"Mr. Barker came to me with a concern," Mrs. Rutley replied. "Not only for the theater but for a pair of young people he was certain should be together. Do you remember when he asked you and Sir Aaron to work together to sell those?"

Louisa nodded. "Of course. It was what brought us together."

The headmistress smiled. "The idea was mine. I knew early on that the knight was the right man for you. I just needed a way to force the two of you to work together, so you would also see what Mr. Barker and I could see. I had already decided to purchase that building. It was far too important to our community, as you learned when you sold every single ticket given you."

"So, if you hadn't made the suggestion..." Emma said.

"They would likely not be married today," Mrs. Rutley finished.

A clap of thunder made them all start. During Louisa's telling of her story, a storm had risen. Rain pelted against the window-panes, and the wind sounded ominous as it blew through the nearby trees.

"And now our stories have been told," Julia said with a pleased sigh. "I can only hope that my daughters will also be able to experience what we all have."

Everyone nodded their agreement, and Louisa sighed. "Although she'll not come to tell her story, I do know a little of how Ruth—"

A sudden shriek filled the air. Had it been the howling of wind? Or perhaps a fox caught in the storm and unable to find shelter. Whatever it was, it had brought with it the distinct sound of footsteps. The others huddled closer to the bed, all eyes on the door. The stomping came to a stop outside the room, and a sense of foreboding filled the air.

The door opened, and a black-hooded man stepped into the room. The cloak moved, revealing black leather boots and brown breeches.

Louisa frowned. Why would Mrs. Shepherd allow a courier into a dying woman's bedroom?

Even as she thought this, however, the figure slowly pulled back the hood to reveal a single lock of red hair.

Emma stifled a cry as she fell against Julia.

Diana whispered, "It's impossible!" just as Jenny said, "But you're dead!"

Despite her frailty, Mrs. Rutley's voice rose above the others. "I knew it was only a rumor."

Tears of joy filled Louisa's eyes as Ruth took another step forward. She stood tall and proud, her still-strong voice piercing the silence. "Even Death himself cannot stop me from fulfilling a promise I made so long ago."

Julia was the first to push forward and throw her arms around their friend, soon followed by Jenny, Diana, Emma, and finally Louisa.

"How did a rumor that you had died start?" Jenny asked.

"And what about Unity and Theodosia?" asked Emma.

Ruth smiled as she removed her cloak and hung it on the back of a nearby chair. "The twins are well and living in America with their husbands. They sadly could not make it." She turned to Mrs. Rutley. "But we can discuss that later. I would guess that our headmistress has been entertained with stories of romance. I suppose it's now my turn to tell mine."

"Yes," Mrs. Rutley said. "That is exactly what I want. Even though I already know it well."

The girls gathered around Ruth, who said, "Then I must tell everything, Mrs. Rutley. Have you a problem with that?"

Louisa knitted her brow. Why was Ruth seeking permission? What did she know the others did not?

Mrs. Rutley nodded her agreement, and Ruth turned to the Sisters.

"My story begins the week after Louisa left. For it was then that Ashton, Lord Lenten, arrived at the school. To fulfill a promise on behalf of Lord Ezra, who wished to see our headmistress ruined for what many believed she had done."

A collective gasp filled the room, and Louisa's mind raced. What could Mrs. Rutley have possibly done?

A flash of lightning filled the room with bright light, followed immediately by a peal of thunder that made the panes in the window frames shake.

Ruth glanced at Mrs. Rutley before saying, "Mrs. Rutley once told us a great storm was coming. And she was right. Lord Ezra assembled an army, and all came to see her destroyed for the death of her late husband, Mr. Phillip Rutley."

Ruth gave a sad shake of her head. "And the captain I loved was among them."

The End

Thank you for reading *Knight of Destiny*!

Read the thrilling finale to the Sisterhood of Secrets series, *Captain of Second Chances*, and learn how Ruth finds love with a captain who had once won her heart!

Coming February 2023!

In the meantime, have you already read Julia's, Emma's, Diana's, and Jenny's story in *Duke of Madness* (book 1), *Baron of Rake Street* (book 2), *Marquess of Magic* (book 3), and Earl of Deception (book 4)?

SISTERHOOD OF SECRETS

And what about Mrs. Rutley? Have you ever wondered about their secretive headmistress's past?

Miss Agnes Fitzimmons and Mr. Phillip Rutley each have a Christmas wish—to marry one another. Yet with financial burdens threatening to keep them apart, it will take a Christmas miracle to have the happily ever after they deserve.

Their story will be told in the Christmas novella *Gentleman of Christmas Past*, which was just released in the *Holiday Regency Anthology* **Naughty or Nice**.

Also by Jennifer Monroe

Sisterhood of Secrets

#1 Duke of Madness

#2 Baron of Rake Street

#3 Marquess of Magic

#4 Earl of Deception

#5 Knight of Destiny

#6 Captain of Second Chances

Secrets of Scarlett Hall

Victoria Parker Regency Mysteries

Regency Hearts

Defiant Brides

About Jennifer Monroe

USA Today bestselling author Jennifer Monroe writes clean Regency romances you can't resist. Her stories are filled with first loves and second chances, dashing dukes, and strong heroines. Each turn of the page promises an adventure in love and many late nights of reading.

With over twenty books published, her nine-part series, The Secrets of Scarlett Hall, which tells the stories of the Lambert Children, remain a favorite with her readers.

Connect with Jennifer:

www.jennifermonroeromance.com

facebook.com/JenniferMonroeAuthor

instagram.com/authorjennifermonroe

bookbub.com/authors/jennifer-monroe

amazon.com/Jennifer-Monroe/e/B07F1MRXDN